THE CURSE
OF CANTIRE

THE CURSE
OF CANTIRE

Walter S. Masterman

RAMBLE HOUSE

The Curse of Cantire ©1939 by Walter S. Masterman
© 2010 by John Pelan
This edition © 2010 by Ramble House

ISBN 13: 978-1-60543-523-7

ISBN 10: 1-60543-523-6

Cover Art: Gavin L. O'Keefe
Preparation: Fender Tucker

Dancing Tuatara Press #8

THE CURSE OF THE MASTERMAN COLLECTOR

It's a rare occurrence when a bibliophile is taken completely by surprise when they set out to collect a particular author. As an example, if one decides to collect the Pelan List as was featured in my long-running column in *Cemetery Dance* they are warned from the get-go that the list is a dynamic document and once a book goes out-of-print and exceeds the ceiling price of $50.00 it gets dropped from the list and is replaced by another title. This list had a very specific purpose, it was intended to be useful to both the novice and the experienced collector as a method to build a substantial collection without breaking the bank and at the same time getting a good overview of the genre with the intent of exposing the reader to a wide variety of horror that might serve as a jumping-off point to assembling a collection in line with the reader's tastes.

An earlier list and one I've heard numerous collectors chase after is Karl Edward Wagner's three lists of the thirteen best horror novels in the categories of supernatural, non-supernatural, and science-fictional horror. Without some understanding of the thinking behind the list(s), Karl's selections seem to be idiosyncratic at best and downright bizarre at worst. Having had a chance to discuss the list(s) with Karl, I can safely say that I don't think anyone (least of all Karl) thought for a second that these were the thirty-nine best horror novels. What they were (and are) thirty-nine books that every horror fan should read in order to get a feel for just how broad the genre really is. Karl utilized his column in *The Twilight Zone Magazine* as a bully pulpit to call attention to books that otherwise might be overlooked by even a very well-read fan.

As an example, I'll cite John Franklin Bardin's *The Deadly Percheron* and Michael Arlen's *"Hell!" Said the Duchess* as two volumes that would likely escape the notice of modern collectors. By that same token, the British thrillers by authors such as R.R. Ryan, Mark Hansom, and Walter S. Masterman would by virtue of their scarcity unlikely to be read by any save those readers diligent (and wealthy) enough to seek out all the titles listed in the Bleiler *Check-list*.

Walter S. Masterman's books reflect the titles included on the Wagner lists in a very interesting manner . . . The Wagner lists can be broken down into three groups: the first, books that are extremely common and inexpensive; the second, books that can be found with some effort and a ready checkbook, and the third group being books that are so scarce that even a collector with considerable resources and contacts throughout the rare book world may only see copies once or twice during their lifetime. The Masterman titles on the Wagner lists (*The Flying Beast* and *The Yellow Mistletoe*) fell into the second group until the Ramble House reissues made them readily available in both hardcover and trade paperback.

Within the Masterman oeuvre we have his series of novels featuring Sir Arthur Sinclair, a sort of cross between Sherlock Holmes and James Bond . . . Sinclair is a brilliant detective, but also a man of action and thus fits in well in both the "impossible crime" venue and the more fantastic scenarios such as those in novels such as *The Yellow Mistletoe*. Of course the Sinclair novels fall into the same sort of grouping, the common, those needing a bit of effort to locate, and the near impossible . . . *The Curse of Cantire* falls into the third category. When three of the most rabid Masterman collectors (myself included) have been chasing after this book for thirty years and coming up empty, one has to consider this a rare volume indeed.

As to the novel itself, many of the familiar Masterman tropes are here . . . A decayed estate replete with secret passages and a family curse, legends of a sinister figure (the Black Abbott) who has haunted the family for generations, and of course the grisly murders that a Masterman fan has come to expect. As much as I'd like to be able to tell you that this is a "lost" fantastic novel with futuristic flying machines, lost races, and mad scientists along the lines of *The Flying Beast*, *The Border Line*, or *The Yellow Mistletoe;* such is not the case; instead, we have a clever mystery novel that echoes his much earlier volume, *The Green Toad.* There are certainly hints of supernatural occurrences, are they legitimate manifestations of a vengeful force reaching from beyond the grave to strike at the living, or the work of a clever criminal hoping to terrorize his victims? Well, that would be telling . . .

I can say this much, *The Curse of Cantire* is a fine installment in the Sir Arthur Sinclair stories, and thankfully not the last appearance of this great detective. Masterman wrote four more novels and I believe that at least two feature Sir Arthur, and for those wondering what becomes of Sir Arthur after the last chronicle by Masterman, he does make a cameo appearance in my forthcoming novel. *The Six-Fingered Hand*. Some months ago (in the introduction to *The Border Line*), we made the promise that more Masterman volumes would appear from either Ramble House or Dancing Tuatara Press; now that one of the rarest of these titles has surfaced, we can be optimistic that coming months may see the remainder of his works brought back into print.

John Pelan
Midnight House
Gallup, NM 2010

THE CURSE
OF CANTIRE

CHAPTER I

A NASTY STORY

SIR ARTHUR SINCLAIR was studying a note he had received by the morning post. It bore the stamped address of the Ordley Hotel, which, as everyone knows, is one of the most exclusive in London. The writing was bold, firm and with strongly crossed *t*'s. There was a vigorous flourish after the signature—"Anthony Montague Musgrave."

The letter informed Sinclair that the said gentleman was going to call to consult him on a matter of great urgency. He added that the strictest secrecy must be observed, but that the emolument would be liberal.

The pomposity of the wording amused Sinclair. He could visualize the writer. He rose and took a reference book from his shelves.

"Musgrave, Anthony Montague," he read, "of Cantire, in Devonshire." Then followed details of the man's career. Colonel in the Indian Army, retired. No issue, etc.

When a member of an old family, as Musgrave undoubtedly had been, serves in the Indian Army, it generally denotes poverty. That in itself was nothing, for most old families are poor, but the Colonel was staying at a very expensive hotel, and spoke of liberal payment for services rendered.

"Cantire?" Some lurking memory came to Sinclair's mind of a tour in Devonshire he had once taken, and he recalled the grim old ruin of Cantire, and the legends that had gathered round it. He had closed the reference book when Buggins, his valet, announced that the Colonel had arrived.

A tall, vigorous man entered. He was somewhere in the fifties, with a prominent hooked nose, grey hair, and a face that showed danger signals to Sinclair's trained mind. The dark eyes were bold and arrogant, and the mouth firm, but the cheeks sagged down like the jowl of a bloodhound, and deep lines seamed the mahogany coloured face. He came forward with an easy elastic step, and removing his grey top hat, placed it with his stick and gloves on a side table.

"I take it you are Sir Arthur Sinclair?" he said haughtily.

"That is so," Sinclair replied with a smile, "and I am addressing Colonel Musgrave, I presume. Pray sit down."

The blustering entrance of the Colonel had obscured his companion, who shuffled forward in a sheepish manner.

"This is Rupert Seften." The Colonel waved his hand almost contemptuously. "It is about him that I have come to see you."

Sinclair took the limp hand of a youngish-looking man, with a weak, indeterminate face, watery eyes, and mouse-coloured hair carefully brushed back from his forehead. In a certain way he might be called good-looking.

Sinclair passed a box of cigars over the desk to his visitors.

"If you don't mind I will smoke one of my own," Musgrave said rudely, taking a gold cigar-case from his pocket.

Seften glanced at the Colonel, and a slight flush came to his face at the brusquerie of his companion.

He took a cigar from the box, with a word of thanks, and removed the band.

Musgrave glanced contemptuously round Sinclair's untidy study. The walls were lined with books over cupboards, and a plain dark carpet covered the floor. Sinclair lit his homely pipe, and leant back prepared to listen.

"Before I say anything about the matter on which we have come to you," the Colonel said, "I must insist on your word of honour that whatever passes between us shall be regarded as strictly confidential."

"Provided there is nothing of a criminal nature concerning either of you," Sinclair said suavely.

"Sir!" Musgrave nearly bounced out of his chair. "You forget to whom you are speaking."

Sinclair gave one of his most genial smiles. "That does not preclude the possibility; the Archbishop of Canterbury might do a murder."

Seften intervened in a lisping voice. "You are right, sir. On our part I assure you there is nothing criminal, and I am sure we need not ask for any guarantees."

In spite of his effeminate appearance, Seften showed a certain quiet dignity.

"The fact is," he went on, "I have been a bit of a waster, and my uncle and guardian packed me off with the Colonel out of the country. We have been away for three years now."

Musgrave cut him short. "My young friend has been the victim of two attacks on his life, and another is threatened. We want something done about it."

"May I ask why you have not been to the official police?"

"I should hardly have done so if such a course had not been impossible. We wish our affairs kept entirely private."

Seften moved uneasily. "Why not tell the truth?"

"Certainly not. I can only go this far: Seften got himself mixed up with a woman, and that was why I was entrusted with the job of getting him away from England."

The speech was brutal, and Seften wilted under Sinclair's eye.

"Perhaps you would give me some details of these attacks," he said stiffly.

"The first occasion was in India. We were staying at Quetta, where my old regiment was stationed. Seften and I were alone on the verandah of our hotel. The native wallah brought us coffee, and I took one sip. Finding it bitter, I put the cup down. Before I could say anything Seften had swallowed half of his, and then spat some out. I dashed for the mustard and gave him a strong emetic, and took some myself, but we were both very ill. The medico who attended us told me he had found strychnine in the coffee, enough to kill several persons, and added that the would-be assassin had overdone it, and we could taste the stuff."

"That is interesting; it suggests amateur work," Sinclair commented.

"In the natural confusion the native escaped, and could not be traced."

"It was a close thing for both of you," Sinclair said gravely. "You had no idea, I suppose, as to the author of the outrage, for I suppose the native was merely a paid tool?"

The eyes of the Colonel hardened to pin points. "None!"

"And the second attempt?" Sinclair asked, after a slight pause.

"After our experience in India we packed up, and crossed to East Africa, where we went on a shooting expedition. It was in Kenya that the assault took place. There were only us two and the native who carried our spare guns. Otherwise we were entirely alone in open country. Someone shot at us from behind, and the bullet grazed Seften's head. He bears the scar still."

"What did you do?"

"Seften was knocked out for the time being, and bleeding badly. While I was attending to him the murderous ruffian got away. It was all we could do to get back somehow to the nearest farm and fetch a doctor."

"What about the native?"

"He was in front of us and could not have fired. We reported the matter to the authorities, but nothing was discovered."

Sinclair tapped his pipe thoughtfully against the fireplace and refilled it.

"Perhaps," he said, weighing each word, "that was because you did not tell them the whole truth."

"We had to avoid a scandal," Musgrave said angrily. "I have told you the whole reason for our wandering life was for this purpose."

"For which, I conclude, Seften's uncle paid the expenses."

"Naturally! I was not going to be a bearleader for nothing, and practically an outcast from England."

Seften had been studying the floor, but at these words he lifted his head, and a flash of anger came to his eyes.

He spoke firmly. "On each occasion, Sir Arthur, we had received a warning that if we did not follow a certain course of action, such an attack would take place."

Musgrave swore beneath his breath, and glared at Seften. Sinclair was watching the Colonel through half-closed eyes, and saw that, in spite of his nerve, he was undoubtedly in a state of extreme terror. Beads of perspiration were on his forehead.

"I can do nothing for you unless you are prepared to tell me more. Who is the lady in the case?"

"That I can't tell you," Musgrave snarled.

"You may call her Mrs. X or Miss Y, for all I care, but you must see that this is the root of the business. Was it money that was demanded—in other words, blackmail?"

"No." Seften spoke quietly. "If it had been, my uncle would have paid: it was more than mere money."

"My dear sir," Sinclair exclaimed impatiently, "I really can't waste my time unless you are going to be more explicit. This is simply beating the air."

Musgrave fidgeted in his seat, and pulled at his grey moustache.

"Let me put it this way. Seften, as I have told you, got himself tangled up with a woman. Had it been just an ordinary intrigue the matter would have been simple, but, like a fool, he married her. That was the reason for our hurried departure from England."

Sinclair's face hardened. "It would have been better if you had told me this at the beginning. Was there any obstacle to their marriage?"

"Not in a legal sense." Musgrave hesitated. "It would have been easier if there had been. But a man in Seften's position must marry in his own social class. This was impossible. His uncle was furious."

"Surely that type of snobbery is a thing of the past. Was there any objection to the woman herself?"

"She was a widow, several years older than Seften, and quite unsuitable."

Sinclair, for all his coolness, was growing angry.

"Look here, Colonel Musgrave. I am fully aware that you belong to an old family, as it is called, but is Mr. Seften some prince in disguise?"

Seften coloured. "My uncle is Lord Wanstead."

Sinclair laughed outright, though his gorge rose at the pair of them.

"Wanstead! I know of him. Started life as an architect's clerk, and then became a contractor. During the war was a food controller and amassed a fortune. After the war he became a speculative builder, and made another fortune during the boom. He first obtained a knighthood, then, passing through the baronet stage, bought himself a peerage, and entered the House of Lords. He was responsible for turning a large part of rural Essex into rows of suburban houses at so much down and the remainder by instalments. And this is the family whose social class the nephew must marry into."

To Sinclair's surprise Seften burst out laughing—the first laugh he had given.

"You have described him exactly. A snob and a bumptious profiteer."

Musgrave turned on him. "You ungrateful whelp. You forget he married my sister, and entered one of the best families in England, and having no children, he adopted you, a penniless brat, and brought you up as his heir."

Sinclair put an end to what promised to become an unseemly wrangle.

"I still can't see why there should be any objection to the marriage. Surely, Seften, you have a mind of your own."

Seften turned white, and something like horror leapt to his eyes.

"When my uncle heard of it he made me promise to leave the country and not see my wife for a year. It seemed reasonable at the time, and, to oblige him, I agreed. He said that he would provide for her, and you understand, Sir Arthur, I haven't a penny of my own. While we were away—Colonel Musgrave and I . . ." he faltered, and laid his head on the table between his hands.

There was a strange brooding silence in the room, and Sinclair scented tragedy as a dog the trail of a rabbit.

Musgrave gave a glance of contempt at the young man, and took up the tale, with a half-concealed sneer.

"While we were away Mrs. Seften was convicted of murdering her child—Seften's child—and then was reprieved. After two years, she was released."

"I remember the case," Sinclair said sternly. "The woman gave her maiden name, and refused to divulge that of her husband. She declared he had deserted her. I can well understand your wishing to suppress some of the facts."

Seften lifted his head, and his face had grown old. "There! Now you have the whole damned story. I knew nothing whatever about it. Colonel Musgrave kept me in wild places, and always on the move, and I learnt by accident, through seeing an old paper with the account in. My wife, I heard afterwards, had gone to my uncle, as she was penniless and expecting a child; he had her turned from the door."

"Ever since her release," Musgrave went on, glad to have got the story told, "she has been trying to get in touch with Seften. His uncle sent his lawyer, offering money, but she refused. She wanted recognition by her husband and for him to take her back after that."

"And so you think these attempts on his life were her doing?" Sinclair asked, restraining himself with difficulty.

"I feel sure of it. My opinion is that some men have got hold of her and are trying to force Seften to recognize her, and proclaim to all the world that she is his wife. One can easily see the object— one day he will be Lord Wanstead."

"You say you received threatening letters?"

"Before each attack, and now again, since we have come to London. This is the latest, which reached Seften at the Ordley, and caused me to write to you."

Musgrave took a paper from his pocket. "Typed in capitals, as the others were."

It was short and concise:

IF YOU DO NOT ACKNOWLEDGE YOUR WIFE AND TAKE HER BACK YOU WILL DIE

Sinclair scrutinized the note carefully. "Highly melodramatic. Were the others similar?"

"Practically the same," Seften said miserably. "You see, Sir Arthur, I would divorce her and give her her freedom, and my uncle would make her an allowance, but on what grounds? She has neither deserted me nor misbehaved herself morally. Then the whole wretched story would come out. She won't divorce me, and there's the deadlock."

"And what do you wish me to do in the matter?"

If Musgrave had known Sinclair better he would have sensed by the voice that a storm was coming, but he spoke eagerly.

"I thought if you would see this woman, and persuade her to drop this preposterous claim, and take a lump sum, the matter could be arranged. She would have to divorce him somewhere abroad without scandal, and, of course, drop these threats. They would both be free, then, to enjoy their lives."

The storm that had been gathering in Sinclair's brain burst out. He rose from his seat and faced the two astonished men.

"Seften, I give you one word of advice, and it is my last. I am sure you will not take it. If there is one spark of decency left in you after three years with this unmitigated scoundrel Musgrave, you will go to your wife and beg her pardon for your conduct. If she still cares for you, acknowledge her, and spend the rest of your life trying to make reparation. You will lose the money your uncle has so generously provided for both of you, and your future prospects will be ruined, but you may become a man."

He turned on the Colonel. "As for you, Musgrave, you are the evil genius who has caused this young man to leave his wife in the lurch. It's no good telling me you didn't know. It is, to my mind, a great pity that the strychnine did not do its work properly."

Musgrave's face went livid, and his eyes blazed with hate. "And you call yourself a detective, you rat!" he fairly screamed.

"I call myself a fairly clean-minded man, and if you don't get through that door at once I shall give myself the extreme pleasure of putting you out. Come! Pack off, both of you."

Musgrave's fists clenched, and his lips turned back like a wolf at bay. He was not lacking in physical courage, but his mind was master of his temper. He knew that a brawl might lead to the police courts, and then the whole beastly story would become public property.

He controlled himself with a desperate effort, and picked up his hat and stick.

"Come along, Seften; there is nothing further to be gained by talking to this person."

The door banged behind them, savagely. Sinclair helped himself to a whisky-and-soda, which he felt entitled to after such an interview, to get the taste out of his mouth.

He turned resolutely to his work, to get it from his mind, but the beastliness of the story stuck, and could not easily be dismissed.

Buggins knocked and entered quietly.

"A lady to see you, sir."

"Ah! Admit her." Sinclair was expecting this.

The woman herself entered closely behind the valet, and Sinclair rose and offered a seat with a feeling of sympathy.

She was exactly as he had pictured her. Tall and slim, with deep brooding eyes, but a firm mouth. There were traces of great beauty now obscured by overwhelming sorrow, which had stamped its marks in the lines on her face, and the grey hair. Her manner was quiet and grave; he judged her in the middle thirties, though she looked older.

"Forgive this intrusion." She spoke abruptly in a low voice. "You have just had two visitors. I followed them here, and have seen them go. One was my husband. Do you mind telling me who the other was?"

Sinclair saw no reason for screening the miscreant. "That was Colonel Musgrave."

"Ah!" she gave a gasp. "I thought I could not be mistaken."

"There is no need to tell me who you are, Mrs. Seften."

"I make no secret of my name. I am Rupert Seften's wife, and can prove it. I am not going to take up your time, Sir Arthur, and I don't wish to know what they have said behind my back. I married Rupert without knowing anything whatever about his family or prospects. I loved him, and that was sufficient, and I thought he loved me. He deserted me without so much as a line of writing, leaving me penniless. I had given up a good job to marry, but I could not take another—"

"You need not go any further," Sinclair said gently. "I know the rest. You did a fine generous act in suppressing his name."

She lifted her tortured eyes to the detective. "At my trial, you mean? I knew then that he was Lord Wanstead's nephew and heir, and it would ruin him."

"He was abroad at the time," Sinclair said musingly.

"He had been sent off by his uncle. What a cur! I only wanted our marriage recognized. I asked for no public announcement nor wished to interfere with his life. When I came out, Lord Wanstead sent his lawyer to say that they would give me money if I would give Rupert grounds for divorce, somewhere abroad, and free him." There was a world of scorn in her voice.

"Forgive me for asking rather an intimate question, but do you still love your husband?"

She answered passionately, "I wish to God I could say no, but that would not be true. I do love him. I suppose we women are all mad—I believe he would have come back to me if they had left him alone. But if Colonel Musgrave has got hold of him there is no chance of that."

"But why, then," Sinclair asked a little sternly, "did you try other methods, and threaten his life?"

Mrs. Seften opened her eyes wide and looked steadily at the detective. "Other means? I don't understand you. I have never communicated with Rupert or tried to do so since he left me. I have some pride left. The last thing I would do would be to make threats."

Sinclair could sense the utter sincerity of the woman. The greatest actress in the world could not have looked as she did. She was not only innocent, but completely puzzled at his accusation.

"Attempts have been made, and in each case a warning note was first sent."

"I know nothing about it. I did not even know where he was, and only knew he was at the Ordley because"—a red flush came to her worn face—"because I am employed there in a humble capacity."

"Then why did you come to me?"

"It was on the spur of the moment. I was afraid they would have asked you to get him out of the mess, as they would put it, and probably suggest that I was trying blackmail. I don't care what happens to me, but you can imagine what chance I should have with my record, if such a charge were brought."

Sinclair knew only too well, and an angry frown revealed his feelings.

"You can get that out of your head, Mrs. Seften. They would not face the publicity, for the whole story would come out, and the papers would make it front-page news."

"You may as well know the rest of my miserable story," Mrs. Seften broke out in a burst of confidence. "I married when I was seventeen, a runaway match, when I was little more than a child. I had one child, a girl, and then my husband divorced me on a trumped-up charge. I need not bother you with that. My life was over, as I thought, and I found a steady job in London. I dared not go home. Then I met Rupert. He was considerably younger than I, as you will have noticed, but he said that didn't matter. He lied to me almost from the first. He told me he was an engineer, and had a job abroad. Then he left me, and I have never seen him again till I recognized him at the Ordley Hotel, and heard him tell the taxi driver to go to you. I followed, hoping to be able to speak with him. It's all over now."

"You have suffered much. I will certainly see your husband and try to get him to see reason. By the way, what happened to your child by the first marriage?"

"My husband was awarded the custody; I never knew. I believe he had her sent to some institution."

"If I can do anything for you, I will do so with pleasure; never mind about money." He saw her hesitation.

"I am very grateful. The Ordley Hotel will find me, but I am there under my maiden name, Mary Rhodes. I could not bring myself to take another. I thought—oh, it's no good now—it was foolish of me, but somehow I always cherished the idea that perhaps Rupert would try to find me, and the police have my address."

She looked at him mistily, not far from tears, and rose abruptly.

"You have been very kind to me—the first kind words I have heard for such a long time. I shan't forget it."

When she had gone Sinclair paced the floor restlessly. The repulsiveness of Musgrave contrasted with the quiet dignity of this woman made a picture he could not get out of his mind.

The story was grim enough—stark reality from real life—but he was certain there was more behind it. The obvious explanation of these so-called attacks on Seften was that they had been engineered by Musgrave, but with what possible object? He paused in his walking. It seemed like killing the golden goose, but was it?

Musgrave was a poor man, and had been living in luxury at Lord Wanstead's expense. Perhaps he imagined that these threats would enable him to go on looking after Seften and drawing large sums from the uncle. He may have intended to extract sums which he could say he was passing on to Mrs. Seften.

At last he sat down, determined to dismiss the matter from his mind, for the time, at any rate.

On the following morning the matter was brought tragically to his notice. He was reading his morning's mail. There was a letter from Mary Rhodes.

Dear Sir Arthur [he read],

After leaving you I took a long walk, and threshed the whole matter out in my mind. After Rupert having consulted you, I am sure he will never come back to me. There is only one solution, and that rests with me. Rupert must have his freedom without any scandal or dragging his name into public. I can see it now. You must believe that I know nothing whatever about those threats to him. Perhaps they will cease at my death. It was good of you to treat me in such a kind manner. I have one request to make. I have destroyed everything that could possibly connect me with Rupert, and all my clothes are marked with this name. The past is buried and over, and when they drag my body from the Thames I ask you not to state what you know, and to burn this letter. Forget that you ever met me. I faced death in the condemned cell, and a living death in prison. My life has not been such that I mind losing it.

The letter was signed in a bold hand, *Mary Rhodes*.

That was all. Sinclair stared at the letter, and then picked up one of the daily papers on his table. A suitcase and coat had been found lying on the bank of the Thames near Greenwich, and later the body of a woman had been dragged from the river. By her clothes she had been identified as Mary Rhodes, and then, to Sinclair's disgust, the newshawk had let himself go. "This recalls the case", etc., and the story of her trial. Poor Mary—they would not let her rest in peace. But surely, if the dead have knowledge, she must have smiled to think that she had kept the real secret to the last, and saved the wretched man she had loved from a scandal that would have branded him as a cur and coward.

Sinclair attended the inquest, the verdict was a foregone conclusion with poor Mary's record. Neither Musgrave nor Seften appeared, as Sinclair expected they would be only too anxious to keep out of it.

The only witness was a brother, who came from Devonshire to identify the body. He was a dark, scowling man of immense strength and appeared to belong to the farmer class. His manner was reticent and almost sulky. Asked by the coroner when he had seen his sister last, he muttered that she had left home at the age of seventeen, and that he had neither seen nor heard anything of her since then. Seeing an account in the papers he had come up to Town. His manner was secretive, and Sinclair, who had a keen sense of summing up character, felt that the man was holding himself in with difficulty, and that a few more questions would have caused him to explode into some revelation that would have startled the court and brought the listless reporters to sudden attention.

The coroner was not observant, and the case was plain and sordid.

He let Rhodes go with a word of sympathy, and he stumbled out of the box, and disappeared before Sinclair could get a word with him.

That was all; but Sinclair could not get the story out of his head. He looked up the history of the Musgraves. They had lived at Cantire for generations, since the time of the Spanish Armada in fact. Gradually they had become poorer. A proud family, they had scorned all form of trade, and clung to the land. The demesne had shrunk in size, as field and meadow had to be sold off, till nothing remained of the once fine estate but the castle, now in ruins, and a small wood and patch of kitchen garden surrounding it. It was a common enough tale in these days. For the best part of a hundred years the castle had been unoccupied. Richard Musgrave, father of Anthony and his sister Julia, had, the account told him, committed suicide in the castle, in direst poverty.

Anthony, according to the family tradition, had gone into the Army, and Julia had married Sir John Seften, afterwards created Lord Wanstead—'for public and social services.'

Then Anthony Musgrave had retired from the Service with the rank of Colonel, and had made an abortive attempt to restore the castle for some reason. This was abandoned, and he had installed caretakers, and charged fees for admission, sufficient to pay the rates and the salaries of the old couple.

Sinclair did not obtain all this at the time, but it is convenient to give it here.

Two days later, as he sat at breakfast, Sinclair was startled out of his habitual calm by an astounding piece of news, and dashed off to catch the Riviera express.

CHAPTER II

MURDER IN THE CHAPEL

MRS. CAMPION STIRRED in her bed. The wind was making such a noise round the ruin of Cantire that it was hard to sleep.

She could hear the trees lashing against the high walls outside, like angry waves against a cliff. Her husband was sleeping quietly through it all, snoring a little at times. The walls of the old castle were too thick to give even a quiver, but the windows rattled like chattering teeth. A more than usually violent gust made her frightened. There was no reason for it. For three years she and Campion had acted as caretakers for the place, ever since Colonel Musgrave had gone abroad, and there had been storms in plenty. But this night there was an ominous sound—as though fiends were at play. She had half a mind to wake Campion, but he would be cross. She lay awake and clenched her gnarled hands. It was impossible that anyone should be about in the castle, and yet she seemed to hear noises and footsteps. Nerves, it must be!

The massive doors were shut fast, and the forty-foot walls were hard to climb. And as she sought the sleep that would not come, there came to her mind the scenes this wicked old place had witnessed. Revels and lovemaking in plenty, and murders too, if the guide-book spoke the truth.

She dozed at last, and the bed creaked as old Campion turned uneasily in his sleep.

A shriek of mortal agony rent the night above the howling of the gale—one wild desperate cry, and then silence. Campion sat up, scratching his head.

"What be that—I heard a cry somewhere, or was it the wind?"

"John—something has happened."

"Must have been outside." He hit his pillow and prepared to lie down again.

She shook him roughly. "It weren't then. 'Twas inside the castle, I tell 'ee. Someone's been murdered."

"I better go and see, then."

The old man rolled out of bed and lit a lamp. He searched for his slippers grumblingly, and then took an old dressing-gown from the back of the door.

"Don't go, John; don't 'ee go. I be fair scared."

"We be paid to look after the castle, ain't we?" he answered doggedly, and took an ancient shot-gun from the corner.

There was a patter of feet, and the door was flung open. A young girl burst into the room, a thin elfin child with a very scanty nightdress reaching barely to her knees. Her eyes were wild and staring, and the black hair swept round her none too clean face.

"What was that," she cried, "an awful yell—somewhere in the court?"

She leapt into her mother's bed and covered up under the old patched quilt.

"I be going to see," Campion growled, and they heard his footsteps stamping across the stone floor of the inner court. He threw round the light of an electric torch he carried, but there was nothing there. The inner court was roofless and the rain swirled round him as he crossed to the further side, and pushed open a rough oaken door leading to the chapel.

The glassless windows let in the driving rain, and the storm raged through the place through a great open rent in the walls where the west door had once stood.

Campion cast the light round the place, but, as far as he could see, it was empty. He was about to continue his search when, happening to cast his torch upwards, he stood stock-still, and horror made his hair rise.

The figure of a man was hanging from a rope, and the body swayed and turned in the wind. The feet were six feet or more from the floor, and he could dimly make out the rope passing into the cavernous darkness above.

A mist rose before his eyes, and his throat went suddenly dry.

He advanced fearfully towards the body, when a single word "Stop!" brought him up sharply. Fear held him spellbound.

"Put out that torch, or you are a dead man."

Campion obeyed instantly.

"You will remain here for ten minutes, and then return to your room. Any attempt to raise an alarm will result in your death."

The old man's mind was fogged; he could not think collectedly. The weird scene in the chapel, and that grisly thing swinging overhead, as though enjoying some devil's joke, combined to have a numbing effect. He sank to his knees in abject terror, incapable of movement.

It seemed hours to him before a faint call came from across the inner court. His wife was calling urgently. Campion started, and taking his torch from the floor, stumbled to his feet. He saw his wife at the entrance to their rooms holding a flickering lamp.

"What's the matter?" she screamed above the storm.

Campion staggered across the court, and up the short flight of stone steps flecked by the rain. He shut and locked the door, and sank down in a chair.

"Murder!" he managed to gasp.

The girl, Elsie, opened her eyes wide, and stared at him. Breathing heavily he recited his tale.

"We must get the police," he muttered, half crazed.

"Not on a night like this, my man," Mrs. Campion said firmly. "Like as not the murdering blackguard will be waiting for you."

"It's nigh on two mile to the village," Campion said slowly, "and a pesky bad night to be sure. But I can't leave that hanging in the chapel."

"You're doing nothing till the morning, Campion, and you can take that from me."

The old man shrugged his shoulders. He glanced at the window where the storm was driving the rain like pistol-shots against the panes. Elsie was watching him closely.

"Who was it, Daddy?" she asked in a whisper.

"I dunno! I couldn't rightly see, and t'other took darned good care I shouldn't see 'un."

"It was the Black Abbot," Elsie declared confidently.

The old couple exchanged glances. "You lie down, my gal, and don't meddle with what don't concern you. There's no such person."

"But, Daddy, I've heard you telling visitors about him. All in black you said, and he jumped out of dark places."

"That's for the visitors," Campion growled. "Isn't there a drop of the whisky that gentleman left here still in the flask?"

Mrs. Campion rose and fetched a large flask from a cupboard, and Campion poured himself out a liberal dose. "My nerves is all o' a jump," he said in excuse.

Campion furtively picked up the flask, and moved to the sitting-room, where he poked the embers into a flame.

"There'll be no more sleep for us tonight," he said heavily.

Mrs. Campion got into the bed with Elsie. "Lie down and go to sleep, child," she said, as Elsie sat up.

"Can't we go and have a look, and see who it is?" she asked, greatly daring.

"Certainly not. Lie down, I tell you."

The dawn came at last, but no cessation of the storm—the worst for years. A faint light filtered through the corners of the ill-fitting curtains, and Mrs. Campion set about making tea. Her husband was sleeping in an armchair, and she did not waken him until the tea was ready.

He dressed slowly, and washed himself crudely in the scullery.

"Better go out by the postern," his wife said. "I shan't open the main gate till you come back."

The old man nodded; he looked dubiously at his shot-gun, and then, picking up a stout cudgel, went out, clothed in an old mackintosh.

He was wet through when he arrived at the 'Green Man' at the village of Barton. Grimes, the landlord, was staring out at the driving rain, thinking gloomily that no one would come that way on a day like this. He saw old Campion hurrying up with unusual activity, and waving his stick.

"Summut's up," he muttered, and went to the door.

As he listened to the tale his eyes grew large and round. He rose from the bench on which he was sitting, and drew cider for both. He felt the situation called for some refreshment.

"Constable Ted Bolt be over at Payning with Sergeant Haddon—best call up there. He'll likely come in his car."

"You call up, Sam—you understand them telephones." Grimes, feeling the importance of the occasion, went to the 'phone, and got through.

"What's that you say? Tell Campion to come to the phone."

Campion began his story, but the voice at the other end cut him short. "Murder? I'll come at once. Wait there for me."

"That be Sergeant Haddon," Campion said when he returned to his seat. "He be powerful short in his way o' speaking."

A quarter of an hour later a car drove up to the door. Sergeant Haddon was a stocky red-faced officer, country born and bred, and not over-gifted with brains. A murder was a rare occurrence in these parts, and he felt the importance of the occasion

Ted Bolt, the local constable, was driving the car, a brawny countryman of few words.

Grimes led them inside from the storm, and poured out cider for both.

"Let's have your yarn," Haddon said, stretching his feet out to the blaze.

"My wife be mighty anxious and worried, Sergeant, being all alone."

"A few minutes won't make any difference, and I 'phoned for the Inspector from Exeter. This is too tough a job for me. Mind, I ought to speak severely to you about the delay in reporting this matter. You should have come at once and knocked Grimes up."

"It were a wicked night," the old man mumbled in apology.

Campion had finished his story when the Inspector arrived. He was a youngish man, recently from London. Tall, spare and with a black moustache and keen eyes, he formed a complete contrast with the local officers. He greeted Haddon with a cheery nod.

"Came over as fast as I could in this beastly weather. A case of murder, eh? Well, we had better get to the castle at once."

He looked with disapproval at the empty glasses on the table.

As they entered the long drive to the old ruin the grim old building stood before them, lowering in the heavy gusts of rain that nearly blotted it out.

The entrance to the drive had once been through a gateway with rooms on each side, but one of these had fallen down, and the other was blocked up and in a state of decay. Part of the arch that crowned the gate at one time, was showing, perilously overhanging the entrance. The gates swung drearily on their hinges.

Cantire was a strange edifice, really more of a fortified manor house than a proper castle. It was a product of the time when castles were obsolescent, and before the unguarded country mansion had come into fashion.

The English Channel was near, and war with France almost continuous. Raids were frequent, and had to be met adequately.

Two strong towers stood at the north and south corners, connected by a high crenelated wall, with machicolations. In the centre was a square tower in which was the main gate, with a portcullis above. A high wall surrounded house and garden at the sides and back. Mere loop-holes showed on the ground floor, but the windows above were large and covered by iron grilles.

The place was not suited for a siege or sustained attack, but was strong enough to repel a raiding party, and form a refuge and rallying place for the peasants when an enemy appeared.

The chapel was on the right, by the side of the north tower, and on the left, glass in the windows indicated the rooms occupied by the Campions. And here was a small but massive postern door.

The castle had never been sacked or burned, but had merely fallen into decay, so that the walls were intact, but the roofs had for the most part fallen down, and the windows looked like empty sockets in a skull. Seen in the rain and under leaden skies, Cantire was depressing. Mrs. Campion had evidently been on the look-out, for the postern door opened as the cars drew up.

This door led into a narrow lane between the castle itself and the outer wall. A solid low door, heavily studded with nails, led into the castle, and winding stairs took them to the Campions' rooms. As the castle was unoccupied, these caretakers' apartments were larger and loftier than any lodge. The woman had done some tidying up, and the place was unusually clean and neat.

Campion offered chairs. Inspector Gillian turned to Mrs. Campion.

"Will you please tell me exactly what happened in your own words, before we go into the chapel. I take it that no one has been there since your husband left."

"Oh no, sir!"

Gillian listened intently while the woman told her tale until she mentioned Elsie's strange fancy. "What's all this about a Black Abbot?" he asked.

Haddon smiled. "An old wives' fable, sir. You always get them in these places, and it helps to interest the visitors."

"All the same, I would like to hear it," Gillian said, turning to Campion.

The old man recounted the story, as he had done many times to visitors. "It's like this, sir. They do say there was a monastery here, afore Cantire was built, and old Henry the Eighth who, as you know, sir, had many wives, and bust up the monasteries, gave this one to a Musgrave, who pulled down the place and built the castle on the same spot, and they do say with the same stones. Some say he murdered the Abbot, and for sure no one ever seed his body. That's where the legend comes from. He is said to have cursed the family, and has regularly appeared to one of them when about to die."

"Stuff and nonsense!" Haddon declared noisily.

"I don't know; sometimes these old legends are of interest," Gillian said seriously.

"Anything more?"

"Well, sir, I do know that when old Mr. Richard died—that were the father of the Colonel who owns the place now—the Abbot came for him. Leastwise," he added hastily, as he saw Haddon's amused face, "that's what they say, though crowner did bring it in suicide for sure."

"One moment," Gillian said. "Surely this place hadn't been occupied for a great number of years."

Old Campion exchanged glances with his wife, and he saw a frown of warning on her face.

"No more it had, sir, but Mr. Richard, like all the Musgraves, was a daredevil, and he insisted on sleeping in the chapel for what he called the fun of the thing. In a camp-bed it were, and they found him dead in the morning, hanging on a rope from a beam in the chapel, and no sign on him, but he was covered over with a cloak—all black—and some professor who came down from Lunnon said it were an Abbot's cloak of the time of the Spanish Armada. No one knew properly why he died."

"All that is most interesting, but I hardly see how it can have any bearing on this murder," Gillian remarked. "We had better go to the chapel, eh, Haddon?"

"I think so, sir," the sergeant said scornfully. He had no use for fairy stories.

"Lead on, then, exactly the same way as you went last night."

Old Campion obeyed, and conducted them down five steps into the inner court, between the towering outer walls in front, and inner ones as high, making a veritable death-trap for any enemy who broke through the massive main gate. In one corner was a table sheltered by a pent roof, whereon were booklets containing the history and plan of the castle, and a visitors' book. Gillian scrutinized the latter sharply.

"No entries yesterday, I see."

"No, sir, none—it were a terribly bad day."

"And is that main gate kept open or shut?"

"We generally keeps it open when one of us is here to see to things; but when no one is here, we shuts it, and visitors have to ring a large bell outside."

"And yesterday? Be careful to remember."

"It were open part of the day, but either me or the missus or our daughter was in this court. When the storm came on, we shut 'un."

They proceeded along the inner court and came to the door leading to the chapel, standing open, as Campion had left it when he fled.

The old man hesitated, but Gillian pushed past him, and entered the dim place. The body still hung from the beam; the head sagging down at a ghastly angle. Gillian spoke sharply.

"Stay exactly where you are, Campion; we don't want any footprints more than we can avoid. Where was the murderer when he spoke to you?"

"I can't exactly tell, sir; somewhere behind me. But I daresn't look, and I were that scared—"

"All right. Hello! Sergeant, there's something here out of the ordinary."

He pointed to the rough uneven floor by the ruined stone altar. The remains of a fire were clearly visible on the ground, white ash and charred sticks. Gillian approached the spot and placed his hand on the ashes. "Warm still. It must have been alight when Campion came in."

"Unless it was lit after he had gone," Haddon observed.

"That is possible, but hardly probable. The murderer would want to make a break as soon as he had silenced Campion by his threats."

"Hadn't we better get that thing down?" Haddon suggested, with a motion of his finger to the grisly thing above them.

"One moment. It can't hurt him, poor devil. I want to have a look first. There are several cigarette-ends in the ashes and round about; bad shots at the fire, I suppose."

Haddon pointed. "There are several here, sir, by the side of the wall, and there is tobacco ash too."

"Someone has been sitting here," Gillian added, "and, if I am not mistaken, on a piece of sacking. On the rubble and sand there is the distinct mark that canvas makes when pressed down."

Further examination revealed four such places, each with telltale cigarette-ends and grease marks, as though from a candle that had gutted in the draught.

Some ghastly scene had been enacted here.

"There were four of them at least," Haddon said in a whisper. The gruesome place overawed him, with the strange moaning of the wind, and that thing swinging above.

"All these must be photographed, and here are footmarks."

The floor was of paving stones, but in places these had been removed, and sand and small stones had drifted into the spaces.

A rough wooden staircase, with a handrail for support, caught Gillian's attention. "What's that for?" he asked sharply.

"There's a room up there, sir, they call the Monks' Room," Campion started glibly. "There is an old winding stairway to it in the north tower, opening just outside the chapel, but it is very worn and damaged so that staircase was erected for the convenience of visitors."

"We'd better have a look," Gillian said; "we have to go up those stairs in any case." He pointed to the rope above them.

One single oak beam crossed the chapel, the only one that remained, but the corbels showed where the others had once been. Over this beam, the rope by which the unfortunate man had been suspended, crossed, and the end was fastened to the top of the handrail.

Gillian ascended gingerly, and he and Haddon examined the Monks' Room. A cursory glance was sufficient. The chapel occupied two stories in height, and the entrance to the chamber was half-way up. Evidently at one time there had been merely an oriel looking into the chapel.

The room itself was dimly lighted, and not large. The walls had been defaced, and the facing stones removed for building purposes. In one corner was a narrow arched door leading to the spiral staircase of which Campion had spoken.

"Better get this down, sir," Haddon remarked gruffly. He did not understand why Gillian had left the body hanging so long; it seemed almost indecent to him. He unfastened the rope with some difficulty, and the sudden jerk nearly tore it through his hands. Gillian seized it, and together they lowered the corpse to the floor, where it subsided in a heap, a ghastly travesty of a Guy Fawkes or a scarecrow.

Old Campion, who had remained by the door, according to orders, gave one stare at the object, and then let off a yell that echoed through the place.

"What's the matter with the old fool?" Haddon said as he hastened down the stairs. Campion did not appear to hear. He had come forward, and was gazing at the still form on the ground with a look of something more than horror.

"Lord, ha' mercy!" he muttered in a shaky voice. "It's Colonel Musgrave himself!"

Haddon bent down and then straightened himself. "He's right, sir. I remember him well. That's Colonel Musgrave, the owner of the place."

Gillian turned sharply on Campion. "Did you know he was here?"

"No, sir, on my Bible oath, we b'ain't set eyes on him for three year or more. We all thought he were abroad."

The face was purple and swollen, and the eyes half protruded from their sockets. But it was not at the face that Gillian looked. On the coat, an old shooting-jacket, a piece of paper was roughly pinned. He stooped down to read the words in the dim light.

"Look at that, Haddon—don't touch."

In typed capital letters was the following

THIS IS NOT MURDER. IT IS AN EXECUTION ON ONE WHOM THE LAW CANNOT PUNISH. HE DESERVED THE FATE THAT HAS BEEN METED OUT TO HIM, AND HAS HAD A PROPER TRIAL.

That was all—there was no signature or ending.

"Melodrama!" Gillian said contemptuously. "The sort of thing one used to read in the old penny dreadfuls."

"There were four of them did it," Haddon said gravely.

"How the devil did they get out of the place?" Gillian commented angrily. "That's the more important thing. Is there any other means of exit beside the main and postern gates?"

"None at all, sir—they must 'a' climbed the wall." Old Campion was shaking with fear and cold.

Gillian issued his orders. "Sergeant, take the car, and go to Payning. Fetch a doctor—though that is merely a matter of form—and a photographer, and bring them here as quickly as you can. At the same time you can order the police ambulance, and inform my H.Q. at Exeter. We've nothing to go on at present, but the roads must be watched for strangers, and inquiries made. I expect that wretched landlord has spread the news already, and we shall have a lot of pressmen here. They are not to be admitted—do you understand, Campion?"

The old man said he did, and hobbled off to let Haddon out, and lock the door behind him.

"I shall have a look round."

When Campion returned he found Gillian examining the visitors' book.

"Tell me," he said sternly, "how long was it between the time you heard that cry and when you got to the chapel?"

Campion thought about a quarter of an hour.

"Come with me and show me over the place, then."

Inspector Gillian was not satisfied until he had completely examined the castle and the small garden within the frowning walls. He searched the old dungeons below the castle, and ascended the spiral stairs in every one of the towers, but not a trace could he find of any visitors.

The forty-foot walls could only be climbed with a very long ladder, and the trees grew close outside, making it almost impossible to get such a ladder into position. Gillian was very thorough in his methods, and knew he had an important case here. The Musgraves had borne a great name in the county in the past.

Haddon returned in the afternoon with the doctor and photographer. The former could merely pronounce that the man was dead, which anyone could see, and that death, so far as he could tell, was due to strangulation by hanging. The rest would be for the post-mortem.

The photographer got busy with camera and flashpan. Haddon had brought provisions with him, and he and Gillian made a late lunch.

The ambulance had come and gone with its grim burden, and the doctor and photographer had packed up and departed. Gillian and Haddon were sitting in the Campions' room, discussing the affair, when a loud knock came at the front gate and the bell jangled noisily.

Several pressmen were hanging around, and Bolt had been stationed in the inner court with orders to admit no one.

"Damn the fellow!" Gillian said, as the ringing continued. Silence fell, and then they heard footsteps approaching, and Ted Bolt came in with a man following him, at the sight of whom Gillian sprang to his feet with a cry of astonishment.

"Sir Arthur Sinclair! Whatever brings you here, sir?"

In his early days at the Yard he had both heard of, and seen, the great detective, and an uneasy feeling came to him Sinclair had come to take charge of the case.

The first words reassured him.

"I must apologize for intruding," Sinclair said with a smile. "I came down here as soon as I heard of the murder, but entirely for private reasons, you understand. I shall not interfere with your work, Inspector, but I am interested in the case."

CHAPTER III

SINCLAIR TAKES A HAND

SMOKING BY THE FIRE, Sinclair listened intently to the tale as Gillian retailed it. Swift retribution had fallen on Musgrave, and Sinclair could hardly bring himself to feel any deep sorrow at his death, awful though the end had been. The terror he had seen on the man's face during the interview had been real enough.

"What do you make of it, Sir Arthur?" Gillian brought him back from his thoughts. "I am not altogether satisfied with the Campions' story. They know more than they will tell, I fancy."

"His story, as far as it goes, holds water, but I'll have a talk with him presently. There is only one point about it that is suggestive. A man does not utter a shriek when he is being hanged. He might have shouted before, but his enemies would have gagged him. I could understand it with a knife-thrust, or some other method of murder, but when a rope is suddenly pulled tight . . . It's strange, and suggestive. You say Campion states that only a quarter of an hour elapsed before he got to the chapel."

Gillian could not quite follow Sinclair's line of thought, but he knew better than to say so.

"Have you wired to the next of kin?" Sinclair asked. "I understand that his sister married Lord Wanstead, as he is now."

"We haven't had time for anything. I must do so, of course. And I suppose I shall have to give something out to the Press. If I don't, they will make up their own story from village gossip."

"Don't make it too sensational. Plenty of time for that later on, perhaps. This Musgrave's father committed suicide in that chapel."

Haddon started. "You knew that, sir? That is a fact, but there are some strange rumours going about."

"Tosh!" Gillian said impatiently. "What would you expect with an old ruined castle, full of legends and superstitions? Of course you'll get rumours. The Black Abbot, a man of gigantic strength, seized him by the hair and dragged him down to hell. We don't want that sort of stuff here."

Sinclair was watching Gillian carefully. "Why so much heat, Inspector? I rather think that you do think there may be something in the rumours."

Gillian laughed uneasily. "It's a depressing sort of place, and I wouldn't care for the job of caretaker myself, I must say."

"I would like to see the chapel," Sinclair said, having gained all the information he required.

They entered the place, less gloomy now that the corpse had been removed, but still far from cheerful.

Sinclair took a quick survey of the place, and went up the winding stair that led to the Monks' Room, instead of by the new staircase. He was some time gone, and when he descended he was covered in dust and dirt. "A nasty place; I would not care to go there at night. The stair ends in the air, where the top of the tower has fallen down. Anyone might fall over without proper care." He was dusting his knees while he spoke, and the two officers failed to detect a certain note of satisfaction in his voice.

His quick brain and trained eyes could see further than the others.

"What's this?" Sinclair went to the corner of the chapel behind the wooden staircase. A huge block of stone had either been detached or fallen from somewhere. Gillian was annoyed that he had not noticed it. By itself it was of no great importance, but Sinclair pointed to a great iron staple, deeply embedded in the stone. It was either for fixing purposes or something had in old days been fastened to it.

"I begin to see how this murder was committed," Sinclair said thoughtfully. The others remained in respectful silence.

"I may be imagining the scene, and be quite wrong. But if the rope had been fastened to this staple and passed over the beam, and the end of the rope afterwards tied to the rail, as a 'blind'—"

"You mean," Gillian said excitedly, "that stone could have been on the steps, and a push would have sent it over, and lifted anything on the other end of the rope?"

"Exactly," Sinclair said grimly; "and if the other thing happened to be a living man, caught in the noose, he would be lifted from the ground and hanged without bother."

"Of course, that is most ingenious, sir," Gillian remarked, "but I don't quite see how it helps our problem."

"It helps materially. Musgrave was a strong man, and would take some overpowering, even if unarmed, which is improbable. Your idea is that there were several men here, and the cigarette-ends and fire bear that out. But that may be all bluff, deliberately staged, and to hide the real fact—that Musgrave was tricked—and that might have been by one man, or even a woman, for the stone had merely to be pushed over."

"But how could Musgrave's head have been caught in the rope?" Haddon asked stubbornly. He did not like theories, being a plain man.

"The place was in darkness," Sinclair continued, as though telling a tale. "Musgrave comes down those stairs one hand on the rail, and perhaps holding a torch to light the way. Someone is behind him. The noose is dropped over his head, and at the same moment the stone is kicked or pushed."

"That's rather fanciful, sir, isn't it?" Gillian said.

"It may be absolutely wrong," Sinclair said calmly, "but I knew a case almost exactly similar to this, and that was the method employed. It is certainly worth bearing in mind, because in that case the question of the so-called trial and the difficulty of several men getting away does not exist. The murderer may not have got away at all."

The chapel was growing dark, and strange shadows crept about the walls. Sergeant Haddon suddenly felt cold, and shivered.

"I ought to be getting back to Payning," he muttered.

"And I must drive to Exeter," Gillian added briskly. "Can I give you a lift, Sir Arthur? We can't do any more tonight."

"I am going to have a talk with the Campions; I have my own car, a hired one, waiting for me,"

Old Campion let the police officers out by the postern. As they stood talking by their cars Haddon spoke of Sinclair: "Bit balmy in his theories, isn't he?"

"Don't you believe it," Gillian replied. "He's got more brain than you and I put together and doubled. He's seen something we haven't, you may depend on it. He speaks as though he *knows* something. Well, I must get off."

Sinclair followed Campion to his sitting-room, where a cheery fire burned.

Mrs. Campion and Elsie rose at his entrance, and Sinclair shook hands with them, putting them at their ease at once.

"This is our daughter Elsie," Mrs. Campion said; "our only child,"

Sinclair stole a glance at the peasant and his gawkish wife, and a curious expression came to his face.

He sat by the fire and lit his pipe, as the old man was smoking.

"I don't mind telling you, Campion," he opened, "you were nearer your death last night than you will ever be till your time comes."

"Lord, sir, were it as bad as all that?"

"I fully believe that if you had not obeyed that order instantly, you would have been killed." He watched the old man's wrinkled face as he spoke.

"I was fair mazed up, sir, and hardly knew what I was doing."

"This was not a common murder for gain, or the work of a madman. The murderer—or as Inspector Gillian thinks, murderers—wanted one man, and they got him. They spared you, because there was nothing against you. Let me advise you not to meddle, or there will be something against you. Is that quite plain?"

Sinclair spoke as though talking to a small child, then his tone changed. "Now tell me what you know."

"I know nothing, sir. I told the Inspector so."

"I am not an inspector, Campion, and not connected with the police force now. When did you see Colonel Musgrave last?"

"We ain't set eyes on him for three year. That's Bible truth, sir."

Sinclair always got on with children. They trusted him at once; and when the party had sat round the fire, he had thrown a cushion on the floor with a smiling invitation to Elsie. She was sitting there, glad enough for the warmth, and leaning her back against Sinclair's knees.

At the question Sinclair felt Elsie's body quiver and stiffen. Slight as it was, it told him what he wanted to know.

"And you are sure you can't tell me any incident, however small, that might have some bearing on the case?"

The old man shook his head. "Nothing, sir. Yesterday, being such a dirty day, we had no visitors at all. We fastened up the door about four, weren't it, Elsie?"

"Who locked the door?"

"Well, sir, as a matter of fact I did," Campion said slowly, as though on guard. "Elsie had stayed out in the court, just to see whether anyone did come, and I was having a cup of tea with the missus. Then Elsie called out to know whether she should shut the door, and I went out and did it. 'Tis a heavy door for a young girl to close for sure."

"A funny thing happened to me some time ago," Elsie said hurriedly—just a little bit too hurriedly—as though she wanted to change the subject.

"The gentleman won't be interested with that foolish story," Mrs. Campion said brusquely.

"On the contrary, I am interested with everything connected with this old castle."

"It was only Elsie had a bad dream, and it frightened her."

"It wasn't a bad dream then," the girl declared stubbornly.

"Let me have it—there is nothing here to frighten you.

The lamp had not been lit, and the firelight cast ghostly shadows on the wall. Whatever fate befell the Campions, it would be a good thing to get a young girl away from this crime-haunted place.

"It was about three weeks ago," Elsie began in a dreamy voice. "I was fast asleep, and the moonlight was shining in the room. I woke up, and saw a man standing there. He was dressed all in black, and had a kind of hood over his head."

Campion gave a rather forced laugh. "Of course, sir, she'd heard all about the Black Abbot that is supposed to haunt this place before a Musgrave dies. It had got on her nerves and she imagined it."

Elsie hid her head on Sinclair's knee and sobbed silently. "Don't go on if you would rather not."

"They don't believe me, sir."

"I do; and I want to hear."

"There was nothing else. I thought he was going to murder me, like the Princes in the Tower."

"That's where it all came from," Mrs. Campion said triumphantly; "she had been learning about that at her school, and it had got on her mind."

"I would like to hear the end," Sinclair said, stroking the girl's unruly hair.

"I couldn't see very much, but he was feeling round the room, and then I could have shrieked, for he came to the bed and pulled the bedclothes down, and I felt his hand at my throat. But he only took off my locket from my neck and then replaced the bedclothes and went out silently."

"So he took a locket?" Sinclair said thoughtfully.

Mrs. Campion broke in: "She found it in the ruins by the north tower, when they were doing some excavations, and asked if she might keep it. It was gold, and had the crest of the Musgraves on it. I believe the child lost it, and made up this tale to account for it. She is not truthful."

Old Campion slowly removed his pipe. "We were going to ask the Colonel whether she might keep it, if he ever came back. I expect he would have given it to her."

Sinclair felt Elsie suddenly straighten her back, and she looked quickly at her parents. He also saw a hard challenging look in the old woman's rheumy eyes. He was sure she was lying.

"Well," he said, "it's a queer story, but I expect there is some explanation. Meanwhile, Elsie, I should try to forget it, if I were you. Nothing has happened since, I suppose?"

"You may well ask that," the old man grumbled. "Ever since, the girl has taken to sleep-walking. I found her wandering in the court in her nightdress. There's no telling where she might get to—like as not break her neck. I've thrashed her till I'm tired of it."

"You ought to be ashamed of yourself," Sinclair said indignantly; "you could be sent to prison for that."

"I didn't hit her hard, sir," Campion protested hastily; "just to stop that nonsense."

"I should have thought the best thing would have been to lock her door," Sinclair said deliberately, watching the two faces before him.

"She made such a fuss about it, or I would have done. She has a silly notion that the man she fancied she saw, came in through the window, and she was afraid of being locked in."

This was becoming interesting, and called for further investigation. The old man slowly got to his feet and lit the oil lamp, with apologies for his forgetfulness.

The light gradually grew bright as the wick caught, and the room was illuminated. Elsie would have sprung up, but Sinclair placed his hands gently on her shoulders.

"You'll have a cup of tea, sir?" Mrs. Campion asked, more cheerful in the light.

"Thank you, I would like one," Sinclair said.

"I must just go and see that everything is fastened up," Campion said. "Excuse me, sir." He shambled out, while his wife went into the tiny kitchenette supplied with an oil stove.

Sinclair leant down and spoke to Elsie, and the girl turned her face, flushed with the fire, towards him.

"Aren't you afraid to sleep without your door being locked?"

Something in the simple words made the girl flush a deeper red. "No, sir, not now," she answered.

"You mean since the murder," he persisted, perplexed by her manner. "Yes, sir. I don't mind now. It's all over."

Mrs. Campion bustled in. "Now then, lazybones, get up and lay the cloth," she said sharply.

The girl rose, eagerly, as Sinclair fancied, and busied herself. Sinclair drank a cup of tea, but refused food. "I must get off," he told them.

"I'll let you out by the postern door." Campion rose as he spoke. "The missus and I are grateful, sir, for your coming to see us in this friendly way. We be simple folk."

There was a tone of relief in the peasant's voice that was not lost on Sinclair.

He shook hands with them, thanking Mrs. Campion for the tea. Elsie's hand, in spite of the fire, was icy cold, and there was a frightened look in her large dark eyes.

The night outside was clear after the storm, which had subsided with sunset. The moon was full, and flooded the drive with light.

The car was standing forlornly where Sinclair had left it, and as he heard the postern door being locked behind him, he glanced up at the high walls, black in the shadow.

There was now no means of getting into the castle, as far as one could tell, by door or window, for Elsie's, as he knew, opened on to the alley-way by the postern.

Sinclair determined to do a little exploring by himself, before the police got busy the next day.

A narrow track led past the castle wall, close to the postern gate, which went to the small patch of kitchen garden behind, which old Campion cultivated. On one side was the towering wall in one unbroken line forty feet in height, without window or loop-hole. The thick undergrowth crowded close, leaving barely room to pass.

Sinclair was about to proceed down the path when a man stepped from the bushes and stood looking at him in the bright moonlight. The light shone full on his face, and Sinclair knew him at once. The massive shoulders and scowling brow betrayed him.

He greeted Sinclair with a surly grunt, looking him up and down with an insolent stare.

"You're a stranger in these parts," he said in a deep voice.

"Just a visitor," Sinclair said with a smile. "Having a look round the old place."

"You've chosen a funny time for that," the man growled. "You've just come out of the castle, haven't you?"

"Yes; I have been having tea with the Campions."

"Humph! Tell me, mister—I heard in the village. They tell me that damned scoundrel Musgrave has been murdered." He gave a hollow laugh as though the matter were a joke.

"He was murdered last night."

"Thank the Lord! I'd like to shake hands with the man who did it!"

There was intense fury in the man's voice, a fury of maniacal hate.

"Your name is Rhodes," Sinclair said quietly.

The man drew back into the shadows as though he had received a blow. "What the hell's that got to do with you? Who the devil are you?"

"My name is Sinclair, but that would convey nothing to you."

Rhodes advanced with his huge fists clenched. "If you're a friend of that swine, I'll swipe you."

"Stop that nonsense, and don't you dare to threaten me," Sinclair said sternly. "I have only seen the man once in my life, and took a hearty dislike to him."

"I'm sorry, mister, but if you had known him you would feel as I do."

"Perhaps I do. I was at the inquest on your sister, Mr. Rhodes, and saw you there."

Rhodes stepped out into the moonlight, and raised both hands above his head, a gesture more potent than any words.

"You see me here," he said after a pause, and in a subdued voice, "a rough sort of customer, and not over respectable, they will tell you. Once I had a tidy farm, and we come of a good country stock. My sister was the only one—there were just her and me . . . She went off to London when she was seventeen without so much as a word, except a line to say she had got a job. We never heard another word from her for years. It killed my father, and Mother was dead already. I see it in the papers. She was on trial for murdering her kid. I went and saw her in prison, and I sold the farm to pay for her defence. Poor lass, it didn't do her any good."

"Did you know the name of the father of the child?"

"Mary wouldn't tell me—she refused to tell the court. But I have my own ideas about that." He brought one huge fist with a crash on the other.

"You were upset, of course, at her death," Sinclair said sympathetically.

"I feared it would happen some day. She was ashamed to come home, and would not let me look after her, as I would have done. I lost touch with her, and when she came out of prison they let her out privately, and I never knew till I asked about visiting her."

"I am very sorry. You must have had a terrible time. When was the last time you saw Colonel Musgrave?"

Sinclair shot the question at him, and watched his face.

"I haven't seen him for three years; not since he cleared out of here, and pretty quick too."

"Why did he go when he had started to restore the place, from what I have been told?"

Rhodes gave a sardonic laugh. "Ask him yourself—he's in the mortuary."

He turned abruptly, and forced his way through the woods in a sort of blind passion, making no attempt to avoid the undergrowth.

Sinclair watched him go. Here was a new complication. If ever a man had cause for murder this man had, and Heaven help the person who came into his savage grip. He walked up the narrow path, his mind rather disturbed by the interview. The walls ended and an open space lay in front of him, like a silver pool in the moonlight. It was little more than a clearing in the woods, and formed the Campions' vegetable garden.

A wire fence enclosed the shining rows of cabbage and broccoli. In the further corner was a clump of thick bushes.

Sinclair was skirting the wall, for any sign of a door or break in the masonry, when he saw a sudden quick movement in the bushes. Someone in white looked out for a brief moment, and then whisked out of sight. Quick as she was, she could not hide in time. The telltale beams revealed Elsie. She must have seen him moving, but could hardly have recognized him in the shadows.

Sinclair was puzzled. He had left the girl with her parents not more than half an hour before, and she certainly had not passed him. On the other side of the castle the undergrowth grew close against the walls, leaving no space for walking. He advanced straight across the moonlit garden, boggy after the rain, to the clump of bushes, but there was no trace of her. Within the ring made by the growths a curious circular depression showed in the ground, like a bowl. In the centre of this was a dark opening like a well. Sinclair stepped to the edge and flashed his torch down. The light revealed a circular shaft, but the brickwork one would have

expected with a well only began about six feet down, and above
that was earth with embedded stones, where ferns had grown. By
flashing his torch he could see the bottom, about ten feet down,
and a mass of rubble and loose stones. The entrance was half
blocked by overhanging bushes, but there was no place where the
girl could have hidden. She must have bolted into the wood while
he was approaching. Not a sound came from the trees, pitchy
black in the deep shadow.

What possible connection could Elsie's presence have with the
brother of Mary Rhodes, or was it a mere coincidence?

Hunger began to assert itself, and Sinclair turned back. He
picked up his car in the drive and went to the 'Green Man.'

CHAPTER IV

LORD WANSTEAD

SINCLAIR WAS STANDING in the inner court of Cantire, with Gillian and Haddon, when a car drove up to the door.

"Here's the very man we want," Haddon exclaimed. "Mr. Hicks, the lawyer who has charge of the property." Two men came forward through the gate, now standing open.

A stout, middle-aged man entered aggressively, and stared at the group in a domineering manner. His nose was large and rugged, and the eyes had that secretive look that belongs to the successful business man. Sinclair knew him at once without being told.

He was obviously Lord Wanstead.

"Let me introduce myself—my name is Sir Arthur Sinclair."

The newly made peer graciously extended a large firm hand. "I am pleased to meet you, Sir Arthur; your name is, of course, familiar to me. And who are these persons?"

He swept his arm round in a contemptuous gesture. Sinclair did the introducing, and Wanstead merely bowed frigidly, as though these minor officials did not interest him.

"This is Mr. Hicks, the family lawyer," he said, and a pasty-faced lean man with thin lips and shifty eyes came forward in an obsequious manner.

"Pleased to meet you, sir."

"We can't stand talking here; show me the place where the murder took place," Wanstead said.

Haddon led the way to the chapel, while Lord Wanstead walked with Sinclair, as though he were the only person with whom he would deign to speak.

"This is a most extraordinary affair. I can't pretend that I feel much regret at his death. From what I have heard from my nephew, he seems to have been an arrant scoundrel."

"I am hardly in a position to judge," Sinclair said coldly.

"I may tell you, Sir Arthur, that my nephew has told me something of his experiences with Musgrave. He made a very frank confession, and I think if that unfortunate woman had not taken her life he might have been quixotic enough to have taken her back."

"I am glad to hear it," Sinclair commented.

They stood in a rather sheepish group in the chapel.

"The body was hanging from that beam," Gillian said in explanation.

"My good man," Wanstead interrupted petulantly, "it doesn't interest me in the least where he was hanging; that is a matter for the police."

"I suppose," Hicks said, speaking slowly, and picking each word, "a thorough search of the castle has been made?"

"Yesterday we did what we could, but with a place like this one cannot say what there may be."

"Of course," Hicks said unctuously, "his lordship will now have the place properly restored, and as it will come by descent—"

Lord Wanstead glowered at him. "We can't go into that now. The property, such as it is, comes to my wife as the last Musgrave."

Hicks shuffled uneasily, and looked at Wanstead with a glance almost of surprise, which was not lost on Sinclair.

Gillian thought that the conversation was drifting from the immediate question in hand—the murder itself.

"Our first job is to find the criminals," he said, "and for that we shall require all the information that we can get."

"You are in charge of the case, Inspector," Sinclair said with a smile. "I think if I were you I would take the opportunity of asking these gentlemen what they know about the late Colonel Musgrave. It's cold in here, and draughty. Why not move into the old dining-hall? I understand Campion has lighted a fire, and we could talk better there."

"You are not suggesting that I should submit to an examination?" Lord Wanstead drew himself up haughtily.

"Certainly; why not?" Sinclair said, quite unimpressed with the conceit of the man. "Musgrave was your brother-in-law. In any case, you will be called at the inquest."

"I will, of course, furnish you with what I know, which isn't much."

"Good. Then I think if you will come first, perhaps Mr. Hicks would wait in the Campions' room."

Wanstead shot an angry glance at Sinclair, but followed him to the old dining-hall. It was a magnificent specimen of thirteenth century work, evidently the refectory of the monks, and left untouched. The roof had fallen in and was replaced with corrugated iron, and the windows lacked glass, but a cheery fire of logs burnt on the great open hearth, and a long oak table ran down the centre.

They took their seats by the fire, and Haddon produced a pocket-book in which to make notes. Gillian turned to Sinclair. "Perhaps you, sir, with your experience, would ask questions." He thought Lord Wanstead would be more tractable with one of Sinclair's reputation and status.

"Colonel Musgrave was your brother-in-law; you married his sister?" Sinclair asked.

"You know that already," Wanstead said stiffly.

"You did not get on very well together, I think?" Sinclair asked quietly, and Wanstead coloured.

"You may put it that way if you like. He fancied his family was something wonderful—always boasting about it, and he hadn't a brass button. He objected to his sister marrying me, because I was in trade, as he called it."

The grievance of years ago was coming up now, and Wanstead had dropped his hauteur.

"Trade! And he let people come here and see the old ruin at one shilling a head. What was that but trade, and a damned poor one at that!"

Sinclair was watching him with half-closed eyes, but he did not interrupt. He had got him where he wanted.

"I tell you, Sir Arthur, the man was impossible with his absurd family pride. And yet he was willing enough to take charge of my nephew, and have a trip round the world at my expense, and did not stint himself, I can tell you."

"And I suppose," Sinclair asked softly, "when your nephew returned, that source of income was cut off?"

The hard look of the business man came to the eyes of the peer, who had paid a cool fifty thousand for that honour. "After what my nephew told me, there was an end of the subsidy."

In Sinclair's clear mind it was poor Mary's death that had removed the need for Musgrave's tutelage, but he kept that to himself.

"I understand that he once started to restore the castle?"

Wanstead gave a short unpleasant laugh. "The fool, yes. He didn't seem to know his own mind. I offered to finance him, and went so far as to make him a proposition that he should live here during his lifetime. He threw the thing up after only a week or so, and then—"

"How long ago was this?"

Wanstead stared at Sinclair. "You are smart, Sir Arthur—it was three years ago, and then, well, let us put it that another job cropped up, but that is known to you, and confidential."

So the bear-leading had caused the termination of the restoration work—or had it? Was Musgrave's presence essential when the work had started? This certainly required some further research.

"And you haven't seen him since then?"

"Never!" Wanstead was most emphatic. "I refused to meet him, and I can answer for it that my nephew has not met or communicated with him in any way since he returned to England and came to me."

To Gillian, much of the conversation was meaningless, but he was content to let Sinclair proceed along his own lines.

"Then it comes to this," Sinclair said urbanely, "you really can't throw any light on the murder?"

"No, I can't, but I should think that someone he has swindled in the past, or wronged perhaps"—he emphasized the words—"has taken his revenge."

"Thank you, Lord Wanstead." Sinclair spoke as though to terminate the interview. "By the way, how did you hear of the murder?"

"Mr. Hicks informed me."

"He wired for you, I suppose? Very wise of him."

"Really, one would think I was being subjected to an interrogatory. If you want to know, I was staying down here, at Payning, at the 'Horse and Hounds.' Hicks told me verbally."

"Thank you, Lord Wanstead," Sinclair said with a singular smile. "Perhaps we can see Mr. Hicks. Haddon, will you fetch him?"

Wanstead bit his lip, but could scarcely object. The object was apparent—that they should not have a chance of talking.

"I shall return to Payning. I must get on the 'phone to London. You will find me there, Sir Arthur, if you want me for anything. I shall stay here for a few days to see this affair through."

Sergeant Haddon entered with the lawyer, who took a seat and lit a cigarette awkwardly.

"Now, Mr. Hicks," Sinclair said genially, when Wanstead had gone, "you are a most important witness. You have known the Musgraves for a long time, I take it."

"Yes, Sir Arthur, and my father before me. We have managed the estate when it was a fine property, but it was sold off bit by bit. Nothing left but this ruin. A sad case for an old family, but all too common nowadays."

He seemed to wish to talk in order to gain confidence, but his shifty eyes roamed round the dining-hall.

"Exactly. And when did you see the Colonel last?"

The pale face went a sickly yellow.

"He arranged for the place to be opened for visitors, and put the Campions in here as caretakers. Then he went away. I have received the money, and paid their wages, and the small expenses for upkeep."

"That is very interesting, but you haven't answered my question. I asked you when you saw Colonel Musgrave last."

"That was the last time—roughly three years ago."

"Come now, Mr. Hicks, I know you are not on oath, and need not say more than you wish to. Wouldn't it be rather curious if Colonel Musgrave came to Cantire and yet did not even call on his lawyer? And with Lord Wanstead, by a mere chance, of course, staying at Payning." Sinclair leant forward and demonstrated with his pipe stem. "And you informed Lord Wanstead of the murder."

"I?" Hicks looked up in genuine surprise. "He informed me."

"My mistake," Sinclair said with a glance at Gillian. "I thought it was the other way round. You are certain you haven't seen Musgrave since he came back to England from his travels?"

Hicks saw the three men staring at him, and the silence grew tense. He gave a nervous laugh.

"You have cornered me, Sir Arthur, but I am not going to tell an untruth even to please Lord Wanstead. I did see the Colonel, as a matter of fact."

"Now we are getting at the truth, but it would have been better if you had said so at first."

"Let me explain. The interview was strictly private and confidential, and I had given my word to Lord Wanstead to regard it as such. Naturally, now that this murder has taken place, it can no longer be kept a secret."

"Will you please tell us the object of the visit?"

"That I must decline to do without his lordship's permission."

"I can't force you, Mr. Hicks, but you're a lawyer, and you are perfectly aware that you will be on your oath at the inquest, and will have to tell the truth."

"I am afraid I can say no more," Hicks said nervously.

"Then I must ask Lord Wanstead," Sinclair said firmly.

"For heaven's sake don't do that! I don't know what to do for the best. You see, it was confidential."

"Perhaps I can help you," Sinclair said. "May I suggest to you that Lord Wanstead came down here to meet his brother-in-law?"

The shot went home. Hicks half rose from his seat. "He told you that?" he exclaimed.

"I think the reason is not hard to guess, eh, Gillian?"

"I am afraid I can't follow you there, sir." Gillian was all at sea.

"Colonel Musgrave had returned to England almost penniless. He was not the type of man who saves. He was in deadly fear obviously. Is it too much to suppose that he wished to make a bargain with Lord Wanstead?"

Sinclair watched the lawyer's face and saw a look of relief pass swiftly across it.

"Yes; that was it," he murmured. "He wanted to raise money on this property."

"He wouldn't get much for this old ruin," Gillian said scornfully.

"Precisely!" Sinclair cut in. "As you say, he would not get much, except from one man: a man who would give a fancy price for it, from snobbery, and because he had immense wealth. A man who wished to live here and become a county magnate."

"Lord Wanstead," Gillian suggested. "I see."

"How much did he give for it?" Sinclair shot the question at the lawyer.

"Five thousand pounds."

"And when was this interview?"

"The day before the murder," Hicks said, his face livid.

"So you and Lord Wanstead met Colonel Musgrave at your office, I suppose?"

"Yes. The money was paid in cash. Musgrave insisted on that."

Gillian gave an impatient gesture—he was tired of the lawyer's shifty ways.

"And did Musgrave tell you where he was staying?"

"He 'phoned me, and made the appointment. I had no idea where he was. He would not meet his brother-in-law."

"So he and Lord Wanstead did not meet," Sinclair remarked.

"It was a most absurd business." Hicks was glad, now the truth was out, to make amends for his slyness. "The whole transaction was conducted through me. I had to walk between my room, where Lord Wanstead was, and then to my clerk's room, where Colonel Musgrave was sitting."

"Your clerk! Was he there at the time?"

"He was with the Colonel, and witnessed the signatures."

"And who is he?"

"A young fellow called Rob Summers."

"Then he heard everything on Musgrave's side?"

"There wasn't much to hear, but of course he saw the money handed over. Musgrave rather foolishly insisted on counting the notes over in front of him. A large sum to tempt a young fellow who's been a rolling stone, and with none too good a reputation."

There was no doubt about the insinuation, but Sinclair made no comment.

"And that was positively the last time that you saw Colonel Musgrave?" Gillian asked with scorn.

"I never saw him again."

"I'd like to see this clerk of yours. Perhaps you would bring him along sometime," Sinclair said.

"He left me. Walked out directly after Musgrave had gone. I haven't seen him since." Hicks showed signs of uneasiness.

"I can tell you where the young rascal has gone." Sergeant Haddon spoke for the first time.

"I would be glad to know," Hicks said with forced politeness.

"He's gone back to live with his uncle, if you want to know— that good-for-nothing loafer Rhodes."

"Birds of a feather, eh?" Hicks said with a smile of contempt.

"Who is this Rhodes? This is all out of my province," Gillian interposed.

"You would know him, sir, if you lived here," Haddon answered; "a huge hulk of a man, once had a farm but lost it all through drink and gambling they say, and now is probably a thief and certainly a poacher. He's always about these woods, but of course old Campion can't interfere, and there's no gamekeeper." He grinned at his joke.

"It looks to me," Hicks said, "as though you won't have to look very far for your murderer. Five thousand pounds are not to be won every day."

"I think that is all, Mr. Hicks, thank you," Sinclair said icily. The lawyer retired hastily, glad to get away.

Lord Wanstead had gone straight to the Campions' rooms, where the old couple were wondering what all this meant to them.

Campion rose respectfully and touched his grey hair.

"I shall not require your services any more," Wanstead said sharply. "You and your wife can pack up your things and go. I am not at all satisfied with the way you have conducted yourselves, but that will be for the police." He threw a five-pound note on the table. "That is in lieu of notice and to cover the expenses of moving."

"It'll be main hard for me to get a job at my age, your lordship," old Campion whined.

"You should have saved up, and I expect you've made a bit out of the visitors here. You'll get the old age pension later on that we taxpayers have to provide."

"Can we stay a day or two just to look round like for a place?" Campion asked anxiously.

"As far as I am concerned you can, but I expect the whole castle will be taken over by the police—you'll have to ask them."

He turned and stalked out of the room.

"I'll see that gentleman, Sir Arthur Sinclair," Campion exclaimed indignantly. "Perhaps he'll likely do summut for us."

He hobbled out of the room and down the steps, going to the old kitchens and buttery, now only empty walls. He entered the dining-hall from behind the 'screens,' just as Hicks was leaving.

"Me and the missus has got the sack, sir," he wailed to Sinclair.

"Wanstead hasn't taken long to assert his authority," Sinclair observed. "Have you anywhere to go?"

The old man shook his head forlornly.

"The police will be taking possession," Gillian said, "but I don't think there would be any harm in your staying for a bit."

"I think they would be most useful, as they know the place inside out," Sinclair agreed. "We'll see what we can do for you later on."

Campion muttered his thanks, but the rough oak door was pushed open violently as he spoke, and a young man entered jauntily. He was a tall, thin young man with a shock of tousled hair, and merry blue eyes, and advanced without a trace of embarrassment to the fire.

"Good morning, gentlemen."

Campion's fists closed and he glared at the intruder. "I told you never to come here again, you rascal!" he shouted.

"I didn't come to see you, grandpa," he said cheekily. "I came to see these sleuths."

Sinclair's sense of humour was tickled. "May I ask your name?"

"Rob Summers," he said with an elaborate bow, "late clerk to the bag of misery who's just left you—Hicks, the lawyer."

"From whom you ran away."

"I didn't run; he gave me the push."

"Don't you believe him, sir," Campion exclaimed angrily. "He's a liar and a varmint, and comes round here after my daughter Elsie, and she's but a slip of a girl, too young for them goings on."

Rob laughed merrily. "Juliet was fourteen. Elsie and I are only pals. Stuffed up in an old ruin with two aged frumps like Campion and his wife is enough to give the girl the jim-jams."

"He takes her to the pictures," Campion raged, as though he were accusing him of murder.

"Why not? It's the only chance for her to see something lively."

"Really, Campion," Gillian said impatiently, "we don't want to hear your grievances. We want to talk to this young man."

The old man was hobbling off, when Sinclair detained him. "One moment, I find this very interesting. You say that this young man takes your daughter to the pictures. I thought you always locked the place up at night."

The question seemed irrelevant to Gillian and Haddon, but a look of disquiet came to Rob's face.

"You may well ask, sir! I wish we knew how the young imp manages to slip out. Time and again we've tried to find out, but she's that artful."

Sinclair stopped him hurriedly. "I expect, like his friend Romeo, he has a ladder. It's the oldest way, you know, Campion."

The old man went off, grumbling beneath his breath, and Sinclair turned to Rob.

"Sit down, my boy; you may be able to help us. Why did you come, by the way?"

Rob's face turned red, and he lit a cigarette to hide it. "I just came to see what was happening I saw old Hicks coming along with that Lord Wanstead, whoever he is."

"I think I understand." Sinclair smiled. "The Campions were very busy, and the gate was open."

"I saw old Musgrave in our office the other day," Rob went on hurriedly, "and now I hear he's been bumped off."

"Mr. Hicks told us that you were there."

"The swine; he deserved all he got."

There was an intensity of fury in the words that caused Gillian to look searchingly at him. "Why do you say that? Have you ever seen him before?"

"I didn't even know who he was till he came into the office."

"And that's the last you saw of him?" Sinclair asked.

"Oh no!" the youth answered readily enough. "I was interested in this funny business, and thought I would follow him. The beggar led me a pretty dance. He went right away into the country, keeping to the woods, and skirting Barton. Then I knew he was making for this place. But he was one too much for me." Rob grinned expansively.

"You lost him?" Gillian said.

"He must have known I was following, and hid behind a tree. Round I came, a proper amateur sleuth, and of course he conked me on the head with a stick he was carrying, and knocked me out good and proper.

His laugh showed Sinclair clearly that he bore no animosity for the blow, and this was not the cause of his hatred.

"When I had got my senses back, he had gone. Slipped it in the woods, I expect."

"How far was this from the castle?" Sinclair asked.

"Couldn't have been far, because when I followed I came out into the garden at the back." He stopped, as though he had said too much, and went on hurriedly: "When I got back, there was a row with old Hicks, and he told me to clear out."

"This is very interesting, Rob, if you don't mind my calling you that. And what else have you to tell us?"

Rob looked straight at Sinclair. "I say; you're smart, aren't you? I have something else, but I don't know how you guessed. I don't know whether it's of any use to you or not."

"Let's have it." Sinclair smiled at the young fellow.

"When I got the push I went to see my uncle, Mr. Rhodes, to tell him. When he heard about Musgrave he fairly went off the deep end for some reason, and, after a bit of grub, he made me take him into the woods where I last saw the brute. He knows these woods very well." He grinned impudently at Haddon, who glared at him. "We had a good old search but couldn't find anyone, but when we came out by the main road who should drive up but old Hicks himself. We hid down behind a hedge and he got out before he reached the drive, and walked up to the gate. You remember the storm was just coming on, and I said what a fool he was to leave the car in the road.

Rob spoke in a careless voice, and was kicking the fire with his foot. He did not see the intense interest his story was arousing.

"What time was this?" Sinclair asked quietly.

"About four, I should think, roughly. He went in through the main gate, and I didn't see him come out. My uncle and I had to do a bolt for it, as the storm came on like billy-o."

"So you think he may have had something to do with this murder?" Gillian asked sternly.

"I expect he did; I wouldn't trust a lawyer anywhere when there's money about, and Musgrave had a cool five thousand on him. Lord! It's enough to make anyone bump a man off. By the way"—he faced round to the officers—"did you find the dough on him?"

"No, we didn't," Sinclair told him, to Gillian's surprise. He thought it unwise to tell the youth.

"Depend on it that lawyer's trousered it. Here, this may be of some use to you." He dived into his pocket and produced a piece of paper. "I took the numbers of the notes before Musgrave had them. Hicks was chin-wagging in the other room with some bloke."

"I suppose"—Gillian was rather annoyed at the free manner in which Rob spoke to Sinclair—"the bank would supply us with them."

Rob grinned at him. "That's where you come unstuck. The other man who was with Hicks brought them with him, and you bet he didn't draw them from one bank. If you search right through England you might find them."

Sinclair thanked him for the list, which he placed in his pocket.

"You know Cantire pretty well, I suppose?"

"When I was young," Rob said loftily, "I used to wander all over the place with Elsie; she was a kid then. Now they won't let me inside, and wouldn't have done today, but the slop at the door let me pass when I said I had an important message for Sir Arthur Sinclair—wonderful what a name will do."

"You'll do, Rob," Sinclair said with a grim smile.

Rob rose, and stretched himself. "Well, I can't stop gossiping any longer. I have an appointment. I'll roll up and see what's happened tomorrow. If I can be of any assistance, let me know. So long."

He waved to the others, and went out.

"Cheeky young monkey," Sergeant Haddon said angrily.

"I don't agree," Sinclair said. "I like his spirit, and he's given us some valuable information."

"It seems to me he's given his uncle away pretty thoroughly," Haddon growled.

"On more important matters than that, perhaps," Sinclair added.

"I don't see that we can do anything more here," Gillian said. "I've got a man here to prevent any press men or inquisitive strangers coming in."

"Then we'll have lunch at the 'Green Man,' if you will honour me."

CHAPTER V

A MIDNIGHT ADVENTURE

SINCLAIR HAD TAKEN his scanty luggage to the 'Green Man,' which he preferred to the garish modern hotels of Payning. It was the type of old country inn that he liked; oak-beamed, with low ceilings blackened by age, and patronized by honest decent countrymen. Once it had belonged to the Musgraves, but the poverty of the family and the spread of the tied-house system had caused it to fall into the hands of a firm of brewers, who were shrewd enough to see that the proximity of the old ruin, if properly advertised, might be a source of gain.

In contradistinction to most brewers, they had sufficient sense to leave it as it was, and made no attempt to 'modernize' it.

Grimes boasted proudly, and with truth, that the place was as old as the castle, and that his ancestors had kept the place ever since the castle had been built. Smuggling was profitable in those days, and now, after many lean years, spoliation of visitors had revived past glories.

Sinclair had partaken an excellent dinner of roast duck and green peas, fresh from Grimes' garden, and had settled himself down in the private room he had taken, to think out this strange confusing problem.

Some facts emerged, as he gazed at the smoke rising from his pipe and leant back in a comfortable armchair.

When Musgrave had come to see him with his tame bear, Seften, he was even then in what is called a blue funk. Sinclair had seen it in his manner, and yet he was no coward, but a strong determined type.

The row with Seften, who had thrown over the traces when Mary's suicide had taken place, had left Musgrave with no job, and probably with little money. So far he could trace the story. He had put himself into touch with Hicks in order to attempt to sell the property to his brother-in-law, whom he would not meet. That was important.

He must have been in a desperate condition to part with Cantire, if the story of his tremendous family pride were true. But had he the right to sell it at all? Was it not entail?

Then he had been at Cantire. That seemed fairly evident, but the Campions knew nothing about it from their tale, and Sinclair was a good judge of truth and lies. But Elsie did, or he was much mistaken, for that telltale jump she had given had betrayed her.

What was she doing in that back garden, and where did she vanish to? Again, what connection had Rhodes' sudden appearance outside the castle to do with this incident?

He picked up the guide-book which he had brought from the castle and read it through with great care. There was a brief history of the place, and the Musgrave family, and a plan of Cantire as it was in early days. And then a paragraph stood out before him, and he read it through again. It seemed innocent enough.

> The garderobe shaft (indoor sanitation), which was found during recent excavations in the inner court, is separated from the living-rooms by a covered archway, the garderobe rooms being in the first- and second-floor levels in the northwest tower.
>
> These rooms are not shown to visitors, as the tower is not considered safe, but the old shaft forms an interesting relic historically.

In itself it was just, as the guide-book said, an interesting old relic, but there flashed back to Sinclair's mind that strange hollow in the ground that was like a well, and not a well. For a well would have been bricked up to the top, but this was not. It had fallen in. The true explanation came to him at once. Centuries ago there had been a cesspool, bricked in, and with a conduit under the walls to the castle, and leading to the shaft mentioned in the guidebook.

That was where Elsie had disappeared then, and if she could get through, perhaps he with his greater bulk could also do so. And on that thought came another. The disappearance of Musgrave, as Rob had told them, close to the kitchen garden.

It fitted like a puzzle. Old Campion's remark about Elsie slipping out to the pictures, and the guilty look that Rob had given. Two facts emerged. Here was a way of getting into the castle, and the Campions knew nothing about it or they would have stopped Elsie's games.

This must be investigated, and the lazy evening before the fire was abandoned. Sinclair changed into a very old suit he kept for such expeditions, and armed himself with a flask of whisky and his powerful torch. He always carried an automatic with him, for there were many who would dearly like to have murdered him.

He went to his bedroom and ruffled up the clothes, as though he had slept there, in case his investigations proved long.

Then, telling Grimes he was going to bed, he quietly slipped out and made his way across the fields, sodden after the storm.

It was bright moonlight, and he made rapid progress until he came to the thick woods, as dark as Erebus. He pushed through the undergrowth as silently as possible, and emerged in the kitchen garden, near the clump of bushes. The ruin looked eerie and grim in the bright moonlight.

He approached the queer depression, and an examination showed that his guess was correct. He had brought a rope with him, but the drop was only ten feet at most, and he slid down easily, finding himself in a sort of cavern, the top of which had collapsed. At one time it had been deep, but centuries of slow disintegration had piled up the debris, and it was hardly more than five feet from the crown to the bottom. On the side nearest to the castle Sinclair found what he had been looking for. Here was an opening—a circular conduit about three feet in diameter. Originally it had been circular, but the continual flow of centuries had made a solid bed on the lower side. Into this Sinclair crawled. The place was dry, and in good condition, but it was back-aching work, and he was glad enough when the conduit ended and he could stand upright in the shaft. There was barely room to turn round, but Sinclair knew there must be some way of climbing it, and his torch revealed a rope hanging down, knotted at intervals.

Sinclair heaved a sigh. It was all right for a girl like Elsie, wiry and light, but he was middle-aged and not used to climbing ropes.

The ascent seemed endless, but at last he stood in a small room, with a domed roof, lit by a loop-hole through which the moon shone.

So far so good. Sinclair sat on a stone seat by the loop-hole and rested.

There was something queer about this business. The guidebook stated that this place had only recently been discovered, but surely the workmen would have investigated the shaft and found the exit. That would certainly have been recorded in the book. The question opened all sorts of possibilities. Round him was the stillness of death; of dead things that had once lived here, and dead stones that had formed this stronghold.

Sinclair had no particular plan in his head. He had found what he wanted, but the spirit of adventure was on him, and he made his way to a low-arched door, which he expected to find locked. Rather to his surprise he found it swung easily on its hinges, and he stood on one of those winding stone staircases that were in every tower. It was very much out of repair, and required careful going. At the foot was a sort of fence of rough boards, but he found these were loose, and easily gained the other side. Turning his torch on the wall he read a notice to say that there was no admission, as the place was dangerous.

A short passage led into the inner court, not far from the chapel.

Here he paused, for a very faint sound came to his ears. It came from the opposite end of the court, where the Campions' rooms were situated. A faint light showed on the short flight of stairs, and then Sinclair saw Elsie, in her nightgown, and carrying a candle, descending the stairs. Her other hand was extended stiffly before her, and a glance showed that her eyes were wide open, and fixed with the stare of a sleep-walker.

She came across the inner court confidently, her bare feet making no sound, and almost touched Sinclair. There was something horrible about her assurance. She never paused, and Sinclair felt a thrill as she passed into the chapel. He followed her closely in case she might wake suddenly. His lips set firmly as she made for the winding staircase that led to the Monks' Room. He expected her to enter the place, but she went on up the stairs, lit dimly at intervals by loop-holes. He followed in dread, for he had already discovered that the staircase ended in the air, where the top of the north tower had fallen down, and there was a sheer forty-foot drop into the yard below.

They had reached the level of the third and highest storey, below the flat roof of the tower, now broken away. Elsie stopped, and Sinclair nearly butted into her. From the position of the loop-holes he calculated that they were opposite the massive outer wall, but with this giddy spiral it was difficult to tell.

Something happened. Elsie's dim white form disappeared, apparently into the thickness of the wall, and a black opening showed where none had been before.

Elsie walked straight in, and the light of her candle showed a narrow passage in the thickness of the walls, which opened into a rough chamber. A glance showed that the place was empty, but Elsie for some strange reason placed the candle down on the floor, and then turned and went back into the passage. She nearly touched Sinclair as she passed. To his horror she started to ascend the stairs.

Sinclair had to turn, expecting a knife in his back, and with no time to study the place. He followed the dim white figure. It was ghastly to see that steady advance towards the yawning abyss. Another step, and she would have crashed down to death. Sinclair sprang forward and seized the girl in his arms. Her eyes seemed to come to life, and horror grew. She struggled violently and gave a cry.

"Elsie," he said firmly, "keep still; you are quite safe."

Her head sunk on his shoulder, and her body went limp. Sinclair's foot slipped, and the stones went rattling down in a cascade. He recovered and managed to wriggle down a few steps, where he stood panting. Then he began that terrible descent. The girl was, mercifully, in some sort of swoon. It was comparatively easy to ascend those old and broken stairs unhampered, but quite another to carry the girl with him, and feel with his feet for the next ledge. He leant his back to the wall and slithered down. All his professional training urged him to investigate that concealed opening, but how could he drop the girl on the stairs?

As his back was pressing against the wall he expected at any moment to fall into the opening, but after going some way it dawned on him that he must have passed the spot, and he realized with sudden foreboding that the door must have been shut, either automatically, or by some agency.

The stairway became easier as he descended, the stones less worn, and at last he stood on firm ground. The rest was easy to a man of Sinclair's strength, and he carried the girl to her bedroom and laid her on the bed. He knew the reaction that follows sleep-walking, and felt her pulse anxiously. Then he tucked her in warmly, and took his seat by her side. He dared not leave Elsie, who was moaning fitfully in her sleep, though he was impatient to explore that strange room. He sat there during the hours of darkness and thought out the new aspect of the problem. So this was the place where Musgrave had taken refuge, and Elsie knew of it. What had happened on that desperate night when Musgrave had left his hiding-place, never to return?

Daylight filtered slowly into the bare room, furnished only with an old wash-stand, a chest of drawers, and one chair on which he was sitting, where Elsie's scanty clothing had been flung.

He rose and walked to the window, gazing down on the alley.

The girl woke and stretched herself with a yawn, and then she saw Sinclair and gave a cry.

"You need not be afraid, Elsie," he said. "I have been watching here for hours."

"How did you get in?" she asked, drawing the bedclothes round her neck.

"I want to talk to you, Elsie, and I want you to tell me the truth. No harm shall come to you, and I shall keep it to myself."

"I don't understand." The girl puckered her eyebrows. "I feel confused. I seem to remember something."

"You walked in your sleep as you have done before. I brought you back to your room."

She stared at him, her eyes wide with terror.

"Elsie, I saw you in the garden, the night before last. Last night I found the entrance and came through that conduit."

Elsie coloured up. "I ought to have pulled the rope up," she said unguardedly.

"Now I want to know all about it; don't be frightened. Did you discover that way yourself, or did someone show you?"

"I didn't discover it—the workmen found it when the castle was going to be restored about three years ago. You can read about it in the guide-book."

"I have read it, but there is no mention of any entrance."

"Oh, please don't ask me, sir, my father will beat me."

"No, he won't, I promise you that. But I must have the truth."

"Well, sir"—she hesitated, and looked at him through her large haunted eyes as though trying to sum him up—"the Colonel was there when the workmen found that room in the old tower, and a French gentleman who had come over to see about things. They turned the men out, saying it wasn't safe, and examined it themselves."

"How did you learn all this, you were not here then?"

"The Colonel told me—oh, what have I said!" She buried her head under the bedclothes.

Sinclair approached gently and laid a hand on the heaving shoulder of the girl.

"You may tell me without any fear, my child. I already know that Colonel Musgrave came in through there and has used it for a hiding-place."

She looked up then in surprise. "You know that, sir. Then I don't mind telling you, only the Colonel made me promise never to tell a soul, but now he's dead I suppose it doesn't matter."

"Not a bit," Sinclair said cheerfully; "go ahead."

"Well, sir, I was playing in that back garden—we had just been put in here to take care of the place. I saw Colonel Musgrave come out of that place where you saw me, and the French gentleman with him. He made me promise then."

"And do your father and mother know anything about that entrance?"

"Oh no, sir. They would have stopped me from using it." A faint smile came to her pale face.

"Weren't you frightened of the Colonel?"

She looked at him with wide-open eyes. "Of course not—as soon as I knew who he was, I wasn't frightened. He gave me that locket before he went, and told me to wear it."

"You are sure it was not he who stole it from you?"

"Quite, sir, and why should he steal it when he had given it to me?"

"And when did you see him again?"

"Four days ago, sir. He came to this room and woke me up. He told me to get him food and bring it to a place he showed me, and I have done so every night."

Light dawned on Sinclair. "It was to that place you took me during the night in your sleep."

Elsie stared open-mouthed. "Did I, sir? And you saw then . . . I had promised never to tell . . ." Recollection came to her. "But I suppose now he is dead it doesn't matter."

"It matters very much," Sinclair said soothingly. "I begin to see. Colonel Musgrave came here to hide, and got you to help him to obtain food. I think I can guess something then. You went to the chapel with food on the night of his murder."

"How did you know that, sir?" She trembled violently.

"Don't be frightened—it's all over now. Just tell me."

"I went to the chapel, and then I saw him hanging, and ran back to my mother's room. I dared not say anything."

"Was there anyone else in the chapel?"

"No, sir, not that I saw by my candle. It nearly blew out in the storm."

"And you shrieked out when you saw what you did?"

"Yes, sir, I must have done, but I was so frightened I don't rightly remember."

That explained one point that had been puzzling Sinclair. It was the girl's cry that had wakened the Campions, and had brought that mysterious person back, to find out whether it had been heard.

"And this hiding-place in the tower; did you know of that?"

"Not before Colonel Musgrave showed it to me. He said that when Cromwell was hunting for Royalists they hid in there. It has a small opening into the chapel, which they call a spy-hole, I think."

Elsie was calmer now, and seemed willing to tell Sinclair all she knew.

"When did you see the Colonel alive last?"

"On the day he was murdered." A look of horror came to her face at the recollection. "My father shut up the outer gates and locked them, and then I slipped up and took the Colonel food. I used to get it in the village and bring it in. He seemed very worried about something, and kept on asking whether I had seen anyone. And he was most particular that I should pull that rope up when I came in."

"But I found it hanging, or I shouldn't have got in."

"Yes, sir, since the murder I've left it there."

"One more question, and then I want you to come and show me that place by daylight. Do your father and mother know anything about the murder?"

"I am sure they don't, sir," she answered firmly.

"Then we'll go now," Sinclair said.

"I'll get dressed, sir," she said, and with charming naïvety sprang out of bed and seized a vest preparatory to slipping off her nightgown.

Sinclair smiled at her, and going out, softly closed the door.

Her dressing did not take long, and she joined him on the little landing. The Campions' door was still fast shut, and they went down the steps into the inner court. Elsie led the way without hesitation up the winding stair to the curve, now lit from the loop-holes in the walls that showed at intervals.

The stones were uneven, and the mortar had fallen away, but even the minutest inspection failed to show a crack or crevice in that dark angle. Without any effort Elsie pushed on one stone, and a piece of the curved wall went back into a cavity, smoothly and without sound. The passage in the thickness of the wall was in front of them, beyond lay the small chamber, and Sinclair drew his automatic and went before the girl. The room was entirely empty, and cold and cheerless.

"Is there any other way out?" Sinclair whispered. Somehow the grim place made him shudder.

"Not that I know of. If there had been, I think Colonel Musgrave would have come by that way instead of through the shaft. But the things have gone."

"What things?" Sinclair asked sharply.

"The Colonel had a camp-bed here and a washing-stand and chair. They have all been taken away." She spoke in an awed undertone.

She led the way to a narrow door in the corner, from which the usual spiral staircase went down. It only had one whorl, and then ended blindly, blocked completely with debris. But there was a small slit through which the inside of the chapel could be seen.

"There is nothing beyond this," Elsie told him. "I believe it went down to the ground once, but that was a long time ago."

It was cold and damp in the place, and Sinclair was glad to return to the entrance, where Elsie closed the door.

"It doesn't close by itself then?" Sinclair asked.

"Oh no, it has to be shut."

They went together to the garderobe room. "I am going out by the way I came," he said. "Mind you, I don't want anyone to know I have been in here. You will keep it to yourself."

"Certainly; and you have promised to keep what I have told you secret." She smiled at him, her confidence quite restored.

"It throws no light on the murderer's identity, and I shall certainly tell no one, but the information will be useful to me. I hope your young friend Rob doesn't know of this entry?"

"Certainly not." Elsie tossed her head indignantly. "He leaves me in the garden when we come back from the pictures or a walk."

"Very well, you had better go back to bed."

Sinclair was a dirty, bedraggled object when he crawled from the conduit.

A figure sprang from the bushes and seized him by the throat. He was half-way out of the place, and still gripping the sides. There was only one thing to do. He let go and dropped back, dragging his assailant with him. The grip loosed on his throat, and Sinclair was on him like a flash. The light did not penetrate down and they struggled in darkness. Sinclair's hand came into contact with a mass of tousled hair, and sudden realization came to him.

"Stop!" he called. "Aren't you Rob?"

"Good Lord!" The grip relaxed. "You are Sir Arthur Sinclair."

"You've got a strong grip, my lad." Sinclair laughed as he felt his throat. "Let's get out of this and explain." The rough, uneven stones were not hard to climb, and both stood panting on the edge, among the bushes.

"What are you doing here?" Sinclair asked when he had got his breath.

"I was going to ask the same question," the boy answered cheekily. Sinclair was too big a man to resent the tone.

"I have been carrying on some investigations on my own."

"Have you seen Elsie? Is she all right?"

Sinclair smiled; so that was the reason for his presence here.

"She is sleeping peacefully in her bed," he said. "You knew of this passage into the castle?"

"That is the way Elsie used to go back after I had taken her to the pictures."

A sudden thought came to Rob. "I have never been down there in my life, so don't get imagining things. I said good night here. But after all that has happened—this murder and so on—I have been watching the castle, and I waited here in case anyone tried to get in or out."

"And you have never seen anyone try to do so? Not tonight for example. It would be useful to me if you had."

"Never. Those Campions won't let me near the place. It's not fit for Elsie to live in."

"You may put your mind at rest on that score." Sinclair smiled at the youth. "Lord Wanstead has given them notice to leave, and they are moving very shortly."

"What a lark! I'll go and help them move."

They were walking briskly through the trees, for the morning was cold and raw.

"Where are you living now?" Sinclair asked.

"I don't know why I should tell you particularly—you are a sleuth aren't you?"

"I was a sleuth, as you call it"—Sinclair laughed—"but I am not in charge of this case, thank goodness, and my interest is purely personal."

Rob stopped dead, and an ugly look came to his face. "You weren't a friend of that blighter Musgrave?"

"I have only seen him once in my life, and then I formed a very bad impression of him. As a matter of fact, I was making some inquiries about him when I heard of the murder."

"O.K., then I don't mind telling you. I'm living with my uncle, Mr. Rhodes—ever heard of him?"

"I saw him the night before last," Sinclair replied.

"I am glad to hear that tecs can sometimes tell the truth. He told me he had met you."

They were plodding across the fields towards the 'Green Man.'

"You had an aunt, didn't you?" Sinclair asked casually.

"Yes, I had once; I don't remember her. She died when she was seventeen—Aunt Mary." The voice was quite indifferent.

"Come in and have some food with me; I'm ravenous," Sinclair remarked when they arrived at the inn.

"Thanks—I say, I'm sorry if I was rude to you. You see, I've always had everyone against me, and only my uncle as a friend, except Elsie, of course, but she is different. I like you, and so does she."

CHAPTER VI

AT THE 'HORSE AND HOUNDS'

THE INQUEST ON COLONEL MUSGRAVE produced nothing of a sensational nature. Gillian was too practical to allow more than the bare facts to be admitted. The body was identified by Lord Wanstead, and Hicks, and old Campion and his wife, were put in the box after a careful warning from the Inspector to give nothing but actual facts, as briefly as might be. Inspector Gillian and Sergeant Haddon added their statements, which, with Campion's, disposed of any idea of suicide.

A vague suggestion was thrown out that Musgrave had become involved with some gang who had murdered him from revenge or to keep his mouth shut.

In the ordinary way there would have been an adjournment, but the police were anxious that a crop of rumours should not be spread about the place, and decided to get it over. The coroner agreeing, a verdict of murder, by persons unknown, was brought in at the first sitting. The story that emerged was plain and straight. Musgrave had been travelling abroad for three years, and had only recently returned.

Quite naturally he had seen his lawyer and gone to Cantire to inspect his old property. There he had been attacked and murdered by hanging.

The villagers shook their heads and spoke fearfully of the Black Abbot, and of former Musgraves who had met with violent deaths, but the Press could discover nothing tangible out of which to make a story.

The inquest was over, and Lord Wanstead had driven to the 'Horse and Hounds,' where he had taken a palatial suite of rooms. He had asked Sinclair to accompany him, to discuss matters, and, on entering the sitting-room, Seften rose, and then turned red as he saw the detective.

"This is my nephew," Lord Wanstead said with a sweep of his hand. "I believe you have met him."

Seften held out his hand nervously, with a quick glance at Sinclair, as though imploring silence about the interview. He had come to Payning much against his wish, at his uncle's order. He looked better in health than when Sinclair had seen him before, and the hangdog look had gone, but he was obviously ill-at-ease.

"This is rather a bad business, Sir Arthur," he lisped.

"Murder is always a bad business," his uncle said sententiously.

"I suppose you have no idea as to the murderer?" Seften asked.

"Please remember I am nothing whatever to do with the case. I merely heard of it by accident, and came down, being rather interested."

Seften subsided, but Lord Wanstead was not so easily satisfied.

"I understand that, but your knowledge is vastly greater than these country bumpkins.' I thought you might have come to some conclusion. You know my wife always declared that the place was haunted, and several Musgraves have been found dead there."

Sinclair smiled. "Most old country houses have their own legends. They tell me there is a certain Black Abbot who has a grudge against the House of Musgrave, and kills them off when he can."

"You surely don't believe that rubbish," Seften said.

"I don't know; queer things happen in this world. But in any case, the last Musgrave has gone now, and so I suppose the curse will end."

The waiter entered with champagne, which Wanstead always took in the morning before lunch, and the thread of the conversation was broken.

When they had sampled the wine Sinclair remarked casually: "I wanted to ask you about that lawyer, Hicks. When we had that talk at the castle there were one or two discrepancies which you can probably supply."

Wanstead's face clouded over. "I have spoken to him," he snapped. "If I had known he was going to tell you about that confidential interview with my late brother-in-law I should have informed you myself."

"I rather wonder that you did not."

"I could not see that it had any possible bearing on the murder, and was purely a private matter."

Seften stared at his uncle in a puzzled fashion, and was on the point of interrupting, when Wanstead went on, "As a matter of fact, I made a poor deal there, for, if I had waited, the property would have come to his sister in any case."

"Whatever is this about?" Seften said querulously. "Property? I thought Aunt Julia was bound to get it."

Wanstead for once was put out of countenance. "It is a matter that does not concern you, my boy, except that, if you behave yourself, you will come into it when I am gone."

"What's the good of an old ruin?"

Sinclair intervened. "I think your uncle's intention is to have the whole place restored and brought up to date." A smile lurked round the corner of Sinclair's mouth. It seemed to him that Wanstead was glad of the change in the topic.

Wanstead gave quite a genial laugh. "Certainly not, Sir Arthur. I wish to have it exactly as it was in the old days. There are maps and plans, engravings and old records. Hicks has them all. They were got out three years ago when my brother-in-law started the work and then left off."

He sipped his wine with evident relish, and told Seften to open another bottle.

Sinclair saw a sort of challenge in Wanstead's look. He did not want to go back to the interview and the purchase of the castle for some reason.

"I have seen some of your houses," Sinclair remarked.

"My dear sir, what one supplies to meet the needs of City clerks, and one's idea of a gentleman's residence, are two different things, and poles apart. All they want is a box to live in, and a garage for their hire-purchased car. I supply what they want."

His bumptiousness was intolerable, but Sinclair passed it over, for he had a sudden idea, and seemed to show interest in the scheme.

"In that case," he said with enthusiasm, "there is only one person who could do the job really well. A Monsieur Guillet, the French architect. He did splendid work at Rheims, and Beauvais, and is almost as great a genius at this kind of work as Violet le Duc."

He watched Wanstead narrowly while he spoke, but the nobleman was unmoved by the name. "I should be glad to get a really good man, and money is no object. I want it properly done. Do you happen to know this fellow?"

"Fellow"—this from a profiteer devoid of all culture!

"I know him very well, and if you like I will see him and ask him whether he would undertake the work. He is extremely busy, and a curious type; he takes offence at the slightest opposition, and wants his own way."

"I don't mind that. I should be very glad if you would get him. There will, of course, be the usual commission for the introduction."

For a brief second Sinclair's anger rose at the man, but he had too much at stake. He controlled himself, and said, "Thank you, I don't take commissions. You can give the money to the Campions if you want to."

"I shall be pleased to do so," Wanstead said, quite unable to appreciate the enormity of his offence.

"Then I think I will get away." Sinclair rose as he spoke.

"I would ask you to lunch, but I want to talk with my nephew," Wanstead said. "I wonder whether you could arrange to be here at three? I have those policemen coming to discuss matters with me, and would be glad of your advice."

Really, there were no limits to this vulgarian. Sinclair gravely assented. It was impossible to snub such a man.

He drove to the 'Green Man,' where the atmosphere was more to his liking than the 'Horse and Hounds' and Lord Wanstead.

He had made quite a friend of Grimes, and the old man took special care to see that his meals were of the best, though Sinclair was easy to satisfy.

He was sitting at the table in his room, enjoying the warm weather that had succeeded to the storm. The door opened, and Elsie walked in. The girl looked more bedraggled than when he had seen her last, but greeted him with a bright smile.

"Sit down and join me; I am all alone," Sinclair said with easy courtesy.

She eyed the leg of lamb and smoking vegetables with a famished look, but, to Sinclair's surprise, took some persuading before she would join him. The small act of delicacy on her part struck Sinclair, and he was surprised when she said she must have a wash. The little hands and feet, and the way she walked, all indicated to him that, whatever her origin, she had little connection with the gross, peasant type of the Campions. When she returned she had combed her wild hair and washed herself. She took her seat quite composedly.

"I have left the Campions," she announced when the first pangs of hunger had been satisfied.

"Indeed?" Sinclair said with a smile. "Was that what you came to see me about?"

"No, Sir Arthur. I wanted a private talk with you, but I thought it might interest you: I have got a job."

Sinclair waited. A slight colour had come to her face, and she was looking down at her plate. "I have moved to Mr. Rhodes' house, and am looking after him."

"Where your friend Rob is living? You will be quite a party. But what have your parents to say about it?"

"I told them," she said with cool assurance, "that I wasn't going to stay on in the castle. I have found out from Mr. Hicks that a girl of sixteen can choose her own place of residence, provided it is respectable."

"Sixteen!" Sinclair was genuinely taken aback. "I thought you were not a day older than fourteen."

"I am not very big, am I? Anyway, I told my parents that, and I don't know what will happen, but I'm not going back there. I want you to back me up."

"And you escaped by the conduit, I suppose?" Sinclair's eyes twinkled with merriment; he liked the girl's spirit.

"They tried to keep me in, and told the copper on duty not to let me out," she said in explanation.

"I shall certainly back you up for all I am worth," Sinclair declared. "That was what you came here for?"

"Not altogether." Elsie fixed her clear eyes on him. "A funny thing happened this morning, before I had that row with them. My father sent me here to change the five-pound note that Lord Wanstead had given him. I went round to see Rob to arrange about coming there, and told him. So he came with me, and saw Grimes, and got him to change it, but Rob said he was certain it was one of those that had been given to Colonel Musgrave, as he had kept a copy of the list he had given you. He said you ought to know, and asked Grimes to keep it till you had seen it."

Sinclair rang the bell, and Grimes came in; he always waited on his distinguished guest himself.

In answer to the question from Sinclair, he produced the note, which was compared with the list Sinclair had kept. There was no doubt about it. Neither Rob nor Elsie knew from whom the money had come, but Wanstead had undoubtedly given old Campion one of the notes, unless . . . Sinclair wondered. There was the possibility that it was not the same, and that Campion had others. He kept this to himself, and dismissed Grimes with thanks, but without any explanation.

"Please tell Rob I am much indebted to him," he said. "And now, young lady, much as I prefer your company, I have to go to Payning to see Lord Wanstead."

"I don't like the look of him," Elsie said candidly, "the way he stares at one—like a great fish."

"Give you two years, and there will be others who will stare at you, my child," Sinclair thought, but he merely shook hands, promising support if needed.

"Ah, here you are!" Wanstead said in a tone of relief as Sinclair was ushered into the sitting-room by a flunky in gorgeous apparel.

Inspector Gillian and Haddon were already seated at a long table, looking a little uncomfortable, and smoking big cigars of Wanstead's providing.

It was like a Board meeting, and Wanstead sat at the head, as to the manner born.

"We have been discussing this matter before you came in," he told Sinclair, "and these two officers say that they have absolutely no clue as to the murderer or, as they say, murderers."

"Why the plural?" Seften asked.

"You haven't heard all the details, Rupert." He turned to the others. "My nephew has only arrived this morning, and hasn't been informed of anything but the bare facts."

"I think we must agree," Gillian said with a sidelong glance at Sinclair, "that all the indications point to several men having been present at this murder, or, as they call it in their insolent piece of paper—'trial' and 'execution.' It was scarcely likely that there was a typewriter on the spot, and that must have been prepared before."

"I quite agree," Sergeant Haddon assented; "the places where the men sat, and the cigarette-ends, showed that clearly."

Sinclair remained silent. He had pulled out his large pipe, and lit it before Wanstead could offer him a cigar.

"Four of them at least," Gillian said firmly. "One may have been walking up and down. We found a lot of confused footmarks, impossible to measure, but certainly of different boots."

"Yes," Wanstead said impatiently. "No doubt you are right in your theories, but what I want to know, as a plain practical man, is how these men got into the castle."

"Perhaps you are not aware, Lord Wanstead," Sinclair said, answering for Gillian, "Mr. Hicks, your lawyer, was seen going into the front entrance at about four o'clock, just before the place was shut up for the night."

Wanstead glared at Sinclair. "Who told you that?"

"His clerk—or rather his late clerk—Rob Summers."

"Pouf! A hare-brained young fellow who has been dismissed by his employer. Fancy taking any notice of such a person."

Sinclair's mouth set hard. Knowing men as he did, he would sooner trust the word of this youth than that of the slimy lawyer.

"Trace up on Mr. Hicks' movements," he said sharply to Haddon.

"But this is absurd!" Wanstead said. "Hicks was with me, if you want to know; we were discussing plans with regard to the castle before I had to return to Town."

Sinclair turned on him like a flash.

"Before you returned to London, Lord Wanstead? May I ask what made you alter your plans and remain here the next morning?"

For the first time Wanstead lost something of his arrogant manner.

"I had intended doing so, but Hicks came to tell me that he had heard that Colonel Musgrave had been murdered."

"Strange!" Sinclair muttered half to himself. "And Hicks told us that you told him."

Wanstead banged the table in the best chairman manner. "Look here, why not say outright that you think I know more about my brother-in-law's death than I have told you? Because I didn't like the man is that any reason why I—"

"Why all this heat?" Sinclair said quietly as Gillian and Haddon were rather overawed by Wanstead's title and position. "I merely remarked that Hicks had said that. No doubt he was telling a lie, but I wonder why?"

"We had better send for him then," Wanstead said incisively. "Haddon, you might 'phone."

Haddon went out at once, and the moment the door was shut Lord Wanstead turned to the others. "I don't know whether it has struck you, but that police-sergeant must have known that Colonel Musgrave was down here. Has he told you?"

"He has said nothing to me," Gillian said shortly.

"Oh, well, he certainly saw Colonel Musgrave coming out of Hicks' office, for he was standing immediately opposite. I saw him myself as I was waiting for Musgrave to get clear before I came out."

Haddon returned to the room. "Mr. Hicks is coming over at once," he reported.

Gillian looked awkwardly at him. The matter could not be allowed to rest there; here was a reliable police officer against whom an accusation had been made. He would have liked to have taken Haddon aside and questioned him, but that was not feasible.

Sinclair saved the situation.

"Do you remember, Haddon, where you were on last Tuesday afternoon?" he asked suavely. "Lord Wanstead thought he saw you on duty near Mr. Hicks' office."

Haddon stared at Sinclair in surprise at the question.

"I wasn't on duty at all that day, sir. I was laid up with a touch of 'flu at home. Here is my record book."

He drew a neat leather-bound book from his pocket and opened the page. "You see, sir, there is my entry. P.C. Hawkins was acting for me."

"You haven't a double by any chance?" Lord Wanstead asked with a touch of irony.

"No, my lord." Haddon drew himself up with dignity. "I am responsible here, sir, and I have only constables—three of them—under me."

"Then I think we may take it," Gillian said sharply, "that Lord Wanstead made a mistake. You have never seen Sergeant Haddon before, have you, my lord?"

"Never, and that was why I recognized him again. It is very puzzling. He was in uniform with the chevrons he is wearing now."

Haddon made no reply—he had stated his case, and was on firm ground.

The lawyer bustled in; he always seemed in a hurry. He looked round rather uneasily at the group, and bowed to Lord Wanstead.

"Look here, Hicks," the latter exclaimed angrily, "these policemen say that you told them that I informed you of the murder of Colonel Musgrave—you know perfectly well that it was you who told me."

Sinclair watched Hicks' face, and saw amazement and then chagrin grow there.

"That is hardly a fair way of asking," Sinclair declared. "It is what we call a leading question, and not permitted in the laws of evidence."

Wanstead turned on him. "Damn it, Sir Arthur, I've been a magistrate for ten years, and I don't want to be told about laws of evidence at this time. Now, Hicks, what have you to say?"

"Yes, my lord—that is right. I must have made a mistake. I remember now, it was I who told you." He stammered through his piece with obvious embarrassment.

"And where did you get the information from?" Gillian asked before Lord Wanstead could interrupt.

"As a matter of fact"—Hicks seemed to be groping round for a plausible tale—"they told me at the 'Green Man.' I had gone out early for a stroll; I don't sleep very well."

To Gillian's surprise, Sinclair said, "That is quite satisfactory; it was evidently a misunderstanding. These things will happen."

Gillian glanced at Sinclair and read a warning in his eyes.

"I don't think we can carry the matter any further just now. I suppose you will be returning to London, Lord Wanstead?"

"I shall have to, but it is very unsatisfactory to find that there is absolutely no trace of the murderers. I shall make a point of seeing the Home Secretary and placing the matter before him. I expect he will order an expert from Scotland Yard down here."

That was more than Gillian could stand. He turned scarlet. "You will excuse me, Lord Wanstead, but you seem hardly aware that Sir Arthur Sinclair was once the most brilliant of the Scotland Yard C.I.D., and we are most fortunate in getting his help here."

"Quite so! No insult was meant, but of course, Sir Arthur is not directly concerned in this—I mean he is, I understand, acting in his own capacity, not officially."

Sinclair was quite unperturbed. "I am sure, Lord Wanstead, I shall be delighted. You will do whatever you think best, as it was your own brother-in-law, and naturally you are anxious to bring the miscreants to justice. It was certainly a murder of revenge for something in Musgrave's past, and, of course, that will all come out at the trial."

Rupert Seften turned white as chalk, and glanced uneasily at his uncle. He furtively licked his dry lips as though he were about to speak, but thought better of it. He knew what exposure would mean.

"Then I think I shall go and see about certain matters. Hicks, I shall want you about the castle. Come along, Rupert."

The whole party rose, and Wanstead swept to the door, where he wheeled round, feeling that he had been perhaps discourteous to Sinclair, who might have influence at Headquarters.

"Please use this room, Sir Arthur, if you care to have a discussion. I shall be delighted to place it at your disposal."

"Thank you," Sinclair said gravely polite; "we shall be glad to avail ourselves of your offer."

When the door shut Gillian fairly exploded. "Damned pompous ass! And a first-class liar, too, if I am not mistaken. Why did you drop the matter of Hicks, Sir Arthur?"

"My dear fellow, if you had had as much experience with Lord Wanstead's type you would not take him seriously. Personally, I found him most amusing. As for that lawyer, I saw no point in going on. He would certainly have denied having been near the castle, and it is his word against a clerk he has sacked—I am putting his case, mind you."

"I see your point—but we don't want the interfering devil going to the Home Secretary."

Sinclair laughed heartily. "That is the last thing he will do. Did you see the way he crumpled up when I mentioned about scandals coming out? He knows a good deal more about this than he will admit, you can take it from me, but no good purpose will be served at this time by going more deeply into it. Lister.."

A discreet knock came at the door, and a waiter entered.

"Lord Wanstead's compliments, and would you gentlemen have some wine with him."

He set a tray on the table, with a decanter and glasses.

"How typical," Sinclair observed. "Any man of breeding would have asked us to join him, but *quot homines, tot sententiae*."

The quotation was lost on the other two, but Gillian poured out the wine without any qualms. "We will drink his health, anyway."

"While we are together," Sinclair said gravely, "let's marshal our facts as far as they go and leave out theories. It is quite possible that the murder was committed by some complete strangers, who had followed Musgrave down here, for he was undoubtedly in hiding. Against this is the fact that such persons were never seen, and it is harder, believe me, to conceal oneself in a village than in the heart of London. Then they must have got away somehow, and that is another difficulty.

"Again, we can't altogether eliminate the question of the five thousand pounds that Musgrave had in his possession, and which cannot be traced. It is a sufficiently large sum to tempt someone to murder, and the rest may be bluff to put us off."

"That is a little—shall I say far-fetched?" Gillian commented, as he sipped Wanstead's good port.

"What I can't understand," Sergeant Haddon said, "is why the Colonel should have sold the place like that; he must have been hard up."

Sinclair took him up quickly. "But did he? Up till this morning I thought as you did, but Lord Wanstead and his precious nephew rather opened my eyes. It appears that the property would have gone automatically to Lady Wanstead, and Colonel Musgrave had no power to sell it."

Inspector Gillian drew in a breath and stared at Sinclair. His brain was quicker than Haddon's.

"You mean," he said with slow emphasis, "that the five thousand pounds was not the purchase money?"

"What else could it be, sir?" Haddon blurted out.

"Blackmail! The lowest of all crimes," Sinclair said, and Gillian nodded his head in agreement. "That opens up a wider question."

"It looks uncommonly like it to me," Sinclair said. "It would account for Musgrave first tackling the lawyer, and then fetching Wanstead down from London. Then there is some secret for which Lord Wanstead was willing to pay that sum in blood money."

Sinclair had a shrewd idea as to what that secret was, but his lips were sealed by his promise.

Haddon joined in, seeing his chance. "But wait a moment, sir. That young clerk witnessed the document, he would surely have seen what was in it?"

"He might have seen a document," Gillian said with contempt, "but a blackmailer will never put his signature to a real statement. You remember the curious way the matter was conducted, Hicks going backwards and forwards, and the two principals never meeting—that smells of blackmail a mile off, eh, Sir Arthur."

"That is so, but then, that involves Hicks being a party to any such transaction, and Heaven help the man who gets into the clutches of that type. He would bleed a man dry."

"Unless he were involved as well," Gillian suggested.

"Exactly; but Hicks is not the man to do a murder. He might shoot a man in the back when he wasn't looking, but not a hanging."

"You will excuse me, gentlemen," Haddon said a little irritably, "aren't we rather wandering from the point? You may be right, but I'm a plain man, and as I see it there's much more likelihood of that black scoundrel Rhodes having done it. He's got the physical strength, and his own nephew knew that Musgrave had five thousand pounds on him."

Sinclair kept his counsel. What would Haddon say if he knew that Rhodes had the very strongest of motives for killing this man, and further, that Rob knew of a secret entrance to the place? Things would look black for the pair of them.

Haddon went on: "I wouldn't trust those Campions beyond my nose. They are a cunning pair, and their dismissal may have been a bluff."

"Phew! We are getting into a tangle," Gillian said, scratching his head. "I can't make head or tail of it myself at present."

Sinclair smiled at the bewildered man.

"It's quite simple," he said. "You see, Wanstead financed the scheme, and the lawyer devised the scheme, while Rhodes and Rob carried it out, and the Campions let them in. There you have the whole thing in a nutshell. Have another glass of Wanstead's port."

He saw the blank faces of the other two staring at him in dismay.

"On the other hand," he continued calmly, "Musgrave belonged to a secret society and betrayed their plans. They tracked him down remorselessly, tried him by rough justice, and hanged him out of hand. That fits the case."

"You are trying to pull our legs, sir," Gillian said stiffly. "I don't think it is very fair. Of course, we haven't your experience."

"My dear Gillian, I am merely trying to demonstrate how impossible it is at this stage to attempt to build up a case."

"At any rate, we can verify the alibis of these people," Haddon growled. "That should be simple."

"You will have a hard job, Sergeant. Hasn't it struck you that they run in pairs? Wanstead says Hicks was with him, and Hicks will of course corroborate that. Rhodes, on the other hand, was at his cottage with Rob, who had come there that day. Rob will confirm this. The Campions will support each other."

"That's all very fine, sir, but I shall go on my own lines if the Inspector will let me. Old Campion never reported the murder till the next morning, and allowed the murderers to get away safely and have a complete alibi. I begin to see it now."

"I should proceed on those lines," Sinclair commented; "one never knows. I am afraid my part in the case is over. I have promised Lord Wanstead to get hold of a French architect to take charge of the restoration of the castle. He is most eager for it to be done, and to take up his residence here as a county magnate. He has offered me a commission for the introduction, and I shall be going to Paris shortly."

Inspector Gillian gave an uneasy laugh. "If I hadn't heard of your reputation, sir, at the Yard, when I was a mere youth, I should have serious doubts about your sanity. You take a commission! And to run off when a case is unsolved is not like you."

"You see, Inspector, we all have different methods, and it may be that my visit may land me nearer the truth than staying here. I shall hope to return and find that you have solved the problem."

"And when do you propose to set out, sir?" Haddon asked, twirling his moustache in secret annoyance.

"I shall see you both again before I go," Sinclair said cheerily.

He rose and stretched himself. "It's very stuffy in here. I must go to the 'Green Man.' "

CHAPTER VII

THE CONSTABLE SEES THINGS

IN ANOTHER ROOM in the 'Horse and Hounds' Lord Wanstead was pacing up and down, his hands behind his back, and his face red with anger.

Hicks was cringing in an armchair like a dog expecting a thrashing.

"I told you it was a damned stupid thing to bring me down here. Why the hell didn't you arrange another place?"

"I am sorry, my lord, but Colonel Musgrave insisted on meeting at my office, and then only if you came down and stayed in another room."

"A pretty mess you've made of it. You told the whole story of our meeting to those sleuths instead of consulting me first, and you kept your clerk in your room with Musgrave."

"I had to have a witness," Hicks stammered. He had another reason he did not mention—he was not going to be alone with Musgrave.

Wanstead stopped his pacing and faced the lawyer. "And you must needs have Rob Summers of all people. Why didn't you sack him first and get someone else? My nephew would have come as witness."

"I thought he would hardly care to meet Musgrave again," Hicks snarled; even he had had enough hectoring.

"I don't pay you to think. Only to obey orders. And then you must needs go to Cantire. Why?"

"It was the only chance of getting in; I could hardly climb the wall."

"Why go at all?" Wanstead fixed his eyes on the lawyer.

"It was necessary to make certain that Musgrave was there," he replied, his face looking sallow in the sunlight.

Wanstead moved his hands restlessly. "You'll want all your wits about you. I don't care a rap for the local police, but Sinclair is a different matter."

"I don't expect he will stay here for long."

"You will have to go to the 'Green Man' and fake up something to cover your lie about having heard of the murder there."

"I'll do my best, but it's risky work."

The door was flung open, and Lady Wanstead entered the room.

She was tall, angular and bony. As a young girl she may have possessed considerable attraction in a masterful dark beauty, but age had hardened her features, and the nose was too prominent. Her mouth was hard and the black eyes had the same arrogant look as her brother's.

She stared at common folk as though to say in Stevenson's words:

"God damn you, did God make you?"

She invariably spoke of the 'lower orders,' and regarded her family as something set apart from commoner clay. The anger died out of Wanstead's face. Bully as he was in business, he was terribly afraid of his wife.

She ignored Hicks altogether, and closed the door behind her.

"What is the meaning of all this?"

"My dear; there was really no need for you to come down. The inquest is over, and it must be painful to you to visit this place."

"Stuff and nonsense! Anthony was my only brother, and the last of the Musgraves. Even if we did quarrel, is that any reason why I should not attend his funeral, and, of course, take over our family property?"

"Quite so, my dear, but the place for the present is in the hands of the police. I have no doubt as soon as you have established your claim—" he got no further.

"My claim! There is no question whatever of claim. Anthony had no power to will it away or to sell it; it comes from my father, not from him."

Hicks coughed awkwardly; he felt in the way.

"Who is this person, John?" Lady Wanstead asked.

"Mr. Hicks, the lawyer who acted for your brother, and his father for yours."

Instead of the explosion that Wanstead feared, his wife held out her hand. "I remember now, as a small child, and you were a boy. Your father was a good man, Mr. Hicks. I trust you have followed his example. He served our family faithfully, and I always recompense good service."

Hicks murmured his thanks, not unmindful of the fact that Lady Wanstead did not possess a penny of her own, except what her husband had endowed her with.

"You will, of course, have all the family papers in your charge. I shall want to have them, and we can then discuss matters."

Hicks met a warning glance from Wanstead.

"His lordship is proposing to have the place restored as it used to be from the plans we have," he faltered.

"I had already decided on that," Lady Wanstead said haughtily.

"The funeral is tomorrow at Barton," her husband said hastily, to change an awkward conversation.

"I saw that you had made arrangements without consulting me. It should have been delayed, in order to give the county families a chance to attend."

Wanstead remained silent. He had hurried it on for that very reason, in order that they might have an excuse for not attending, as he was certain would be the case.

"And have these policemen caught the murderer yet?"

"I am afraid they have no clue. They are not very bright. Perhaps it might be as well if the murderer were not discovered." He met his wife's gaze steadily, and she bit her lip. The family name must not be smirched by any vulgar revelations in the press.

"I came down in the car," she said. "I shall now call on the Rector, and then go to Cantire."

"We are going to Barton; perhaps you could give us a lift."

"Barton." Her voice softened at the name. "I remember Barton when I was a child. All our family have been buried there. The church is almost a family chapel."

Sinclair passed through the hotel lounge as their car drove off. Rupert Seften had hidden himself when he saw the terrible form of Lady Wanstead enter the place.

He was nervously pacing the floor waiting for Sinclair, and came forward eagerly.

"I am glad to see you, Sir Arthur, I wanted a talk."

"What is it about?"

"You haven't told my uncle all that took place at that interview?"

"Certainly not: I told you at the time it was confidential."

"Of course, I fully understand that, but I thought after what had taken place here, you might have—"

"Broken my word, you mean? I never do so."

He turned to move away, but Seften followed him like a dog.

"My uncle made me come—I didn't want to," he whined.

"I am afraid that does not interest me. Look here, Seften. I gave you advice at our last meeting. Had you gone at once to your wife, her life might have been saved. I don't want your confidences, and the only excuse of any sort I can find for your conduct is that I believe you were under the influence of Colonel Musgrave."

Sinclair stood by his car, anxious to shake this person off, but Seften persisted. "My uncle wired for me four days ago, but honestly I funked it."

"What for?" Sinclair asked, his interest aroused.

"I don't know what he wanted me for, but he told me he was going to settle matters with Colonel Musgrave—those were his words—and I wanted to keep out of it."

"Well, you have kept out of it. What are you afraid of now?" Sinclair said sternly, knowing what the answer would be.

Seften trembled violently, and looked up the road as though he feared that someone might appear like an avenging angel.

"Mary's brother lives here," he whispered.

"You'll have to face that, and make your peace if you can."

"But, Sir Arthur, if he killed Colonel Musgrave, as they say he did, he'll kill me for a certainty."

"I really can't waste any more of your time, I have to get back to Barton, to the 'Green Man.' "

Seften's heavy face lit up. "Could you give me a lift? My uncle has gone there."

It was difficult to refuse, much as Sinclair was disgusted with the man. "All right, jump in."

He drove in silence to the inn, and Sinclair stopped the car.

"I can only advise you," he said, "either to see Rhodes yourself, or to clear out of the country and make a fresh start somewhere."

He stopped speaking as he saw Seften's face. He was staring at a huge figure that came towards them. Seften looked round for somewhere to hide, but Rhodes had seen Sinclair and came towards him, waving his hand.

"Hello! You are just the man I wanted, Sir Arthur. I expected you would be back here soon. I can't find those two young blighters anywhere. They are up to some mischief. You haven't seen them?"

"I had the pleasure of entertaining Elsie to lunch, but haven't seen her since then. I haven't seen Rob anywhere."

Rhodes shook his huge head. "They are up to no good." There was a deep anxiety in his voice, altogether out of proportion to the mere temporary absence of the two.

Sinclair turned to Seften. "Let me introduce you to Mr. Rhodes—this is Mr. Seften, Lord Wanstead's nephew."

Seften shrank back as though expecting a blow, but Rhodes, to his utter astonishment, merely held out his huge hand with a grin. "Pleased to meet you."

Seften managed to shake the hand and mutter, "How do you do?"

Rhodes turned away, as though the name conveyed nothing to him. "Well, I suppose I must go up to the castle, likely enough they'll be there."

He slouched off without another word, and they saw him shambling up the road in great loping strides.

"He—didn't know me!" Seften said in sudden relief. "Mary never told him."

Sinclair felt a sense of utter disgust. He could not refrain from saying, "Don't be too certain." He left the car where it was, and went in to the inn without further words.

Lady Wanstead was more human in these surroundings. Her family had owned the 'Green Man,' and there had been a time when her father had taken up his residence here for a short time with the two children while he was disposing of the last of his property except Cantire itself, in order to get the money to send Anthony to Sandhurst.

She had roamed these woods and climbed over the ruins of the castle with her handsome brother, then only fifteen. Grimes was most deferential, having a doglike devotion to her father's memory.

Lady Wanstead insisted on being told the whole story as far as Grimes knew it.

Lord Wanstead took a bold line: "It was from Mr. Grimes that we learnt about the murder," he said quietly.

"Me, my lord . . ." Grimes said in surprise.

"Not directly, but Mr. Hicks, who had come out to Barton on some business of mine, overheard you talking about it. You were with Campion, I think."

"It may be," he said doubtfully. "I don't remember seeing you, Mr. Hicks."

"I was passing"—Hicks tried a long shot. "You and Campion were having cider together in the bar."

"Well, I never," Grimes said with a forced laugh, "and I didn't know there was a soul about. I hope you won't mention about that, sir."

"That's all right," Lord Wanstead said haughtily. "No tales out of school."

"You will excuse me, my lady—I have quite a lot of people here." He bowed politely to Lady Wanstead, and went out.

"What on earth is all this?" Lady Wanstead exclaimed when the door was shut. "Why are you so anxious to prove that Mr. Hicks heard of the murder from Grimes and Campion?"

"No reason except that one of those detectives seemed rather inquisitive, and I wished to hear from Grimes that Mr. Hicks had done so."

"But Grimes said nothing of the sort," she declared firmly.

"He was so upset, I expect he has forgotten. It is of no importance. Shall we go to the castle now?"

Lady Wanstead was a shrewd woman, and had the family brains. She said no more on the subject, but was certain there was more in it than appeared on the surface.

A small crowd had gathered round the gates of the drive, which were closed, and a constable stood barring entry. The grim place looked silent and deserted.

"Just open the gates, officer," Lady Wanstead called out.

"Sorry, ma'am, but no one is admitted."

"If you are addressing me, you will say my lady—I am Lady Wanstead, and the owner of the place. Open at once."

The bucolic officer scratched his head.

"Those are my orders, my lady," he said doggedly.

"They do not apply to me, nor to my husband, Lord Wanstead."

She was growing red with anger, and two small boys tittered noisily.

"Mr. Hicks," she said loftily, "tell this person to open—you are a lawyer and know how the law stands on the matter." The constable saw Hicks, who was sitting with the driver, and touched his cap. He knew the lawyer by sight, and was afraid of the Law. Perhaps he might have obeyed, but at that moment a car dashed up and Sinclair stepped out with Inspector Gillian.

"What's all this?" he asked. Gillian came from the back.

The constable saluted.

"We wish to go in, and this man refuses," Lady Wanstead said.

Sinclair was unmoved. "He was quite right to do so. He had strict orders. Only Inspector Gillian can give permission."

Lord Wanstead saw that he must save his face—the crowd had drawn close, and were gaping at them.

"He was quite right," he said with an assumption of heartiness, "but after our conversation this morning, I was anxious to see exactly the state of preservation, with a view to the restoration."

"Exactly—Gillian, I think you might let them in."

Something in Sinclair's face made the latter nod to the constable and the great iron gates were thrown open. The two cars went up the drive, and halted at the massive gateway.

"There is another officer inside on duty," Gillian said sulkily.

He had received news of the greatest importance, and had come to investigate. The last thing he wanted was the presence of Lord and Lady Wanstead.

The bolts were withdrawn, and the main gate unlocked. Constable Ted Bolt stood in the doorway, and then saluted. Lady Wanstead stepped over the threshold of her ancient home.

Leaving the unbidden visitors to themselves, Gillian beckoned Sinclair, and they followed the constable to the Campions' rooms after the gate had been carefully fastened. Gillian turned to the constable.

"Now what is this I hear from the constable on night duty?"

"All I know, sir, is that when I took over this morning, Wells was fair scared. He said that he had, acting under your orders, sir, taken the keys of the main and side gates after locking them up. He patrolled the castle all night, it being cold, and when he came in here for a rest and a warm, he thought the Campions had gone to bed. In the morning, hearing nothing of them, he became suspicious, and found their bedroom door unlocked. They were nowhere in the place and their beds had not been slept in. Clean gone, and goodness knows how they got out of the castle. I had a look myself, sir, but could find no trace."

"This rather complicates matters. We shall have to get on their track. I wonder how far that tale of theirs is true. It looks fishy to me."

"If they had just moved in the ordinary way, they were perfectly entitled to do so, and there would have been no mystery about it."

Sinclair said thoughtfully.

"They haven't taken a single thing, as far as I can see, sir."

"And that's all you have to report?" Gillian said.

"Yes, sir. Except one small matter, hardly worth your notice."

"Let's have it, Bolt," Sinclair said as Gillian was turning away.

"About two hours ago or so, that young Campion girl came to the door and wanted to come in. She said she wanted to see her father and mother, which was reasonable enough, and of course I couldn't tell her they weren't here, so I tried to put her off. She's a cheeky young piece, and told me I was a fool, and that she would speak to Sir Arthur Sinclair about it."

Sinclair smiled. "I am flattered."

The constable addressed Gillian. "Beg pardon, sir, but would you ask Sergeant Haddon to take me off this job and put another man on?"

"You had better ask him yourself, he will be here presently."

"Why do you want to be relieved?" Sinclair asked.

"There are things here I don't like, sir, and that's straight. A man I can deal with, but when it comes to things that are not human . . ."

"Damn!" Gillian swore. "These country yokels make me tired. Just because there are a lot of old tales floating about."

He wheeled round angrily and marched off to the chapel, where he heard Lord Wanstead talking loudly. Sinclair stayed for a moment.

"What things, Bolt?" he asked in a kindly manner.

"Well, sir, it's difficult to say, but Wells told me on night duty last night he saw something black with red eyes. He swears it flew like a bird, and he's not nervous. Even today I fancied I heard all kind of noises, and went to see, but there was nothing there. Gets on my nerves it does, sir."

"I'll see Haddon myself. If the Campions are gone, I don't think a night duty will be necessary."

The constable thanked him, and Sinclair strolled leisurely to the chapel.

Wanstead was in full blast. "We shall want this chapel as nearly like the original as possible. You have a picture of it, Hicks?"

"Yes, my lord, an old engraving."

"That north tower looks none too safe; I see the top has fallen."

Lady Wanstead was not in the chapel, but looking up, Sinclair saw her at the head of the staircase leading to the Monks' Room.

The light came from the glassless chapel window, and fell full on her face, leaving her body in shadow, and Sinclair saw Colonel Musgrave staring down at him. The illusion was extraordinary. Shorn of those trappings that distinguish a woman's figure from a man's, the face alone remained, and the likeness was uncanny. The next moment she moved and the impression vanished. But Sinclair had seen something else that had given him a shock.

"I suppose," he asked casually, "there are no secret passages or old hiding-places such as one reads of in books?"

"None that I ever heard of," she answered with a firmness that made Sinclair have doubts. She was just too emphatic, and the stony look she gave him was one of defiance.

"So she knows of that place," Sinclair said to himself.

It was the most extraordinary situation Sinclair had come across, and puzzling. Here in this very place the murder had been done, and neither Wanstead nor his lady showed the remotest interest in the matter nor any desire to find the murderer. They were merely interested in the restoration of the castle before the late owner was even buried.

They moved into the withdrawing room, open to the sky, and with the socket holes and fireplaces of the solar that had once been above it, showing in the walls.

The small enclosed garden showed through the ragged hole where once had been a door.

"It is going to be a long job repairing this, my lord," Hicks remarked.

"I think I know by this time how to make people hustle when I want building done," Wanstead replied crisply.

An interruption occurred. The constable, a stout_y built and sturdy man, entered the chapel behind them, holding with a firm grasp Elsie in one hand and Rob in the other.

Rob was lithe and active, and Sinclair could see at once that he could easily have wriggled free, but would not leave Elsie to face the music.

"Caught 'em, the young rascals. Just trying to sneak out of the front gate—thought I wasn't there, they did."

"What is the meaning of this?" Wanstead exclaimed, surveying the pair with an arrogant stare.

They both looked very dirty and ragged, and more like a pair of tramps.

"Who are these persons?" Lady Wanstead asked.

Sinclair had been watching Rob carefully. His usual jaunty manner was gone, and he was certain that the reason was not just because they had been caught. There was a look of positive horror in his eyes.

Before the outraged constable could reply he said quietly, "This is Elsie Campion, daughter of the two who were caretakers here, whom you dismissed, Lord Wanstead, and this lad is the late clerk of your lawyer, whom he dismissed. I know them both."

Wanstead looked exceedingly uncomfortable. Here was the young man who had acted as witness to Musgrave's signature, and, although he had never seen him before, there was no telling what he might blurt out. His eyes met those of Hicks, and he read the same alarm there.

"It's my opinion they are up to no good," the constable said.

"I cannot see that they are doing any harm, Bolt," Sinclair said. "You could hardly prosecute them for trespass when the girl lives here. You refused her admission."

"What puzzles me—" the constable began, and Sinclair knew he was wondering how they got in, a question he did not want discussed.

"I know them both, Lord Wanstead," he said, "and if you will allow me I will have a word with them."

"Do by all means—I can't be bothered with a pair of gutter-snipes. There is nothing here to steal."

Bolt released them reluctantly. Neither had spoken a word, and Elsie had kept her eyes on the ground.

Gillian was frankly puzzled; he was beginning to understand Sinclair, and was certain that something of importance lay behind this trivial incident.

Sinclair turned to Elsie and Rob. "Will you both go to the sitting-room and wait for me? I would like a word, but shan't keep you long."

"I've had enough of this," Gillian said impatiently. "These people seem to think of nothing but the restoration of this old ruin, and the late owner not yet in his grave."

"If I were you, Inspector, I should go with them. One never knows what may slip out in conversation, and keep your eye on that lawyer."

"If you think that, sir"—Gillian lifted his eyebrows slightly—"I wonder you don't do it yourself; you get on better with these people."

"I have a much more important job on hand just now," Sinclair said in a manner almost solemn, that sent a shudder down Gillian's back in this sombre place.

CHAPTER VIII

THE FATE OF THE CAMPIONS

THE CAMPIONS' ROOM had a deserted appearance. The furniture was still there, and there was a fire in the grate, which the police officers used, but those small things that make a home had been packed up, ready for moving.

The two young people were huddled over the fire, and Sinclair took a seat between them in a friendly manner, and lit his pipe.

"Let's hear all about it, Rob."

"Elsie told me that she had lunched with you, sir, and she had told you about that fiver."

"Yes; and I was going to make some inquiries about that."

"Elsie came to see her parents, but the sleuth wouldn't let her in, and she came and told me."

"That I heard from the constable."

"Something terrible has happened, and I hardly know how to begin," Rob burst out, as though he had been holding himself in with difficulty.

Elsie took up the tale. "We didn't mean to tell you, but now we must. You know about my habit of sleep-walking: well, last night it seems I did it again, and was making straight for the castle, when Rob, who had followed me, grabbed me."

"That was a dangerous thing to do, but go on," Sinclair said gravely.

"I got her back, sir, and she was in an awful state. She was certain something had happened to the Campions. It must have been a sort of a dream."

"Where was your uncle?"

Rob seemed confused. "He wasn't at home," he said shortly.

"Very good, go on."

"This afternoon, when Elsie couldn't get in, we decided to try the old conduit you know about, sir, and we crawled up there."

"Don't!" Elsie put her hands before her face and sobbed.

"At the bottom of the shaft," Rob said in a half whisper, "the bodies of Mr. and Mrs. Campion are lying dead."

"You are sure?" Sinclair said, drawing in his breath quickly.

"I stepped on something soft, and flashed my torch. Elsie wouldn't look, but I examined them as well as I could. There is no doubt about it."

"They must have fallen down somehow, but I didn't know they knew about that entrance," Sinclair said soothingly.

Elsie looked up, her face tragic in its horror. "They were murdered, Sir Arthur, I am certain of it."

"The rope was still there?" Sinclair asked sharply.

"Of course; we climbed up. Elsie wouldn't go back—the bodies were lying half in the shaft, blocking the way."

"I wanted to escape somehow," Elsie said. "I felt I simply couldn't go down that long, dark tunnel with those bodies behind me."

"Then you came out and the constable caught you."

"He wouldn't have caught us," Rob said contemptuously. "We heard you talking, and were coming to see you when he grabbed us."

"We mustn't jump to conclusions, Rob, but this is a very serious matter. You must be guided entirely by me. You must not breathe a word to anyone about this. Remember, Rob, Elsie's life may depend on that. I am not trying to frighten you. As soon as possible I must get her away. I don't like this sleep-walking."

Rob looked Sinclair fairly in the face. "Then you think they were murdered?"

"That I shall try to find out. If they were, it was because they knew too much. Now you two had better get off to your uncle's cottage. Leave this to me. I shall make a point of seeing you both, but, Rob, don't let Elsie out of your sight, do you understand? Fasten her window at night, and sleep on a mattress outside her door."

"I'll do that, sir," Rob said grimly. "My uncle's got a revolver, and I'll borrow it."

Sinclair conducted them to the front gate, and Ted Bolt, rather unwillingly, let them out.

Then Sinclair returned to find Gillian.

He found the Inspector in the old dining-hall, writing notes in a book.

"Where are the Wansteads?" Sinclair asked.

"They made a move, quite suddenly; Hicks, that lawyer chap, said something to Wanstead that I could not catch, and he seemed quite upset. He told Lady Wanstead they would come again, and went straight out."

"Where were they?" Sinclair asked sharply.

"In the garden. Hicks had looked up at the north tower, or what is left of it. I saw him start, and then he whispered to Wanstead. I looked myself, but couldn't see anything except a loop-hole in the wall belonging to one of those circular staircases that seem to be in every tower."

"So they went," Sinclair said thoughtfully. "You heard nothing more?"

"Only Hicks turned to Lord Wanstead as they were going out, and said 'not a trace—that's one good thing.' "

"You are sure those were the words?"

"As far as I could make them out. Then his lordship told the officer he was going."

"Come with me, Gillian, I have some very grave news for you."

He led the way to the foot of the garderobe room and removed the loose boards.

"That is marked unsafe." Gillian held back.

"We must risk that—others have been here, as you shall see for yourself."

They climbed to the first room, in which Sinclair had stood before, and Sinclair pointed to the shaft.

"I am going down there," he said, "but I don't want to answer any questions yet. You will want to ask quite a lot."

The knotted rope was suspended from a strong staple just inside the shaft, so that in that dim place, without a light, one would not see it without previous knowledge. Sinclair laid hold on this and swung himself over the coping.

"Whatever is the meaning of this?" Gillian asked in wonder.

"You shall know soon," was the grim response as Sinclair's head disappeared down the shaft.

Presently, from the depths below, Gillian heard a voice faintly, "Can you come down?"

The Inspector was not very pleased at the idea, but if Sinclair could calmly descend, he could not hang back. He spat on his hands and lowered himself over with secret qualms.

At last he felt hands touching his boots. "Steady now, and I will guide your feet."

He stood in that narrow place, wondering where he had got to. Sinclair flashed his torch, and Gillian gave a cry in spite of himself. Two bodies lay at his feet; he was almost standing on them.

"These are the Campions," Sinclair said. "Both are dead. I can't ascertain anything else till we get them up. We must tie the rope to each in turn, and I will pull them up. Only I wanted you as the officer in charge of the case to see them *in situ*."

His voice echoed eerily up the shaft, though he spoke in a hushed tone. "I will hold one up if you will tie it. The rope isn't long enough otherwise."

"Wouldn't it be better to go and get a longer rope?" Gillian had an intense distaste for his task.

"I don't like the look of these walls. There are nasty cracks. The sooner we get it done the better." He gave a tug to the rope, and there came an ominous sound. Some loose rubble and stones pelted down, and there was a strange rumbling sound from above.

"Quick." Sinclair dropped the rope and fairly pushed Gillian into the conduit as an avalanche of stones came crashing down. He had barely time to take cover in the confined space. "Crawl down for God's sake," he shouted, and Gillian, half numbed by the suddenness of the catastrophe, scuttled into the darkness.

Sinclair lay panting behind him as the whole inside of the shaft crashed down with a deafening roar, blocking the entrance and flowing out into the conduit.

The darkness and the horror were too much for Gillian. He could not turn. "Are you hurt?" he asked with a catch in his voice.

"Just in time—another second and I should have been crushed to death." Sinclair gave a cheerful laugh.

"But, man," Gillian almost shrieked, "we are buried alive!"

"Not quite as bad as that—there is another entrance; crawl along, my boy, and be thankful you are alive."

A gentle prod acted as a goad, and Gillian crawled along the conduit, now growing stuffy as one end was effectually blocked up.

The tunnel seemed interminable, but at last Gillian emerged into the old cesspool and was able to ease his cramped back. Both men were pouring with sweat and grimy as colliers.

"Let's get out of this," Sinclair said, and climbed out of the place, giving a hand to Gillian.

The blessed light of day was above them, and they lay on the grass by the clump of bushes to recover.

"What in God's name is the meaning of all this?" Gillian exclaimed, indignation struggling with the respect he felt for Sinclair.

The latter spoke slowly, seeming to pick his words with care. "I can't tell you all of it, but I had information from Rob Summers that the Campions were there."

"How did he know?" Gillian growled.

"There you go! You must accept my word that I am entirely satisfied that he found out in a perfectly innocent way. He came and told me. That was the reason for his presence in the castle. He knows no more as to how the bodies came there than you and I do."

"Then he knew about this funny sort of tunnel?"

"He knew, but he had never been through it before that I know."

"Then I suppose the girl knew, as they were together."

"Elsie knew, but her name must on no account be brought into this. There is no need. We found out for ourselves, and I have already been through this conduit and climbed the rope."

Gillian sat up and stared at his companion. "You know best, sir, but to my mind there's too much mystery about it altogether. Why should we not say exactly what did happen?"

"Because, my friend, we don't want another murder on our hands. I am afraid for that girl's life, and that is why I ask for your silence."

"If that is the case, of course I shall do as you wish, but does that mean that you know who the murderer is?"

"My dear fellow, if I did I would tell you at once. I am not wishing to work without you. I haven't the remotest idea at present, but that there is a murderer needs no demonstrating."

"Then you think the Campions were murdered?"

"If this had not occurred we might have had some evidence, but their bodies are now crushed beyond recognition, and we may never know the truth. There are obviously three possibilities. The first is that the Campions committed suicide. They may have fallen down the shaft by accident, or they may have been thrown down either before they had been murdered, or after, though I could see no actual wounds on them."

"Each of your theories presents difficulties," Gillian said judicially.

"Don't I know it? I have had several talks with these two, and I cannot imagine them committing suicide; they are the last people to do it. Next, why should they fall down there when they did not know that there was an exit?"

"You know that?"

"I know it for certain. They also knew the place was not safe, so why go there when they could have walked out of the place, as they had every right to do? No, it's not so easy. As to murder, there was an officer on duty all night, and he was relieved this morning. That seems equally improbable."

"It's pretty tough."

"There is one thing of great importance to us. If they were murdered, and I am assuming that for the moment, the murderer did not know of this entrance."

"You're right, Sir Arthur. They would hardly have hurled the bodies down there if they had known."

Sinclair nodded. "You still use the 'they'," he commented with a smile. "Evidently the old shaft appeared merely as a blind hole into which bodies could be dropped with impunity, but there is a further point here, and one that may give us a clue. Someone seems to have known that that tower was rocky, and might fall at any time."

Gillian shuddered. "Don't let us speculate further on that. The fall might have been deliberately planned."

"Come along." Sinclair sprang up. "We must get back to the castle, to reassure the constable, or he may think we have come a cropper."

They walked round to the front entrance, where Ted Bolt was preparing to lock up and go to Barton. He had heard the rumbling sound and seen no trace of the two detectives, and was scared out of his wits. He was genuinely pleased to see them alive, though in a shocking condition.

Seeing that the constable was considerably shaken, Gillian allowed him to lock the place up and come out by the postern, bringing the keys with him.

They went up the road towards Barton in Sinclair's car.

A shout behind them made Sinclair stop, and the sound of running feet behind him made him turn. Rhodes was running towards them and asked for a lift. He had emerged from the woods and was black from the boughs.

He turned fiercely on Ted Bolt. "Here, what have you been up to, trying to arrest my young nephew and that girl?"

"Jump in if you want a lift," Sinclair said, "but don't start quarrelling. I am answerable for them."

"I am glad to hear it," Rhodes said sulkily. "Of course, you didn't know where they were when I asked you, did you?"

"I did not," Bolt said.

Sinclair put in the clutch. At the cross roads, Rhodes got down. "Thanks for the lift. And one word of advice, Mr. Detective. Don't try messing about in that castle—it isn't healthy. You can take it or leave it."

They saw him slouching up the road in the direction of his cottage.

At the inn Gillian got busy on the 'phone. The shaft would have to be dug out, or the whole tower demolished. The fall may have loosened the entire structure. It would be a long job.

Sinclair retired to his room and changed. When he came down, Grimes met him in the hall, full of apologies. The place was full with sightseers and newshawks, and the landlord had ventured to put Lord and Lady Wanstead into Sinclair's private room, where they were having a scratch meal. He trusted that Sinclair would not mind. Having reassured him on that point, Sinclair entered the sitting-room.

His reception was most cordial, and a complete change, which put Sinclair on his guard. Wanstead apologized for the intrusion, and requested Sinclair to join them. Hicks was not there, but Seften had joined his uncle and aunt.

A place was laid for him, and Lord Wanstead insisted on a fresh bottle of old burgundy being brought. The whole atmosphere had cleared.

"I think we have seen all we want to at the castle," Lady Wanstead opened when Grimes had brought steaming roast beef.

"I am glad to hear it. You will now be able to get busy with the restorations," Sinclair said, falling into their mood.

"The sooner the better—my wife is very keen on seeing the thing started. It all depends on you now, as soon as you can get hold of that French architect and persuade him to come."

Sinclair sensed that Lord Wanstead and his wife were watching him, as though hanging on his reply. Seften showed a jaded indifference.

"There is nothing to keep me here. I was only on a visit. This affair is in the hands of the county police, and perhaps there will be a Yard man sent down if they have any difficulties over the solution."

"Then you could start at once?" Lady Wanstead said eagerly.

"My dear," Wanstead observed, "Sir Arthur is a very busy man—we can't expect him to give up his time at our behest, at a moment's notice."

"I can go quite easily—tomorrow if you like."

"That is very kind of you." Wanstead leant back in his chair as though he had just done a successful deal with a business rival.

"No expense must be spared—make what terms you like with M. Guillet, and, of course"—he laughed—"if you really want me to give what would have been a perfectly fair commission to the Campions, I will certainly do so."

Sinclair finished his excellent roast beef and wiped his mouth carefully before he spoke.

"The Campions will never want your help now."

"You mean that they have bolted?" Seften asked languidly.

"I mean they are dead."

"Dead! Good gracious—whatever happened to them?" Lady Wanstead asked the question. "I can't believe it."

"There is an old shaft," Sinclair said, speaking slowly. "Mention of it is made in the guide-book. It leads from a room in the north-west tower. It appears that they had gone down there, or perhaps the old man had, and his wife, fearing what actually happened, followed him. Then the wall must have collapsed and buried them both alive."

Wanstead's ruddy face had gone white. "But this is terrible. I can't understand it. Do you think they could have committed suicide?"

"Of course there is that possibility. Inspector Gilian is having them dug out, but it is risky, as the wall has given way."

"What a thing to happen. When do you suppose it took place?"

"That is impossible to tell," Sinclair said evasively. At the back of his mind one thought was insistent. Neither of the Wansteads had asked the obvious question—*how did Sinclair know the bodies were under the fallen debris?*

"There is a sort of tunnel or conduit from the shaft under the walls of the castle, which comes out in the garden. Did you know of that, Lady Wanstead?"

"Never," she declared emphatically. "The whole of that tower when I was a child was blocked up, and I believe opened when my brother decided to make the place into an exhibition."

"That bears out what the guide-book says," Sinclair said calmly.

Lord Wanstead ordered port and filled a glass for Sinclair. Seften seemed to rouse himself sufficiently to help himself.

"By Jove," he observed, "then that is probably the way by which the murderers got in. That ought to help clear up the mystery."

Wanstead seized on this suggestion with a clutching eagerness.

"I think you are right, Rupert. That certainly helps matters. Of course, they must have got in that way. There is no other, is there, Sir Arthur?"

"Only the front gate!" Sinclair said dryly, and Wanstead laughed at what he evidently considered a joke.

Sinclair soon afterwards took leave of his hosts, promising to let them know how he got on.

Seften followed him into the hall.

"Excuse me, Sir Arthur, may I have a word with you? It's been awfully decent of you to keep that interview secret from my uncle and aunt."

"You didn't follow me to tell me that," Sinclair said coldly.

"No, sir, I didn't. I've only just now got the story of this murder from my uncle. I couldn't say anything in front of them, but don't you think it just possible that the same people who attacked me might have finished old Musgrave off? I've been thinking it over, and of course the attacks might have been aimed at both of us; the poisoned coffee for example, and the shots. There were two, you remember. I sometimes suspected that there was some gang at work. Musgrave always slept with a loaded revolver under his pillow, and seemed watchful."

"It was quite evident to me, when you detailed that story, that such might have been the case," Sinclair said shortly.

"I am only throwing out a suggestion. He may have got mixed up with some secret society or other. What do you think? Am I talking rot?"

Sinclair remained in thought for a moment, and Seften was on the point of turning back.

"I think there is something in what you say, but I must ask you not to talk about it to anyone. It may be disastrous if you do. You might even be the next victim, and pay the penalty for opening your mouth too much. That's all."

Seften winced at the snub, and returned to his uncle and aunt.

Sinclair found Gillian and Sergeant Haddon at the police station.

"Glad to see you, sir," the former said. "We seem to have got into a proper tangle over this case."

"Well, I hope you will have disentangled it by the time I get back."

The two officers looked blankly at the detective. "You are not leaving us?" Gillian protested.

"I am off to Paris to see an architect about restoring Cantire to its former state."

"So you said, sir. But are you serious?"

"In deadly earnest. I leave this problem with you, and it will give you an interesting investigation."

"Of course we know," Gillian said, "you were only on a visit, but we had hoped to have had your advice."

"Perhaps I may learn more in Paris than you here," Sinclair said cryptically. "As to advice—since you ask for it—go easy with those digging operations. They are risky."

"We shall take the utmost care, of course, by shoring up the tower and soon." Gillian was utterly bewildered.

"That is hardly what I meant," he said gravely. "Let the men work in pairs, and have a constable on the watch all the time within sight of the workers. Don't attempt to work at night on any account, and be on the look-out."

Gillian shifted uneasily. "Why not at night?"

"The powers of darkness are abroad then," he said solemnly.

"Really, sir," Haddon interrupted, "you'll give me the jimjams. There are rumours enough going round about the castle. I didn't think that you, sir—"

He got no further. Sinclair spoke earnestly. "I am convinced there is something there that we have not yet discovered. Something that is active and strong, and will stick at nothing. Beyond that I can't go at present."

Gillian stared at Sinclair as though he had suddenly gone mad.

"You may open up more than you bargain for, and the results may be disastrous. That's all I can say."

"Can't you tell us what to do?" Gillian asked. "It all seems so vague."

"I can tell you what not to do. Keep that story of this afternoon's adventure as concise and commonplace as possible, and don't mention Elsie. Then, don't hurry over your excavations."

"They will have to be, from what I hear."

"I found that Lord Wanstead and his good lady were occupying my room at the 'Green Man.' Now why? Wanstead has his own suite at the 'Horse and Hounds' here, and a dinner after his own heart. Yet he dined there."

"I don't know! It seems very simple to me. Lady Wanstead knew the place when she was a child."

"No, Gillian, my friend, it's not so simple. He stayed there deliberately to see me. And the reason? I'll tell you. He and his lady were extremely anxious that I should go to Paris as soon as possible."

"They wanted to get you out of the way, I expect," Haddon said respectfully.

"Yes. They wanted to get me out of the way, as you say," Sinclair said, with peculiar emphasis on the words.

Sinclair held out his hand to each in turn. "Carry on; perhaps I may be back sooner than you think, but hold your horses."

He went off to get his bag from the 'Green Man.' Rhodes was having a frugal supper with Rob and Elsie in their small kitchen, by the light of an oil lamp. A cheerful fire burned on the old-fashioned cottage hearth.

The sound of a car stopping outside made Rhodes look up suddenly and seize a thick cudgel. He walked to the door, and flung it open defiantly. Sinclair stepped inside with a smile.

"Am I disturbing you?"

Elsie jumped to her feet with a cry of welcome.

"Come in, if you want to. I was thinking maybe it might be someone else," Rhodes said in a less surly tone, and shut the door.

"Well, what are you doing about it?" he said, sitting with his head on his arms and glowering at Sinclair.

"Inspector Gillian and I were trying to discover the whereabouts of the Campions, and found a place that was boarded up, and in a chamber up one flight of stairs there was a peculiar shaft, with a rope in it. We went down there to investigate, and were nearly trapped by a fall of stones."

Elsie's eyes grew large with fear. "Did you find anything there, Sir Arthur?"

"Yes—the bodies of the unfortunate people. They must have fallen down."

Rhodes snarled impatiently. "Do you think I'm a fool? These two told me all about it. What's the good of coming that cock-and-bull yarn?"

Sinclair spoke very deliberately. "Because, Mr. Rhodes, that is the official version, and no other must be told. Do you take my meaning?"

"I suppose you police have got something up your sleeves."

"I mean just this, that neither Elsie nor Rob must appear in this. I hope that is clear, and you must help me."

The surly frown on Rhodes' face lifted. "If it's that way, I'll tell any old thing you wish."

"I am leaving for Paris tonight," Sinclair said, as though in answer to Rhodes' words.

"You are not going to leave us, Sir Arthur?" Elsie cried.

"Yes and no. It depends on Mr. Rhodes and you two."

Rhodes glared across the table at Sinclair, as though he read something into the words.

"What is it, mister?" he said aggressively.

"A rather strange proposal, and one prompted only by the wish for Elsie's safety. This queer habit of sleep-walking is growing on her, and may lead to serious consequences. I think she ought to get away from here, and I want your permission to take these two with me to Paris."

Rhodes face went a dusky red. "I'm not Elsie's guardian."

"Rob is your nephew. I will be responsible for them, but you must help. If they come, you must on no account tell anyone that they have gone with me."

"What a lark!" Rob exclaimed joyfully. "We'll go, eh, Elsie?"

"I haven't any clothes," the girl said simply.

"You need not worry about that. We shall go to London first, and you can get some there. I will look after them, Mr. Rhodes, and it will not be for long."

"Take 'em by all means. As for keeping my mouth shut, I'm not so fond of the cops as all that. They can go to hell for all I care."

"Then we'll come," Rob said. "When do we start?"

"At once. I have my car ready, and my bag is inside. I have told them at Payning that I am off, so that's all right. Go and do your packing."

"That won't take long," Elsie said almost gaily. The thought of the adventure had brought colour to her face, and her eyes shone with excitement.

When they had gone to do their scanty packing, Rhodes turned to Sinclair. "I can't follow your game, mister, but I can see you mean well by them. I am not going to let you pay for Rob at any rate. I take no man's charity."

He slouched to a cupboard in the corner and took out an old wallet. "Here you are—pay out of that." He flung some notes on the table.

"As you please, Mr. Rhodes; I will keep a careful account." Sinclair knew that one unguarded word or a refusal would rouse this man's stubborn pride. He placed the notes in his pocket.

The two returned and took a hurried farewell of Rhodes, who even so far unbended as to kiss Elsie and shake Rob's hand.

He waved to them as the car drove off into the night.

They stopped for food and a few hours' rest at Taunton, and before Sinclair turned in he drew the notes from his pocket, and also a certain list of numbers he had retained. He compared them closely. All the notes that Rhodes had given him were on the list.

CHAPTER IX

THE FALLING TOWER

THE FUNERAL OF COLONEL MUSGRAVE was attended only by the villagers, who came out of curiosity. He had been a stranger and a wanderer on the earth, and the place had been so long nothing but a name that no one of those whose fathers had known the Musgraves thought it worth attending.

The old family vault was opened, and the aged rector mumbled through the Office for the Dead. There were no tears and only a gorgeous wreath from Lady Wanstead, ordered especially by her husband from London.

The assembly broke up in silence and adjourned to the 'Green Man.'

The Wanstead party took possession of the sitting-room which Sinclair had vacated, and his lordship ordered champagne, as suited to the occasion. Hicks had been invited in, as the family lawyer, though Musgrave had left no Will, having nothing to leave. The five thousand he had received from Hicks had vanished into thin air.

The lawyer looked more than usually sallow, and Wanstead noticed that he furtively filled his glass when he thought he was unobserved.

"Well, now that is over we can get to work properly," Wanstead said.

The wine had inspired the nobleman with a spirit of geniality, together with that reaction that always comes after a funeral, even of someone well beloved, and makes the mourners feel ashamed that they can actually laugh.

"You have those plans here, haven't you, Hicks?" he asked.

The lawyer took a black despatch-bag and was about to open it.

Lady Wanstead rose. "I don't think I care to discuss this matter. After all, Anthony was my brother, and it's rather ghoulish. I am going to Payning. Will you drive me, Rupert?"

Seften was glad enough to get away, and they went out together.

"Thank goodness," Wanstead exclaimed, and taking hold his brand new morning coat, tore it off and tucked up his sleeves. "I can't get used to the damned things," he told Hicks. "When I had to go to be sworn in as a Privy Councillor, as every peer has to, I thought I should have died in that Court dress. As for the sword, I nearly tripped over it."

They were busy over their plans when Grimes announced that Inspector Gillian and Haddon wished to see him. Lord Wanstead told the landlord to ask them in, and to bring two more glasses and another bottle.

The officers were surprised to see his lordship in shirtsleeves, and in a much more genial mood than they had seen him before.

"Sit down and help yourselves. What can I do for you gentlemen?"

"You heard, my lord, about the discovery of the bodies of those caretakers, the Campions, by Sir Arthur and myself?"

"Of course—I suppose they were really there?" Wanstead said carelessly.

"I am afraid there is no doubt, but the bodies have been buried, and I wanted your formal permission to have them dug out. It will be a ticklish job, as the whole tower may come down."

"You are quite right, Inspector, it must of course be done. But it is a pity you could not wait till the architect comes over from France. Sir Arthur Sinclair has gone to see him."

"So that is the reason for his sudden departure. He left last night."

Lord Wanstead lifted his glass and watched the bubbles floating upwards. "Yes," he said complaisantly, "the finest architect in France—a M. Guillet."

Sergeant Haddon spoke for the first time. The wine, and the unexpected geniality of the nobleman, had inspired confidence.

"Guillet, my lord! I remember him very well. Funny sort of bloke, and rather fussy."

Wanstead managed to set his glass down without spilling it, but his face had grown grey under the natural red.

"What's that you say? M. Guillet has been here before?"

"Why, yes, my lord," Haddon stammered, struck by the sudden change in Wanstead's manner. "He was here three years ago, when the late Colonel Musgrave started to restore the castle, and then stopped—we all thought perhaps his funds had run out."

There was a silence in the room that was almost tangible. Hicks' face had gone the colour of chalk, and he sat down heavily on the sofa in the corner.

Haddon noticed nothing. He went on: "His name stuck in my memory because it was so like yours, Inspector."

Wanstead gulped down a glass of champagne and swallowed hard.

"I suppose," he said coldly, "Sir Arthur Sinclair was not here then, at the same time?"

"Oh no, my lord, I never saw him in my life till this case cropped up. I am sure we should have heard of it if he had been."

"What is your opinion of the case, Inspector?"

"As far as we have gone, my lord, I think we can be fairly sure that the late Colonel Musgrave became involved in some secret society, or mixed up with gangsters, and they hunted him down and took their revenge.

"And does Sir Arthur Sinclair hold that view?"

"It's difficult to tell with him, my lord, he's a dark horse. One never knows when he is bluffing or pulling one's leg; but he did say that he might get more information by going to Paris than by staying here."

Wanstead's hand gripped a chair hard, and the knuckles went white. He shot a glance at the inert form of Hicks, and then turned incisively to the police officers.

"Thank you, Inspector. You may certainly try to get the bodies out. I am not sure when M. Guillet will be here; perhaps he may be too busy. I shall come and see how you are getting on."

Lord Wanstead had not risen to the position he held without very strong will power and remarkable self control when in a tight corner.

He waited till the door had closed on the two police officers, and then turned to Hicks in a perfect frenzy. "You miserable rat. Why the hell didn't you tell me that this Guillet had been here before with Musgrave?"

"But, my lord, I hadn't the remotest idea that you were going to send for him, or I would have warned you."

"Stop! Let me think—of course it was Sinclair who recommended this man to me, and I, like a fool, fell into the trap."

Hicks appeared to be talking to himself; his staring eyes were fixed on vacancy. "Three years ago, and he left off the work quite suddenly—he *knows*."

A shudder shook the frame of the business magnate. "To think that I, like a fool, urged Sinclair to go, in order to get him out of the way. Do you think Sinclair knows anything?"

"Depend upon it, he must have guessed." There was a despairing note in Hicks' voice. "He's very deep, Sinclair, in spite of his seemingly quiet ways."

Wanstead spoke—harsh and domineering.

"You must go to Paris at once—do you understand? At once. Take a special 'plane."

"I, my lord?" the miserable being stammered.

"I said so, didn't I? Here is money." He snatched a heavy wallet from his pocket and threw down a wad of notes on the table. "That will be ample for your expenses. No delay, mind. Take my car to the airport. It is waiting for me at the door. Try to prevent them from meeting at all costs. I have his address here"—he searched in the wallet and produced a card—"here you are, Bellevue Hotel. Wire me how you get on."

"And Guillet, my lord?"

"If the mischief is done, and they have already met, you must try to find out whether Guillet has told him. If not, possibly the danger may be averted. Guillet must not come here. I shall cable Sinclair that I have changed my mind about him. No! You had better tell him. It might sound fishy."

Hicks rose slowly to his feet. He was calmer now, and his keen lawyer's brain had grasped the situation. He faced Lord Wanstead with the courage of a coward strung up by fear and avarice.

"I am to leave my business and undertake this journey, at considerable risk, and perhaps danger—for what?"

"You miserable cur. I will pay you well—haven't I paid you already, you Shylock?"

"I have all the documents at the bank," Hicks said, apparently irrelevantly.

Lord Wanstead positively snarled. "You rat! Sit down there and write an order for the bank manager to deliver them to me."

"There is evidence there, among the papers," Hicks said with a cunning smile.

"I see. And you think that if I should destroy it you might have a hold over me for blackmail. Is that it?"

"I never thought of such a thing," Hicks protested volubly. "I merely wanted to warn you that they might be dangerous things to have in your possession."

In obedience to the overbearing profiteer, Hicks wrote the necessary note and handed it to Wanstead.

"The price I shall want for this can be discussed when I return," Hicks said silkily. "I'll get away at once; just a bag for necessities."

Lord Wanstead helped himself to another glass of champagne.

A knock at the door made both men start, as guilty men do at the least thing.

Gillian entered and saluted.

"What is it, man?" Lord Wanstead asked testily; his nerves were on edge.

"Beg pardon, my lord, for intruding, but this affair is getting too much for me."

In a deathlike silence Wanstead licked his lips and waited. His eyes strayed in the direction of Hicks, who was standing by the door.

"Them two, young Bob, your late clerk, Mr. Hicks, and that girl of the Campions."

"What about them?" Wanstead shouted. The man was so long at getting to the point.

"They have done a bunk," Gillian said primly. He was annoyed at the change in his lordship's manner.

"Done a what?—talk the King's English. You mean they have gone off somewhere together?"

"I don't know about going off," the Inspector said stiffly. "Rhodes says that he hasn't seen them since yesterday afternoon when they went to the castle. I asked him myself. He's a surly beggar, but I think he was telling the truth. He seemed upset about it."

"You think they may be still in the castle?"

Gillian was tired of devious ways. "I think it's more than likely they've suffered the same fate as the Campions," he said gravely.

"Sinclair sent them off to the Campions' room to wait for him," Wanstead said. "That's the last I saw of them."

"No one seems to have seen them after that."

"Very well. Hicks, you had better get away; I shall expect to hear from you shortly. Inspector, you had better get your men to work, as you suggested. I shall make a point of coming to the castle this afternoon. I have one or two things I have to do." He glanced significantly at Hicks, who slunk out.

"If you don't mind, my lord, I'll get on the 'phone at once. The gang of men are all ready, and the sooner we get to work the better."

When Wanstead was alone he set himself to study the plans with a minuteness that showed more than a mere archaeological interest. He breathed a sigh of relief when he had finished his studies.

Grimes announced that his car had returned, and, carefully stowing the plans into the despatch-case, he left them in charge of Grimes.

Lady Wanstead was waiting for him at the hotel, with the news that she was returning to Town at once. Now that the funeral was over she had no further interest in Cantire, the very sight of which brought back painful memories.

"I am taking Rupert with me."

"By all means. I don't want him hanging round here, you know, my dear, with that hulking brute Rhodes here. You will have to look round for a wife for him. You and I are not as young as we were." After lunch he saw them off at the station and then drove up to Cantire.

At the castle a busy and rather grim scene was being enacted.

Mindful of Sinclair's warning, which he did not understand, Gillian had stationed two constables to watch carefully while the men were at work. A stocky foreman, whose name, Bullen, seemed to suit him, was supervising the work.

The great doors were wide open for the passage of beams and baulks for shoring up the walls, and Bullen informed Lord Wanstead that the whole of the northwest tower, in which was the shaft, was in a shaky condition, and dangerous in its present state.

The men had made an attempt to remove the stones and rubble that had blocked the shaft, but as fast as they pulled out stones others fell from the sides. It was like a crumbling sand castle.

"It will take a good week to get this done, my Lord," Bullen said, scratching his head. "No one should have gone down that shaft at all. I told that Frenchman three years ago, when we discovered it, that it ought to have been covered over. 'Twas madness to my way of thinking."

"Perhaps it may have been madness," Wanstead commented. "There is some suggestion of suicide."

"That's a different matter; but if I were going to kill myself I'd choose some cleaner way. There's always the risk of not finishing the job and lying there with broken legs or something like that."

He eyed Lord Wanstead as he spoke, as though he wished to convey more than the mere words indicated.

"You were employed on this work before then?" Wanstead asked sharply

"Aye. By the late Colonel Musgrave and yon Frenchie. We cleared the place out a bit and found that shaft, and then the work stopped. I thought the Colonel had run out of money, he went off in such a hurry. One of my best men was killed as it was."

"Killed! What do you mean?" Wanstead glanced round the grim walls in sudden fear.

Bullen pointed to where the north tower reared itself into the sky like a vast decayed tooth, broken off and serrated at the top. "He fell off there, my lord," he said briefly, and closed his lips tightly.

"I'm going to have the whole place restored properly. I expect you and your men will get the job."

Bullen shook his head. "See here, mister," he said, forgetting the respect due to a member of the Upper House. "We are doing this job for the police, under orders so to speak, and the sooner it's done the better I shall be pleased, but I'm not going to do any more. And it's my opinion that you'll have to get men from Lunnon or some other place. None of my men will do it."

"What rubbish!" Wanstead exclaimed angrily. "What's your reason? You must have one."

"I've studied my Bible, my lord, and I recollect reading there about someone trying to build a tower, and they was stopped because they should not have done it. It's my opinion there's something in this castle that'll stop us doing any restoring work."

In spite of the bright sunshine a chill feeling came over Wanstead which he could not shake off. "You've got hold of some old wives' tales from the villagers," he said, with more vehemence than he had intended. "If you feel like that, I'll have to bring some sensible men from London. I employ hundreds of them."

"That's as may be. Bring 'em by all means." He turned his back on Wanstead and went off to supervise the men.

Lord Wanstead was learning the age-old lesson, that rank and title by themselves only earn respect from the sycophant and the snob.

Colonel Musgrave, in direst poverty, and without a handle to his name, could have commanded these men by a mere word and they would have obeyed him cheerfully. It is a bitter lesson that profiteers either learn or are so thick-skinned that they never notice.

Gillian joined him, having brought Haddon with him.

"I shouldn't stand there, my lord," he said cautiously, "there's always danger of falling stones, and that tower looks none too safe."

Wanstead turned on him in fury. "Damn it all! You're as bad as the others. Every blessed person here seems scared out of their lives. I've been in the building business"—he stopped at that; it was a matter he did not care to mention now that he was a baron. At the same time he moved into the garden, through the broken entrance from the roofless withdrawing room, where he had been standing.

He stood with Gillian on the little lawn inside the high walls. A crash behind him made him wheel round quickly.

A large stone had fallen on the exact spot on which he had been standing, and had broken into fragments.

"You see, my lord," Gillian said quietly, "my warning was not foolish."

"What the hell are those men up to? Fetch that foreman."

Gillian glanced up to the frowning tower, and there was a peculiar look on his face. "There are no workmen up there, my lord. It must have been loosened by the wind."

"There isn't a wind, you fool," Wanstead snarled, and then saw that fear was making him behave in a childish manner.

"It would be better to have that whole tower down," he said in a calmer voice. "I don't want to run any risks with compensation to widows."

"If I had my way," Gillian said savagely, "I'd pull the whole place down to the ground. There's no Musgrave left to carry on the name, and no good will come of trying to restore it."

"That, I am afraid, is a matter I don't care to discuss with you, Inspector," Wanstead said pompously. "As soon as the police have finished their investigations, and either found these bodies or proved they are not there, I shall take over. You forget my wife is a Musgrave."

A strange confirmation of Gillian's words followed. A rumbling sound was followed by a cloud of dust rising from the interior of the building, and workmen came running out excitedly.

They gazed up at the north-west tower, and Bullen came forward, frowning heavily.

He addressed the Inspector. "This isn't good enough. I'm darned if I'm going to risk the lives of my men, even to get a couple of mouldy corpses out of yon place."

"What do you suggest?" Gillian asked soothingly.

"Why, get a gang, of housebreakers and pull the tower down. That's the only way. We've shored it up, but the inside's rotten. If you ask me, I believe it was that storm loosened the masonry."

Lord Wanstead intervened. "If you propose to do that, I must insist that each stone be numbered so that it can be replaced in its proper place. That has been done in many cases."

"That's your look-out, mister; I'm calling my men off."

"Is that the real reason?" Gillian asked shrewdly.

"You can take it how you like. I don't like the place and that's straight. Let his lordship, who's used to his own houses falling down, get someone to do the job."

He strode off to inform his men that they would leave the work.

"Impertinent devil," Wanstead remarked. "These country bumpkins get beyond themselves. Can't you compel him to finish?"

"I'm afraid not."

"Then you'll have to wait till we have taken the place to pieces before you know about the Campions and their fate. They must be dead bones if they are still there."

"I was thinking more of Rob and Elsie," Gillian said stubbornly. "She knew more about this place than anyone, and they may be somewhere in the castle."

"Oh, of course." Wanstead's manner changed. "That is important. I must get the plans of the castle and go thoroughly over them. One never knows with these old places. Still, they must get food from somewhere, and I suppose if they did hide here they can always come out again." He stopped abruptly, with Gillian's keen eyes on him. There was a puzzled look in them, almost of suspicion.

"Mr. Guillet will know, perhaps, when he comes. He went over the place with Colonel Musgrave," the Inspector said.

Lord Wanstead stood rooted to the spot, a dull flush on his cheeks. He licked his dry lips and made a sort of clicking sound. Gillian watched him closely.

By a strong effort of will Wanstead pulled himself together.

"Yes, of course," he said, with a forced smile, "Guillet will be most useful. We must wait for him to come."

There came an ominous rumbling sound such as forebodes an earthquake.

The workmen came rushing wildly from the building, scattering in every direction. For one moment they saw the top of the high tower shake and lean forward, and then the whole mass crashed down with a noise like thunder, falling stones flying outwards and the masses of ancient stonework flinging themselves to earth. Great fissures yawned and cracked before their eyes. It was an awful but thrilling sight, suggestive of some film with human beings in imminent danger. The whole mass rolled over, and where the tower had stood nothing but a cloud of heavy dust rose like a haze in the air. Deep silence followed.

"My God!" Bullen shouted, and made a dash forward, his first instinct being for his men.

"Come back, you fool." Gillian laid a strong hold on his coat. "There may be some more coming down."

The foreman, his face tensely set, called the men to him, and gave a deep sigh of relief when he found that none were missing.

"We heard it coming," one of them panted; "must have been rotten."

The cloud of dust slowly drifted away, and where the tower had stood nothing but a gigantic heap of rubbish mounted up like a vast slag-heap by a mine.

"That's torn it," Bullen said gruffly. Relief that no one had been killed was mixed with anger that he should have been put on to such a job.

"I'm calling my men off," he told Gillian. "We can't do anything more here. If the place belonged to me, I'd have it all down. 'Tisn't safe for anyone."

He gave an angry look at Lord Wanstead, who was leaning against a broken bit of stonework on the lawn.

"You will have to go out by the postern gate," Gillian said heavily. "The inner court is half full of rubbish."

"You bet I am." Bullen gathered his men together, and Gillian and Lord Wanstead saw him talking volubly to them.

"I am afraid that destroys all hope of finding the children," Lord Wanstead said, and something he could not keep from the tone of his voice roused the Inspector to fury. He turned on the other.

"You devil! I believe you are positively glad."

Before Wanstead could reply, he turned on his heels and strode after the retiring workmen.

A curious expression came to the face of the nobleman as he stared at the pile before him.

He started, finding himself alone, and hurried down the side alley to the postern gate.

His empty car stood in the drive—the rest had gone.

CHAPTER X

IN PARIS

SINCLAIR WAS SITTING ALONE in the lounge of a quiet little hotel near the Place de l'Opéra, where he always stayed. It was not the Bellevue, which name he had deliberately given to Wanstead. He was enjoying the atmosphere of Paris, and waiting with what patience he could for the arrival of Guillet who was on his way back from Carcassone, where he had been putting some finishing touches to that amazing mediaeval stronghold.

He had taken Rob and Elsie round the usual sights of Paris, and now they were out exploring on their own.

Three days had passed since their hectic journey from Rhodes' cottage; three days of wonder and enchantment to the young folk.

Paris always had a charm for Sinclair, as to everyone gifted with imagination. Not the Paris of the tourist, especially staged for English and American visitors, cheap, tawdry and unworthy of the City, but the real Paris which is quite distinct, and more exhilarating than any other city, save only Vienna of the old days before the war.

London is dull, heavy and Mammon-ridden. One can smell money in the fog-laden atmosphere. The close-packed City, with its greedy merchants, and the dreary buildings of the West where the said merchants spend their money on expensive flats and more expensive women; its clutching hands, ultra snobbery, and restrictions on all the amenities of life.

But Paris takes life as it should be taken, as something joyous and fleeting. The spirit of *carpe diem* pervades the place. One does not quarrel or wrangle here, because life is too short. One meets friends in passing in carefree manner, because one may never meet them again. No one can be depressed in Paris who knows it truly, for the French hide their sorrows as they hide their money.

A tall handsome man with a black moustache and beard entered the lounge, and came forward with a smile of welcome.

Monsieur Guillet was at the height of his fame, forty years of age, but youthful and vivacious. He had lived his life to the full, as his quick flashing eyes and rather full lips indicated. With the coveted *Legion d'Honneur* ribbon in his buttonhole, and immaculate clothes on his lithe figure, he might have passed for a film star. Sinclair and he had known each other for many years, and there were secrets between them which would remain hidden.

"*Mon brave!*" he said, extending a delicate artist's hand to the detective.

Sinclair ordered a Kümmel for his friend and a more robust whisky for himself.

After an exchange of courtesies, Sinclair approached the subject of Cantire. "Are you very busy at present, Bertrand?"

Guillet extended his hands with a brief shrug.

"I have a job after your own heart. Restoring an old English mediaeval castle to its pristine beauty."

Guillet's eyes became eager and then clouded over. "But the English—they have no taste. They will not give me what you call the free hand."

"In this case," Sinclair declared solemnly, "I can promise you that you will be able to do exactly what you want. The walls are nearly entire, and there are plans and pictures of the place as it was. Also money is no object."

"For me it is."

"I promised the owner I would try to get you, as the only man in Europe who could make a job of it."

Guillet looked at Sinclair with piercing black eyes. "But you, my friend, what are you doing *dans cette galère*, eh?"

"I am interested, and I am going to get a commission."

The Frenchman dug him in the ribs. "Ah, a commission for the great Sinclair, that is good. My friend, you are too deep for me. But who is the rich owner—some profiteer?"

"His name is Lord Wanstead."

Guillet shook his head. "I do not know him."

"He has recently come into the property, through the death of his brother-in-law." Sinclair carefully watched his friend's face as he said: "The former owner was Colonel Musgrave, and the name of the castle is—"

He got no further. "Cantire," Guillet snarled in anger. "Nevair will I go to that place again." He got up and threshed about the room.

"I happened to recall," Sinclair went on, unruffled by the excitement of his friend, "you once told me in conversation that you had gone there—when was it, about three odd years ago?—and started the work. That was why I mentioned your name to the present owner."

Guillet sat down, his anger having died down as suddenly as it had risen. "Forgive me, *mon ami*; the memory of that awful man and the place makes me what you call see the red."

"I came over here to ask you for information on that very matter. Musgrave was murdered—found hanging in the old chapel."

Guillet crossed himself. "*Mon Dieu!* I am sorry for him in the next world."

"I agree with you, but I would like your story."

"It was, as you say, three years ago. This Colonel Musgrave called on me at Rheims where I was carrying out some work for the Government."

Guillet leaned forward and spread his hands in a dramatic gesture.

"He was what you call a haunted man. He had on his back the black dog."

"What exactly do you mean by that?"

"I cannot tell; he was in fear of something, that I am sure. Who knows? Some ghost of the past, perhaps."

"What did Musgrave want?"

"He required of me, Bertrand Guillet, to go to this Cantire in Devonshire, and to repair the castle."

"What, restore the whole place?" Sinclair asked eagerly.

"That was his request. He said that he would pay me—a great sum, and I consented to go for a few days to look at it."

"Well, what did you think of it?"

"Superb." The artist spoke in the man. "It would have been a fine piece of restoration, a perfect mediaeval stronghold of the fortified chateau. But no! The Colonel Musgrave paid for my fare, and we started the work.

"For one week only we worked. He talk of much money somewhere in the castle, but I think this bluff—eyewashes. Then one of the workmen fell from the tower, dead as a stone."

Something in his manner made Sinclair say, "Fell!"

Guillet touched Sinclair on the knee. "I had none of the proof, but he was thrown from the tower. I said to the Colonel, but he said pouf, nonsense. But there was no money, and we could do no more. We did find an old garderobe and a passage to the garden behind. That was all."

"Who found that—the workmen?"

"The workmen found the interesting old rooms and cleared them out. There was the shaft common to such places. The Colonel turned the workmen from out the room, saying it was not safe, and together he and I explore. The conduit was not broken. We arrive at the other end and dig the rubbish away. Ther the Colonel ask me to say nothing about it. What could I do?—he was the master, I was employed. He fastened the place up, why, I know not!"

"And you stopped the work. I suppose it was because there was no money."

Guillet shrugged impressively. "It was not that, *mon vieux*. There is something there I do not like. Something of no good."

"Come, Bertrand; you are not superstitious."

"I know not, but I who have been in so many queer places, horrible vaults underground, with bones of killed men! One learns there are more things than we think of, as your poet says."

"I wish you would be more exact; you are so confoundedly vague. What was it?"

"I know not! The Colonel come to me, shaking and fearful. He had seen something, but he was a brave man, not a frightened boy. He say, 'Come, Guillet! We clear out of here damn' quick.' "

"So you returned to France."

Instead of replying, Guillet went on half to himself, "There was there a nephew of the Colonel. He was very frightened. He was missing and we searched—that Colonel Musgrave and I. We found him in a vault half dead and nearly strangled. There were on his throat marks of bones, and a skeleton was lying beside him."

"He had been attacked, you mean!"

"He knew nothing of it! He had gone down without a light, foolish that he was, and that was all he knew."

"I can begin to piece it together," Sinclair said. "That was when Musgrave and Seften started on their travels together. Well, Musgrave has gone now and Seften is scared of the place. I have an idea why."

"You ask me, do I go back there?" Guillet remarked. "I say one part, 'Yes, go, as the Colonel is dead,' but the other part say, 'Bertrand, you are a great fool; do not go.' "

"That means you will come. Think of your genius and what you will do."

"I will go." Guillet struck an heroic attitude. "Together we shall be brave."

"Good." Sinclair summoned a waiter for a renewal of the artist's glass. "This man, Lord Wanstead, has any amount of money. You will have what you call a free hand."

"Tell me—there is some story about your visit here, is it not so?"

"It's too long to tell now. You shall hear it, and perhaps you can help me."

Guillet laughed boisterously. "That is good—I, a poor artist, should advise the great Sinclair."

"I mean it, my friend. You were at Cantire when certain events took place, and you may be able to tell me quite a lot of useful things."

The door opened noisily, and Rob and Elsie burst in, and then stopped. "Sorry, Sir Arthur, I didn't know you were here," Rob said. "We lost our way, and had quite a job to find the hotel. And do you know who we saw?"

"I haven't the remotest idea." Sinclair smiled, but his voice had a trace of anxiety in it.

"Mr. Hicks!" Elsie said with a grimace. "Fancy his being in Paris!"

"Are you sure he didn't see you?

"Yes," Rob protested; "we took care of that. He was on the embankment, near that Pont Nuff, or whatever they call it. We saw he was talking to one of those cops with the funny cloaks."

Guillet had been staring at the pair with a strange look in his black eyes. He sat up straight at the name.

"Mistaire Heeks, but surely he comes from Payning, near to Cantire?"

"That is so," Sinclair observed shortly. "But let me present two young friends of mine, Rob Summers and Elsie Campion. I brought them on a holiday with me."

"Stop!" Guillet put his hand to his head. "Into what chasm are you driving me, my friend?"

He spoke in French, and the two young people wondered if all foreigners were as mad as this one obviously was.

Elsie presented a very different picture from the ragged gipsy of Cantire. She had visited a hairdresser for the first time in her young life, and had been clothed respectably.

Her face was flushed from walking, and her large eyes were brighter and less sunken than before. Guillet was gazing fixedly at her until she became embarrassed and turned her eyes away.

Sinclair watched in silence till Guillet rose politely and bowed.

"*Pardonnez moi!* It was a vision from the past. Campion! No, I do not know it. And yet . . ."

"I have seen this gentleman before," Elsie said steadily. "I saw him with Colonel Musgrave—you remember, Sir Arthur, I told you about it?"

Sinclair nodded. "Monsieur Guillet is coming to Cantire to supervise the restoration of the place. He started it with the late Colonel."

"I wonder what Hicks is after," Rob said, and then a bright idea came to him. "I know! I'll bet he heard that this gentleman was to do the work, and came out here to get in first. What a lark!"

"It may be that," Sinclair said indulgently.

Guillet looked at his watch. "I must return to my apartments. You will come and dine with me tonight, Sir Arthur, and we can continue our conversation so interesting."

"Very well. I have the address. There are several points that we can clear up."

He glanced at the architect, who nodded gravely.

Sinclair gave up the afternoon to Rob and Elsie. It was a treat for him in his rather lonely life to see the enthusiasm of the young people, seeing places familiar to him for the first time.

Elsie seemed to have thrown off all her worries, and Rob, with his happy-go-lucky nature, would have enjoyed himself anywhere. Cantire had faded into the background until brought sharply back by the sight of Hicks.

After they returned, he gave them strict instructions not to go out again, and took a taxi to Montparnasse, where Guillet lived by himself. It was a ramshackle old house, with a large studio, and fronted with high palings. Several of Guillet's friends had dropped in to dinner in the casual manner of Montparnasse, and it was only when they had gone that Sinclair and his host adjourned to the studio, where a bright fire was burning, and papers and drawings littered the floor. Here they felt at home, as two bohemians.

With pipes lighted and sitting in deep armchairs they resumed the conversation.

"My friend," Guillet said, when he had heard the whole story, "you have led me into what you call the wasps' nest."

"Hornets, my dear friend, but no matter—in what way?"

"Read that"—he thrust a paper into Sinclair's hands. "Slipped under the door when I returned—brought by hand."

It was a single sheet on which was typed,

DO NOT ATTEMPT TO RESTORE CANTIRE.
YOUR DEATH WILL RESULT.

"Strange, Bertrand, how our friend loves capital letters. Warnings were sent to Seften when he was with Musgrave, and a paper pinned on the dead man at Cantire, and now this—all capitals."

"I don't understand," Guillet said, "but if they think that Bertrand Guillet"—he drew himself up to his full height—"can be stopped for threats—pouf! I shall go now certainly, for there is some secret, and we shall find it together."

All of which sounded very heroic, but Sinclair, who knew the man, was certain that the 'we' was the deciding factor. Alone he would not have gone. Like most men of artistic natures, he was no hero.

"Do you think, *mon brave*, that the man Heeks has done this?"

"How long is it since you left your house?"

"I have not been here since morning."

"Then it may possibly have been Hicks, but he would not have done it if he had seen Elsie and Rob, for he would know they would tell me that he was in Paris."

"Elsie! Of course, the little girl. It is of her that I would speak. When you introduced her to me that name—Campen?"

"Campion," Sinclair said, waiting.

"It was at Cantire that I saw those Campions—peasants, were they not, of the clod hopper?"

"Yes, they were certainly that." Sinclair smiled.

"My friend, you disturb me. You bring back the past. I have seen her many years ago—perhaps twenty."

"She is sixteen," Sinclair remarked slyly.

Guillet waved him aside. "You detectives have no imagery—I spoke in figures. The face, the hands and feet, and those eyes. It must have been her mother. So young, so charming."

"Where did you meet her?"

"Here in Paris—where else? I have often wondered what happened to her."

"And you think that Elsie is the daughter of this friend of yours?"

"She was not a friend—so cold, so frigid, no one could be a friend to her, and proud. She disappeared." He sighed, leaving Sinclair with the impression of Daphne fleeing from an over-zealous god. The skeins of the tangled wool were slowly unwinding before Sinclair's mind.

"Wait, I will show you." Guillet dashed impetuously out of the room, returning with a miniature in his hand. It was tinted, hand-painted, and oval in shape, as though it had fitted a case.

Sinclair gazed earnestly at the face of the young girl depicted there. Then he returned it to Guillet.

"I rather guessed this," he said with a curious smile. "But there is something missing—some strange link."

"One that you hope to find at Cantire, eh?"

"Perhaps; or I may be quite wrong in my ideas. The Inspector may have solved the problem before we get back, and then there will be nothing else to do."

"But to restore that so beautiful place, and make it fit for the Lord Wanstead to live in."

"I must go. I ought not to have come to see you, but we are staying at an hotel, and all should be right."

"You fear something, my friend—no, I do not mean that—you fear nothing, but you are alarmed for others, is it not so?"

"For Elsie—yes, I am, but that boy has his head screwed on the right way."

"Head screwed! You frighten me,"

"Figure of speech, Bertrand." Sinclair took his hat and coat and a powerful stick he carried.

"Tomorrow we start," Guillet said as he shook hands at the door.

Sinclair stepped out into the night. The small garden was full of bushes, in a double row to the old high iron palings, so common in Montparnasse. The light from the front door made a pathway of light before him but only rendered the rest of the garden blacker.

Sinclair was facing his friend. "By the way," he said, "bring that miniature with you; we shall want it."

Something stepped swiftly from the darkness and drove a knife into Sinclair's back. He staggered forward into Guillet's arms. It happened in a second, so blindingly quick that Guillet saw only the light flash on the upraised knife and heard the dull thud of the blow.

"*Mon Dieu!*" he cried, and dragged Sinclair into the hall, where he lay panting on the floor. Guillet gave one look into the night and then closed the door.

"My poor friend!" he exclaimed, quite helpless in an emergency. "Are you badly hurt?"

"Only badly winded." Sinclair tried to smile, but his head fell back. Guillet ran for brandy and poured it into Sinclair's mouth with a shaking hand.

"Steady, Bertrand—don't drown me," he said with a feeble smile. "Help me into your sitting-room."

He rose shakily to his feet and, leaning on the arm of the other, limped into the room and sank on the lounge.

"Help me off with my coat."

Guillet could only stand and wring his hands, but at the command seized Sinclair's greatcoat and removed it, gazing fearfully at a ragged tear in the back.

"But this is terrible, the knife went right through you!"

"Not quite, Bertrand, as you shall see." The coat and waistcoat came off with difficulty, and beneath was a steel waistcoat of fine rings like mail.

Guillet's face expanded into a smile of delight. He would have embraced his friend, but Sinclair held up his hand. "I got off lightly—I always wear this when there is any danger. It has saved my life several times, but it has given me a devil of a bruise and shaking up. It also knocked the wind out of me."

An examination of the back beneath the waistcoat revealed a suffused bruise, turning black, from which drops of blood were exuding.

"We've lost him," Sinclair said. "There's not a chance now. Did you see who it was?"

"Nothing—the assassin was behind you, and you fell forward. My mind was only on you. *Il est mort*, I thought like the lightning."

Guillet's man proved a more useful person in an emergency. He had been a soldier, and soon fetched hot water and lint and rendered first aid effectively.

Guillet wanted to get a doctor, but Sinclair would not hear of it. He was anxious to get back as soon as he could, and the valet 'phoned for a taxi.

"When I have gone—not before, Bertrand—you will call up my friend Morcet at the Sûreté. Don't say anything over the 'phone, except that you wish to see him at once, and mention my name. Tell him about this when he comes, but, mind you, I want this kept between ourselves. It is undoubtedly part of the same plot, and I don't want it to get into the papers on any account."

"You may trust me, *mon ami*—I will be discreet. Then we shall come together, and see how you are."

The valet announced that the taxi was ready, and Sinclair was helped into it, still feeling rather sick and giddy.

The chauffeur drove with that ferocity for which the Parisian driver is celebrated.

Sinclair's worst fears were realized when he arrived. The entire staff of the hotel appeared to be massed in the hall while Rob was trying ineffectually to curse at them in the few French words he knew.

The arrival of the detective caused the distracted *maître d'hôtel* to give an expression of relief. He came forward to Sinclair and asked him to translate what the raging English youth was trying to convey.

The hubbub was deafening, everyone trying to explain at once. Sinclair called for silence, and told Rob to follow him into the dining-room, then empty.

"Now, let's have it," he said sternly.

"Elsie's gone, sir."

"What exactly do you mean by gone? Has she run away?"

"She has been taken by force; I am sure of it." He calmed himself somehow, and spoke coherently.

"I went to bed, and saw her as far as her room. I heard her turn the key in the lock. I couldn't sleep, and so dressed again, and thought I would wait for you. I passed Elsie's door, and saw that it was slightly open. I tapped, but got no answer, and so pushed open the door. I was afraid of that sleep-walking again. When I switched on the light there was no one there. I ran downstairs and found the front door had been opened and the night porter was fast asleep. I roused the devil up and he seemed half dazed, but shook his head."

"What did you do?"

"First I rushed out into the street, but of course I don't know this place at all, and there were so many turnings it was hopeless. I couldn't ask a policeman or anyone else, not knowing the lingo, and there was no one about in any case. It was hopeless, so I came back, and roused these people, and tried to explain. I took the boss man by the arm and dragged him to Elsie's room and showed him it was empty, but the damned ass only shrugged his shoulders and jabbered away in French. They have got her, Sir Arthur."

He poured out the story in a torrent of words.

"All right, Rob. Keep your head now. I can examine these people, and, as a matter of fact, I have a detective from the Paris Scotland Yard coming round."

"You know something, then?" Rob asked eagerly. He grabbed Sinclair and the latter winced, his face twisted with pain.

"What's the matter, sir? You look as white as a ghost."

"Someone tried to murder me, but that story will keep for the present."

The whole staff were examined by Sinclair, and a thorough inspection made of the hotel, but, as was to be expected from the telltale door, there were no signs of the missing girl.

A feature of the case that Sinclair did not like was that she had gone out fully dressed. It would have been much easier to trace a girl wandering in her night attire—in fact she would have been stopped. Either she had never taken her clothes off, or had dressed again. The manager explained that he thought Sinclair had taken the young lady with him.

Meanwhile Sinclair despatched Rob in a taxi to Guillet's house with orders to bring him and Morcet back to the hotel as soon as the detective arrived.

By the time he had sent the staff back to their beds and quiet had been restored the car drove up. Already the bare facts had been reported to M. Morcet, and he, with characteristic energy, had issued orders on the 'phone for a thorough search, and Rob had furnished a description.

That, he told Sinclair, was all he could do at present. Railway stations, roads and airports were being watched, but this was mere routine, as he felt certain in his own mind, from what he had heard, that the girl had merely wandered off in her sleep, and the greatest danger was that she might have fallen into undesirable hands.

He greeted Sinclair as an old comrade. Both had grown grey in the services of their respective countries at similar work.

He had gone at once to Guillet's house and made a rough examination. Beyond a few blurred footmarks and some broken boughs, where the assassin had tried to smash his way through the bushes, there were no other indications.

They discussed the matter far into the night. There was no possible doubt that the chain of events were linked together. Someone was afraid that Sinclair was finding out too much, and he had to be removed. The key lay with Elsie. In a blinding flash something came to Sinclair's mind, sharpened with the pain of his back, as sometimes happens with men of keen intellect.

Elsie knew the truth. He did not doubt that she was honest enough, nor would mere fear prevent her from telling them, but she knew without knowing. It sounded a paradox, but in his mind he could visualize that she might have said something that would have revealed the whole truth. It was the fear lest she might have done that which had caused the attack on his life, and perhaps— here was mere speculation—the disappearance of the girl.

His musings were interrupted by Rob, who had been restlessly pacing up and down the room where they were sitting.

"Can't we do something?" he asked fretfully for the fourth time. "We are all sitting here like a lot of old women, and Elsie may be wandering about this blighted city or worse."

"My dear Rob, Morcet has set the whole of the machinery of his organization to work, and they can do far more than we can. If it were of the slightest use, I would go with you, but we may have news."

Guillet was despondent. His artistic mind was mercurial, and the attack on his guest had upset him. He feared the worst, and secretly cursed Sinclair for ever coming and bringing a horde of assassins in his track.

He sat gazing moodily into the fire and sipping his favourite anise.

Dawn had almost come when Morcet returned from the telephone to which he had been glued for hours.

"I have news for you, Sir Arthur. It may be good or bad, as you take it. The young girl is alive."

"You have found her?" Rob cried.

"Patience, *mon gar*," Morcet said; he did not like interruptions.

"It has been reported that a private airplane left Le Bourget about four o'clock this morning—that is three hours ago. There was a man and his daughter, the girl answering to the description of your young friend in every way. Their papers were quite in order, and no trouble had been made. There was also a pilot— English. They had come from Lyons."

"That may have been a blind," Sinclair said.

"It was, as you say, a blind, for no such 'plane left Lyons. It has been checked."

"But after all," Rob said, "how did they know the girl was Elsie?"

Morcet fixed his eyes on the young man.

"You evidently do not understand the methods of the Sûreté. Monsieur Guillet furnished me with the photograph of the mother of the young girl. It was instantly copied and distributed to all airports. There was not quite time, and the copy arrived at Le Bourget after the 'plane had left, but it was quickly done."

Rob stared stupidly at the famous French detective, and then turned to Sinclair.

"What does he mean—Elsie's mother?"

"I return you the original." Morcet handed the oval picture to Guillet who, at a sign from Sinclair, gave it to Rob and watched the youth. He saw wonder and puzzlement grow on his open face, and then a look of fear.

"Where did this come from?" he said haltingly.

"Monsieur Guillet once met Elsie's mother. You see the likeness, don't you?"

"Of course; but the hair is quite different, and the clothes and so on."

"You don't understand the police methods. You gave a description and Guillet, being an artist, made a rough sketch, altering the hair and other details, and from that they made a photographic copy. That, and the fact she could not talk French, helped."

"But surely she did not go of her own will?"

"My officer says that she appeared very tired and sleepy, and spoke to the man, her 'father,' in English,—only a few words," Morcet said.

"And the man, monsieur?" Sinclair queried.

"It was difficult. He was wrapped up well, but his face agreed with the passport. An obvious disguise. Too much hair."

"We start for London tomorrow, Bertrand my friend, as arranged."

"For you I will come," Guillet said heroically, "but not for another."

"But Elsie," Rob said angrily. "What about her?"

"Keep calm, my boy. I don't fancy she is in any great danger. Some time ago a mysterious person entered her bedroom and stole a locket from her neck. He might have strangled her, or abducted her then. He did neither. I believe this is the same person, and if so the object is not murder."

"Then where are we going?"

"Back to Cantire—there lies the key to the mystery."

CHAPTER XI

THE HAUNTED CASTLE

FOR ALL HIS STRENGTH OF WILL Sinclair found that he could not possibly travel back to England on the day after the attack.

The steel waistcoat had saved his life, but the strength of the blow had severely damaged the muscles beneath and caused a large contused wound.

A council of war was held in his bedroom. Rob was frantic to get off as soon as possible, and chafed at the delay.

Guillet, not being so vitally interested, was only anxious for Sinclair's health, and, if the truth were known, for his own skin.

"You are impetuous," he told Rob, "but where are you going? Without the great Sinclair you will accomplish nothing."

"But Sir Arthur said we must go to Cantire."

"I said the key to the mystery lies at Cantire," Sinclair corrected him. "I do not see that you, by yourself, can do anything there. It will take our combined efforts. If you turn up there without Elsie, what can you say? That she has been kidnapped?—but that is just what I don't want said. You will find your position very awkward, and be sure that Gillian will turn you inside out."

"Then are we just to wait here and do nothing?" Rob said, passing his hand through his mop of hair angrily.

"Let me explain," Sinclair said patiently. "It is a fight now between us and our unknown enemy. One false move may be fatal. The French police are watching this place, and no one can come in here without being carefully inspected. The manager has been warned that neither he nor any of his staff must say a word about me or you, or my state of health. They may think that I am dead. All the better if they do. The enemy—as we have no name to call him or them—will be puzzled by our silence and inactivity."

Guillet spread his hands. "Sir Arthur is right, as always he is. Of all that has happened here, we will make a blank, is it not so?"

"Very well put."

"I will write to this my lord and tell him that I shall come to repair his damaged castle, but I am at present busy. I shall come soon, because Sir Arthur has asked me to come *trés rapide*."

"Excellent, Bertrand; and Rob shall write to Rhodes, who I think can be trusted. You will merely say that we are hung up here, and ask for news, every detail of what has happened. Say nothing of Elsie. He would very likely go and tackle Wanstead himself and make a scene."

Rob seemed mollified now that he had something to do. He went off to write the letter.

"What do you arrive at in all this?" Guillet asked when he and Sinclair were alone.

"It is quite obvious that the girl of the miniature is Elsie's mother. There can be no mistaking that. The gang of murderers, or one of them—we don't know which yet—feared that you and I should meet, for this very reason. But there is more in it than that. Elsie must know something, and they feared she had told us, and that with your picture the truth would come out. My movements have been followed and they tried to get rid of me, and at the same time to abduct Elsie and keep her mouth shut."

"But she went willingly, from what Morcet says?"

"I have already found that she is under some powerful influence."

"You must rest, my friend; such a blow with me would have been a shock very grave. I should have been in a hospital, or perhaps the morgue. You are coarse."

"I suppose you mean tough," Sinclair corrected him with a smile.

"*Bien!* Tough, like a log of wood."

Three days afterwards answers came from Rhodes and Lord Wanstead, but as the news they contained referred to events that had taken place at Cantire since Sinclair's departure, it is best to return to the scene of action.

Hicks turned up at Payning on the day after Sinclair's attack had taken place. He went at once to see Lord Wanstead at the 'Horse and Hounds.'

Wanstead was torn between two courses. He was anxious to get back to London, where his business had got into arrears, and to see the last of Cantire for some time, and on the other hand he felt that he must first see this man Guillet and put the work in hand at Cantire. There was also another reason which he would not impart even to Hicks.

"What's the news?" he asked abruptly as Hicks came in with the air of someone afraid of a drubbing.

"I do not think that Sir Arthur Sinclair will be able to return here for some time," he said guardedly. "He met with an accident."

"An accident! How did you manage it?" Wanstead said bitingly.

"I? It was nothing to do with me, my lord, I can assure you."

"All right, Hicks, perhaps it is wise to keep your own counsel."

Hicks gave a scarcely veiled glance of hate at the impassive red face, and bit his lip. "I heard of the accident from one of the waiters at his hotel. Sinclair had been to see the architect Guillet."

"You allowed them to meet!" Wanstead stormed.

"I could not prevent it. It was not my fault. You gave me the wrong hotel."

"I gave you the one which Sinclair told me."

"Exactly," Hicks said contemptuously. "He gave you the Bellevue, but he was too clever for us. He thought someone might follow him. He never went near that hotel, but is staying at l'Etoile, a small place near the Place de l'Opéra. I had the greatest difficulty in finding him, and Guillet was away in the South of France."

"How serious is this injury?" Wanstead demanded.

"I could not find out. I had no time."

Wanstead assumed his favourite attitude when thinking out a business deal. He placed his hands behind his back in a Napoleonic fashion.

"Things might have been worse," he said at last. "While you were away I arranged to get all those documents from the bank, and have them safe. The plans and drawings I shall leave with you. The rest I take with me."

"You may leave that to me," Hicks said with an ugly laugh.

"Something has happened during your absence something of great importance." He searched the lawyer's face with a boring scrutiny. "The whole of the north-west tower at Cantire has fallen down, and there is nothing but a gigantic mass of stones and mortar."

"Then the Campions will take some digging out." Hicks smiled.

"Campions! Who the hell cares about them. But that black

scoundrel Rhodes says that Rob and Elsie were somewhere hidden in there, and if so . . . "—a gesture finished the sentence.

Hicks sprang back as though he had received a blow. He tore at his shirt, and for a moment turned away. He dared not show the look of astonishment on his face.

"Well, man, what's the matter? You don't think I blew it up, do you?"

"No, my lord." He tried to laugh. "Of course, if the poor wretches have been buried alive . . ."

"It is sad, but fortunately neither of them has any other relatives to mourn their loss, except that fellow Rhodes."

"Then I think we may fairly look forward to getting the place properly done up without disturbance," Hicks said cryptically.

"I think," Wanstead said at last, "I had better not meet this Guillet after what has happened. I shall leave the whole matter in your hands. I shall return to London, and this architect can get busy. You can arrange everything." A grim smile played round his mouth.

"Very good, my lord. I will see to everything."

There was an undercurrent of relief in his voice.

"I will send my nephew down to see how things are progressing. I believe, from what Lady Wanstead writes, that there is some chance of the young waster becoming engaged and settling down."

"I am pleased to hear it, my lord. I suppose there is no chance of the old affair cropping up?"

"Colonel Musgrave is hardly likely to tell, and I don't think that fellow Rhodes will be anxious to bring the story up again. He may want something to keep his mouth shut."

Lord Wanstead returned to London in the afternoon, and the news was received with pleasure by Sergeant Haddon, who had taken an intense dislike to the noble profiteer.

Cantire was locked up, and the keys were with Sergeant Haddon. He had kept a man on duty at night outside the place, as a matter of form, since there were two dead people inside. Gillian had agreed to wait till Wanstead's men arrived, and that was dependent on the coming of Guillet.

So for a moment there was a lull in the proceedings and quiet rested on the village.

Night was coming down on Cantire. The western sun threw the towers into relief, dark and sinister. The fading light of evening gave the ancient place a grim and unreal appearance.

Ted Bolt paced up and down the drive, far from happy in his job. A strange mist was rising from the damp woods, and gradually enveloped the walls and towers like a shroud. Doubtless, had Bolt been versed in the English poets, the words 'Childe Roland to the dark tower came' would have come to his mind, but the Government does not include Browning in the curriculum of a village school.

A silent figure flitted across the drive, making for the woods, and Bolt felt his hair rising on his head. Duty was duty, and he called, "Who's that?" perhaps a little shrilly.

The slouching figure came forward towards him. "Hello, Ted."

"Oh, it's you, is it?" Bolt said in unmistakable relief.

Rhodes laughed. "Yes, it's me. You are in charge here, so to speak? Have a cigarette?"

The constable hesitated between duty and inclination, and then accepted the offer and puffed contentedly.

"Lonely sort of job here at night," Rhodes observed.

"I've known better." Bolt suddenly realized that he was forgetting his duty. Rhodes had placed on the ground a basket he had been carrying.

"What are you doing here?"

"Me? Just strolling round. Interesting old place by night."

"Here, that won't do, you know. What have you got in your basket?"

"A corpse I cut up into small pieces," Rhodes said with a laugh.

" 'Ere, stop that. You've no right here at all, you know. Answer my question in a sensible way."

"I was telling the truth. I am taking home my supper, a rabbit and a few other bits and pieces. You can look if you care to."

"This ain't your way home."

"It was a fine night, and I just went for a walk before going home."

"Now then, John Rhodes, don't come them games on me. You was going to the castle with that food."

"Yes, I thought the ghost might be hungry. Have you seen him peeping out of that window where old Campion used to live? Horrible red eyes he's got, and shows his teeth when he grins at you."

"Stow that nonsense," Bolt said angrily, but his glance strayed to the blackness where Cantire stood.

"Well, I must be trotting. What time do they relieve you?"

"When the sergeant comes with the next man on duty," Bolt

said non-committally.

"Oh, look there!" Rhodes cried in alarm. "There at the window."

Bolt clawed Rhodes' arm. "Where?" he asked fearfully.

"Had you that time," the other said with a laugh.

"None of them jokes—they fair give me the jitters."

"How would it be if I took your place for a bit and you have one at the 'Green Man'?"

"None of that." Bolt stiffened up. "I see your little game, Rhodes. You want to get me out of the way, and you're up to no good here. Now then, march."

Rhodes picked up his basket. "I hope the goblins don't get you."

"Here—one minute. What's this I hear about young Rob and Elsie? Sergeant told me they had gone."

Rhodes spoke in a sepulchral voice. "Gone sure enough. They ventured into that castle and the ghost got them."

"Get off, or I'll take you."

The man disappeared so quickly that Bolt shuddered. The darkness had swallowed him up, and he did not even know in which direction he had gone.

"I shall report this," he muttered. "Trying to scare me, indeed."

All the same it was eerie work and he was half sorry he hadn't kept Rhodes talking a bit longer, just for company.

He marched to the ruined gatehouse at the end of the drive, as far as possible from the castle, and peered up the road. Visibility was bad, the fog wraithes were crawling and swirling. He pulled out his large turnip watch with an illuminated dial. Ten o'clock, and at that moment he heard the village church clock at Barton boom out the hour.

He turned reluctantly, and went back along his beat towards the black castle. He wasn't going to be scared by any ghosts.

He was quite close, could dimly make out the great gate, and then he looked up, and the marrow in his bones froze as he said afterwards.

The window of the Campions' room was just above him. Something moved there behind the glass, he was sure. Fear and curiosity struggled for the mastery. He took a step forward, and uttered one awful cry into the night. A skull was peering out at him. He saw the white grinning thing pressed against the glass. He did not wait to see more. He was tearing down the drive as though the thing were chasing him, in a perfect frenzy of fear, and ran bang into the bulky stomach of Sergeant Haddon who was coming up with the relief.

" 'Ere, what's all this?" Haddon gripped the man strongly. "What 'yer mean, shouting out like a baby and running?" Indignation was mixed with a certain amount of nervousness.

"In the window there . . . staring out at me it was!"

Bolt gasped, still clawing the indignant sergeant.

"What, you fool? 'Ere, let go, will you?"

"A skeleton, leastwise a skull. I saw it plainly."

"Skull—bunkum," Haddon said uneasily. "Come along of me and show me."

The three men marched up the drive, gathering confidence from numbers. Haddon boldly flashed his torch on the windows and on the front of Cantire.

"There ain't nothing there; you ought to be ashamed of yourself, behaving like a baby."

"All right, Sergeant, go inside and have a look round," Bolt said in a surly voice, stung by the words.

"I haven't got a key or I would, just to show you," Haddon declared untruthfully.

The relief constable was far from happy.

"Look here, Sergeant," he said, clearing his throat. "How would it be if Bolt stays with me, and I'll stay when his turn comes. 'Tis a powerful long walk to the village, and mighty dark."

"You can arrange that among the two of you," Haddon said, thinking that it would save him coming again.

"What about it, Jack?" the other said hopefully. Bolt thought of what he had seen, and his next spell all alone. "That'll suit me fine. I don't mind going on."

Haddon left them, and trudged back to the 'Green Man.' He was far from satisfied about this apparition. There were many strange stories floating round Cantire, and he was country bred and superstitious.

He was glad to see the lights of the 'Green Man,' which Grimes had obligingly kept going for him.

CHAPTER XII

THE DOOR THAT WOULD NOT OPEN

THE FOLLOWING DAY Sinclair arrived with Guillet. They came by car, and drove straight to Hicks' office. Seften was with the lawyer, having been, as he said testily, ordered by his uncle.

He was not pleased to see the detective after the snubs he had received, but Guillet greeted him as an old friend. He turned to Hicks, showing no signs of mistrust. "Ah, Mistaire Heeks; I am pleased to meet you again, and to find you your old self—not one day older. And Payning is too unaltered. We shall go and put the castle into so good repair you will not know it again."

He inquired after old acquaintances with a volubility that took the breath away.

Seften saw that Sinclair was a sick man. He remained sitting in silence while his friend rambled on—by arrangement.

"I am very sorry to hear you have met with an accident," he said sympathetically.

"I strained my back," Sinclair said shortly.

"They are beastly things to get over. I suppose you didn't meet Mr. Hicks in Paris?"

The innocent question brought dead silence. Guillet ceased talking and looked on the floor.

Seften noticed the sudden embarrassed position, and looked at Hicks. "I am sorry: I seem to have put my foot into it. Was your visit secret, Hicks?"

"Who told you I had been in Paris?" the lawyer hedged.

"Why, my uncle. He said he had sent you out to see Sir Arthur Sinclair and expected you to come back together."

Hicks was cornered, but his lawyer's mind saw a way out. He forced a smile. "I am afraid that was Sir Arthur's fault. He gave an address of an hotel to Lord Wanstead, at which he said he would be staying, but they had never heard of him there, and I was unable to trace him."

"And what did Lord Wanstead want of me, to send you after me?" Sinclair inquired blandly.

"Merely that he thought it wasn't worth your while staying there on his account, and he thought a letter would do." He saw the look of incredulity on Seften's face. "I had some other work to transact as well, so I was killing two birds with one stone."

Guillet made matters worse. "I do not understand—you have been killing two birds? Who were they?"

"Just a figure of speech, Bertrand." Sinclair laughed. "I am quite sure that Mr. Hicks hasn't been killing anyone, birds or human beings."

"Devilish fishy," Seften muttered under his breath, and Hicks flushed angrily.

He turned to the Frenchman, as though to change the conversation.

"Lord Wanstead has instructed me that he gives you *carte blanche* in the matter of expense. You remember these old plans?"

"Perfectly I do recall them. The late lamented Colonel Musgrave showed them to me. It is terrible his so sudden death, and murdered as well. You have not found the miscreants yet, Mistaire Heeks, no?"

"The police seem to be completely baffled."

Guillet was turning over the plans with the interest of an expert. He picked one up, and held it out to Sinclair. It was a yellow parchment drawing, beautifully executed, showing a ground plan of the castle.

"This is the very plan that made us to discover the garderobe shaft and rooms," Guillet said. "The Colonel took little interest, but to me, Bertrand Guillet, it was a find of the first order."

Sinclair examined the plan. "Very well done," he said listlessly, "and to think that if you had not found that, perhaps the Campions might have been alive today," he moralized in a husky voice.

He leant forward towards the table while he spoke, and his hands sought Guillet's, giving his a squeeze of warning. His quick trained eye had seen something more—something of which even the architect had not seen the significance.

Hicks was diving into a case for the engravings which would give the perspective of the place. With a rapid motion, Sinclair seized the plan and stuffed it into his pocket. Guillet understood the action and rose to his feet. "Shall we go to the castle, Mistaire Heeks? We shall see what damage has been made?"

"I'll fetch Sergeant Haddon if you like," Hicks said. "He has the keys of the place. Inspector Gillian is in Exeter."

He went out, and Seften, who had been staring out of the window, approached the table. "I say, I'm awfully sorry, I'm afraid I put my foot into it, but I thought that Hicks must have seen you, as he went for that purpose."

"He evidently missed me. I never saw anything of him, nor Guillet either," Sinclair said carelessly.

Hicks returned with the sergeant, and a constable who was driving his car, and Seften got in.

"I'll take Guillet with me," Sinclair said, "and follow on. I have to call at the 'Green Man.' "

Guillet turned to his friend when they were alone. "You have discovered something, is it not so?"

"I believe I have," Sinclair said dryly. "We will go into that when we get to the castle."

Sinclair deposited his bag with Grimes, who gave him a warm welcome, and greeted Guillet, whom he remembered very well on account of the strange drinks he had been compelled to obtain for him when staying there.

"You are not in a hurry?" Guillet ventured to protest.

"I want them to get there first and have a look round."

"You are too wide for me."

"Deep, my friend. Come, we can go now."

Cantire was sleeping in the sunlight, and peaceful now. An old ruin can change its expression like a human being, according to its mood. It looked now mellow and smiling, and full of benevolent good nature. The party were waiting in a group by the main door for Sinclair's arrival.

"You haven't gone in then?" Sinclair said in seeming surprise.

Haddon looked uncomfortable, and the constable remarked:

"It's all right in the daytime, sir, only at night—"

"What's that?" Sinclair asked sharply.

"One of my men, sir, Ted Bolt, got a dose of nerves. Thought he saw a skull glaring at him from the Campions' room."

"Really. When did this happen?"

"The night before last, sir; but it's all hocus-pocus. I had a look myself, and there was nothing. By the way, that man Rhodes was hanging around with a basket of food. He said it was for his supper."

"I am afraid a skeleton wouldn't have much use for food," Sinclair said gravely.

They went to the postern door, and Haddon inserted the key, or at least tried to, but it would not go through the lock. He fumbled with the lock, and then examined it carefully.

"Somebody has been playing the fool here," he exclaimed angrily. Sinclair got slowly out of the car.

He too examined the lock, and his face became grave. "Undoubtedly the keyhole has been stopped from the other side. The gate is about three inches thick, and iron bound, as far as I remember. It would take a charge of gelignite to open it."

His eyes sought those of Guillet. "The main gates are completely blocked by fallen stones," he said thoughtfully.

"I locked this door myself," Haddon said, "and sealed it. The seal is intact, so no one can have gone in this way."

"Or come out," Sinclair said quietly.

"The fire escape seems the only chance," Hicks suggested. "We could climb the walls then, and a rope would do the rest."

"Before we resort to that," Sinclair said, "it would be as well to have a good look round and see whether there is any place where an active man could climb. I will sit in the car for a bit if you don't mind. I am not very strong yet."

Guillet looked anxiously at his friend—it was not like Sinclair to complain.

Haddon was astonished at Sinclair's suggestion, for he knew that the detective had thoroughly examined the walls.

Hicks looked at Sinclair in a puzzled fashion, and was about to speak. Then he thought better of it and followed Haddon, who had taken Sinclair's words as an order. He had turned towards the path leading to the kitchen garden, and Guillet followed them. Seften was left with Sinclair, hardly knowing what to do.

"Take the constable and go round the other way," Sinclair said. "You'll have a job, as there is no path, but it's the most likely spot. I will look after the place till you come back."

"Is it necessary?" Seften said sulkily. "It's an awful mess round there."

"You can please yourself," Sinclair said coldly. Seften darted one glance at Sinclair, feeling that it was merely an excuse to get rid of him. "All right then—come along, Officer."

Sinclair was alone at last. He drew the plan he had confiscated from his pocket and studied it carefully. Spreading it on the seat of the car, he orientated it with a pocket compass, and traced the towers and gateway. He had an uncanny instinct of being able to concentrate on a piece of work and yet have all his senses active.

A slight grating noise reached his ears and he looked up quickly. Then he leapt from the car without any appearance of fatigue and knelt by the keyhole. Daylight showed through the aperture, and Sinclair inserted the key hastily. It turned stiffly and he pushed open the massive door. The alley on the other side was empty, and only the shaft of light fell across the old walls.

The inner side of the door showed that an iron plate could be moved on a swivel, a useful device to prevent anyone from opening the door from the outside with a duplicate key if the plate were turned. Sinclair closed the gate behind him and locked it. Then he went back to his car and leant back on the cushions.

Someone had closed that gate from the inside, but, what was of greater importance, it had been released while the party were scattered, obviously with the purpose of showing that there was no one inside. So much was clear. A more pressing question was whether Elsie were in the castle. Sinclair would have investigated. It was not fear that deterred him, but the dread that, if he did, some harm might come to the girl.

For some queer reason this mysterious person had left Elsie unhurt when she had been awakened at night and her locket stolen, and again when she had wandered in her sleep.

The others straggled back, to find Sinclair apparently asleep in the car. Both the constable and Seften were black with forcing their way through the thick undergrowth on the north side.

The others had merely gone round the path, and so into the garden.

"There's no possible way into the place," Hicks said crossly. He had gone only a short distance, and sat on a tree-trunk to wait.

"It will have to be the fire-escape," Haddon said.

"Well, here's your key." Sinclair threw it to him. Haddon was a stubborn man, and hated to be beaten. He approached the door for a last trial. "Good Lord," he shouted, "it turns!" He flung open the door, and turned his red face to the others. "What a lot of damned fools we were wandering round the place. Must have got caught or something."

Guillet smiled, and caught Sinclair's eye. The latter gave an unmistakable wink.

"Well, we can get in now," Seften said, looking ruefully at his blackened clothes. "Spoilt a good suit for nothing."

They went warily into the garden by the alley, and looked up at the ruin. "*Mon Dieu!*" Guillet exclaimed. "What a catastrophe!"

"My uncle is sending down a gang of workmen from London," Seften told him. "They will act under your orders and clear it up."

Guillet opened the bag he had brought, containing the plans, and made his way to a small table and bench where teas had been served in the summer. "Leave me now"—he made a gesture of dismissal. "I shall study the problem with these."

"We can't leave you here alone very well," Haddon said doubtfully, "not after the things that have happened in this place."

"I shall remain," Sinclair said.

"I'll leave you the key then," Haddon said, "only don't get locked in by mistake, sir." He laughed at his own joke and either an accident, or the robust laugh, set loose stones in motion, and they came trickling down the heap like evil snakes crawling over the rubble.

"Let's go," Hicks said. "I can't say I like this place."

"And now, *mon brave*," Guillet said when he and Sinclair were alone, "you must tell me the story of the lock that opened so mysteriously."

"I rather suspected that someone had fastened that plate, which I had observed before. I thought if I sent you all off, and if my theory were right, someone might have been observing us and would place back the plate, to convey the impression that no one was inside. You see, I am right."

Guillet stared at his friend. "Then there is someone here, and he is watching us perhaps!"

"You are not afraid?" Sinclair laughed.

Guillet looked uneasily round. "I am brave"—he patted his chest—"with the great Sinclair, but he might shoot us, like the partridges you so often make the target."

"I think not, but I have something more important to tell you. I daren't bring it out now, as we may be under observation, but that plan I put in my pocket."

"Yes, of course, I am all attentions."

"It was just a ground plan and there was nothing special about it, but it showed the chapel where the murder was done."

"Yes, yes—I remember that chapel," Guillet said.

"To an ordinary observer there was nothing special, but where the altar used to stand is now just a stone table—solid. Here the draughtsman has put a small mark, and the words, very finely written, *'ad cryptum'*—do you follow?"

"Then there is a crypt?" Guillet said in a puzzled tone.

"My dear fellow, ever since I came to this place I have been worrying my head as to how the murderers got into the castle. The discovery of that shaft sidetracked the whole thing. That seemed the obvious way, but it did not satisfy me. If Musgrave had known of another entrance he would have used it, and only he and you and Elsie knew of that shaft, as far as we know. He would not have been caught like a rat in a drain if he had been aware of any other way in."

"Then you think that there is some way?"

"It is suggestive. I have made a study of old castles, though not as deeply as you have done, and I have known such entrances for emergencies. A crypt would be an ideal place, as retainers and others would be afraid to visit it."

"Then we shall explore, eh?" Guillet rose to his feet in excitement.

"Not so fast, and for goodness' sake sit down and just keep quiet. I don't know how far the chapel has been affected by this slide, or whether the entrance has been blocked up, but I should hazard a guess that the way is clear, or why did the plate on the lock turn?"

"Then we just wait," Guillet said in a tone of disappointment.

"We may endanger the life of Elsie," Sinclair said gravely. "We must come at night. The main thing is to discover the entrance if such exists, and here we have valuable information. If there is a connection with the crypt, the passage will not be a long one, and will be somewhere near to the chapel. It was useless for me to search all round the castle, and, to tell you the truth, I had hoped you would have discovered this passage, if it exists, when you started restoring. The Musgraves have been buried in Barton church for three hundred years, but before that there is no trace. As likely as not the former ones lie in the crypt, and it became full. But this is speculation and will not do."

"You will tell me your plans?"

"Certainly. At present you will stay here, while I just have a look round; I am not going to do any research work—but through the south part which has not been affected by the collapse."

The south-west tower contained the old guardroom and quarters for the men. A twisting stairway led to the flat roof, and it was quite intact. Beyond that were the huge kitchens and offices with wine cellar and buttery, and opposite to that the ancient dining-hall. Sinclair knew this part well. He came out into the inner court, which presented a strange spectacle. It was half blocked with the fallen masonry, but one could crawl over the heap at one place, and beyond was the entrance to the chapel, still uninjured. The chapel itself was also complete, but Sinclair did not dare to make any explorations, as eyes might be watching him. He returned to the inner court and ascended the stairs to the Campions' old rooms. It was not without a thrill that he approached the door, for it was from this room that something had shown itself to Bolt. And then like a flash he remembered that the thing had been a skull. A skull from the crypt! Then the skull had been taken from the crypt. Sinclair drew his automatic and pushed open the door. The place was just as the Campions had left it, but the keen eyes of the detective noted an absence of dust such as one might have hardly expected after such an interval.

The kitchen and bedroom were also deserted, and yet clean. The grate was empty, not even a sign of having been used, and that again was strange. Sinclair put his hand down and smiled. The bricks of the open grate were still warm. He went into Elsie's bedroom, but here there was a different tale. Cobwebs were there and thick dust. He dared not linger any longer or suspicion might be roused. He returned to Guillet, who was absorbed in his work, reconstructing on paper with the aid of his maps and the remains of the castle.

He looked up at Sinclair's approach. "Well, *mon ami*, you have found a ghost?"

"Nothing! The place is deserted. Let us go."

~ ~ ~ ~ ~

Black Rhodes was glooming over his fire when the latch clicked, and young Rob sauntered in. By Sinclair's orders he had got out of the train at Summerton, the next station to Payning, and walked by unfrequented ways to the cottage.

"So you have come back, eh?" Rhodes scowled. "Where's Elsie?"

Rob coolly took a seat. "I'm going to tell you."

"Then be quick about it."

Rob recounted as much of their adventure as Sinclair had permitted him to.

"What the devil should anyone want to kidnap Elsie for?" Rhodes said in a tone that denoted that he was afraid of an answer.

"I don't understand it, but Sinclair seems to think she is back here at Cantire. I don't know why he says so."

"What's to be done now, then?"

"Sinclair said I was to stay here until I heard from him, and that he did not want anyone told that I had come back."

"He's got some damned cheek."

"He told me to tell you that Elsie's life perhaps was at stake, and that if it were known that I had come back without her there might be trouble."

"I'll give him half an hour," Rhodes said savagely, "then if he don't turn up, I'll go to the castle myself."

Less than ten minutes elapsed when there was a knock at the cottage door and Sir Arthur Sinclair walked in, followed by Guillet.

CHAPTER XIII

THE ATTACK

THERE WAS A GREYISH LOOK about Sinclair's face, and Rob had never seen him so stern. He was clothed in a loose shooting-jacket and riding-breeches and leggings, as though bound on some expedition.

Closing the door carefully behind him, he came to the fire, with a nod to Rob and Rhodes.

The latter stared at Guillet and then held out his hand grudgingly. "I remember you; you came here before with that blighter Musgrave."

"Monsieur Guillet is a friend of mine. He was here doing some reconstruction work for Colonel Musgrave three years or so ago," Sinclair said with slow emphasis.

"What about Elsie?" Rhodes asked churlishly.

"It is about her that I have come. Rob, I know, I can trust, and I believe I can rely on you, Rhodes."

"That's as you please. It all depends what you are up to."

"Draw up to the table; I have something to tell you," Sinclair said.

His serious manner impressed the others and they obeyed at once. Sinclair drew the plan from his pocket and spread it out. "I want you to understand that we may be entirely on the wrong track. If so I take the full blame. I have given a lot of thought to this problem of Cantire. Every indication points to the fact that there is some way into the place whereby one can come and go without being seen."

Rob started to speak, but Sinclair raised his hand. "I know what you are going to say, Rob; that you know of such an entrance. That is completely blocked up now, and yet there is something in the castle still. Of that I am convinced."

"I went up to see myself," Rhodes interrupted. "That blanked copper spotted me, and I couldn't find out."

"I heard the story. You had some food in a basket."

Rhodes laughed harshly. "Food be damned! I had a long rope, with grappling irons at the end. I hoped to catch them on the coping and swarm up. Then I could have let the rope down."

He spoke quietly, but Sinclair gave him a look of appreciation he always felt for a brave man.

"You meant to get in alone?" he said.

"It was no good trusting those perishers, the police. They are useless. If you hadn't turned up I was going tonight."

Something of his meaning dawned on Sinclair, but Rob was quite in the dark. "You knew someone was there?"

"I knew Elsie was there," was the astounding answer.

Rob gasped. "And you said nothing about it to me?"

"Certainly not; it was no one's affair, and if I had told that policeman he would have thought it another ghost or something."

Sinclair leant forward. "Let's be quite precise now—and never mind the police. I am working on my own, and I quite agree with you. When did you see Elsie?"

"The afternoon of the day the ruddy copper stopped me. I was up there, having a look round, and I saw her at the window, where the copper thought he saw a skull or something. She looked straight at me, but showed no sign of recognition, and then she disappeared suddenly. Now I ask you, Sir Arthur: if I had said anything, they would have said I was crackers."

"I agree with you," Sinclair said. "They all thought that Rob and Elsie had been buried in the ruins, and would have thought it was a ghost or your imagination."

"You were right, Sir Arthur: you said you thought she had come back to Cantire," Bob said.

"Sir Arthur is always right," Guillet interposed.

"I am very glad of this, Rhodes. It confirms my theory, and makes an ally of you. Now let me explain briefly. If we revealed all we know and suspect, to the official police, they would undoubtedly order a search of the whole place and so on. What would be the result? I am sure that at present Elsie's life is not in danger, from what you have told me, and from other circumstances. But if this person is rendered desperate, and cornered, he will not hesitate to kill her. Don't forget that he can do it without any suspicion attaching to himself. The place is already a ruin, and he has only to put the girl in such a position that he can upset some more of the masonry, and bury her underneath."

"Good God!" Rob clenched his fists.

"The only chance is a surprise attack when we can take him suddenly. Your idea of the rope may be very helpful. Now for a moment let's study this plan."

Sinclair unfolded the plan that had formed in his head as he had told Guillet.

"The woods are very thick on the north side," Rhodes remarked. He had dropped his surly manner, and they were all keyed up with excitement at the prospect of the adventure.

"That is true," Sinclair agreed. "But there must be a way out, and if someone had been bursting through the undergrowth, there must have been a track left. I could not find any trace there. The woods are impenetrable."

"If I may offer the suggestion," Guillet said diffidently, "I have had the experience of castles and ruins in France. There would not be a short passage for—what reason—the garrison is besieged. Observe, they want water, and food. Perhaps they wish to escape from slaughter. I ask you of what use would a short tunnel be to come up among their foes waiting for them."

"There's a lot of sense in that," Rhodes said with a laugh.

Guillet placed his long thin finger on the plan. "Sir Arthur suspects the crypt, and I am one with him. It is common for both escape and for storing money safely. But from the crypt a passage may lead here, or here, or there"—he demonstrated with his finger. "*Ecoute!* From experience I say such a passage would long ago have become chock-block, as you say. Either it was repaired at much labour, or there is another made from it, nearer home."

Rhodes had been listening intently. Something of his rough manner had disappeared under the influence of Sinclair, and he spoke in a frank open tone.

"Look here, mister, when you first came here, nosing round, and I met you, I thought you were just an ordinary sleuth. From what Rob has told me, you're a white man, and here's my hand on it." He held out his huge hand, which Sinclair took in a firm grasp.

"None of us are as black as we are painted," he said.

"Now," Rhodes went on, as though the ice had been broken, and he could speak freely. "You seem as keen as I am on getting the kid out of that place. I've told you why I wasn't going to the cops, and for some reason you don't seem over anxious either."

"I am not," Sinclair said emphatically. "A frontal assault on the castle would be a disaster. There is some way of getting in and out, I am convinced of that. Now, if the police went there, and forced their way in, the murderer would undoubtedly escape, and would either take Elsie with him, or worse. We must employ guile, not force, in this case."

"Now I'll tell you," Rhodes suddenly broke out. "I was damned glad to hear that Musgrave had been done in, and I wouldn't have lifted a finger to find the murderer. But now, it's different. I've seen him."

"*Mon Dieu!*" Guillet exclaimed.

"I saw him in the woods, near the entrance to the drive. I didn't see who it was, only a shadow like. But I am sure it was him."

Sinclair went to the fire and lit his pipe with a spill. He was thinking hard. The others were poring over the plan, seeking some light. It seemed hopeless to attempt to find the exit if one existed.

"Wait a moment," Sinclair said, with a quiet note of satisfaction that made the rest relapse to silence.

He sat down and placed his elbows on the table. "Guillet, my friend, you have given me an idea. I was told when I first came here that the castle was built on the site of an old monastery, when Henry the Eighth of that name handed over these monasteries to his friends. There is an old legend about the Abbot cursing the Musgraves, and although we can discount all that, these stories generally have some substratum of truth. The castle was constructed largely from the stones of the monastery, but mark this— the foundations remained."

"Ah, *mon gar!*" Guillet exclaimed, but the others stared in bewilderment at Sinclair.

"The passage was known to the Abbots—they usually had them for their own purposes, not always clean ones. Give me the bag, Bertrand."

Guillet produced his plans and drawings, and Sinclair ran through them, discarding one after another. Then he gave an exclamation.

"Here we are at last." He smoothed out a very old parchment plan on the table, scribbled over with faint lettering in mediaeval Latin, finely written. The building was in the centre, and the grounds and farm buildings were scattered round.

Sinclair's eyes were glued on the plan and he held it up to the light. "See here." There was a faint circular mark drawn with a pair of compasses, and a tiny dot where the central prick had been made over the exact spot where the chapel now stood.

"Someone else was on the same track," Sinclair said. "A clever brain has been at work here. Whoever it was, had some information as to distance which we have not, or why enclose this round space as though somewhere on this line the passage emerged?" It was too abstruse for Rob, but Guillet saw the point, and followed the line round with Sinclair. It cut through the gates which now stood at the entrance to the drive, and on the far side through some old farm buildings long ago demolished. Otherwise the circle merely passed through field and woodland.

"One of these two—the question is which?" Sinclair said.

Guillet seized a sheet of paper from his pocket and rapidly sketched a picture of the entrance to a monastery. "Here is the usual system—certainly in France. There is a high wall to keep off the intruders, but at the gate there is a house for the porter, where he can rest to answer the bell of beggars or those seeking for sanctuary. So as far the good. This small house was pulled down when the monastery was destroyed by the wicked Musgrave. Now there is the gatehouse, of two sides, one in ruin, and an archway, now fallen!"

"There is a sketch of that," Sinclair said. "I saw it. It's exactly as you say."

"Then we approach the verity. In the room not yet destroyed is the entrance." He dropped his pencil with a gesture of triumph.

It seemed a very weak argument to Rhodes, who scratched his head thoughtfully. "You may be right, you two, but I still prefer my own method of getting over the wall."

"We shall try both, Rhodes. Here is the plan of campaign. We must divide our forces. You and Rob will climb the wall at the back with our help, and you must wait for us. Everything depends on that. If you start trying to find out things, it may lead to disaster. When we have seen you over, Guillet and I must investigate this place, and see whether our theory is right. We can do nothing until we have verified this. Then we will proceed along this passage if it exists, and get into the castle. Rob knows the inside, and you will try to get to the inner court near the stairs going to the Campions' old rooms."

"Why?" Rhodes asked.

"I have reason to believe that his room is being used. When I went there today the fire had only been extinguished a few hours, and you remember it was from this room that you saw Elsie, and Bolt saw his ghost. Elsie's room has not been used, so I conclude she is in the Campions.' "

"What about that secret chamber you told me about, where Elsie took you?" Rob queried.

"That's the crux of the whole matter, my boy. You see, since the murderer, or one of them—we can't speculate on that now— was away in Paris, the northwest tower has completely collapsed, and that hiding-place with it. As I see it, Elsie was brought here, and would have been hidden in there, but the assassin must have been furious when he found it no longer existed. What would he do? I put myself in his place. He turned that plate in the gate to make himself safe from a sudden entry through the postern door, and used the Campions' rooms, ready at any moment to flee to the crypt if necessary. Then he gave the impression that there was something not human there, to prevent too close investigation by the police at night."

"That sounds all right as you put it, Sir Arthur," Rhodes said, "but it's all theory, isn't it?"

Sinclair smiled. "Not altogether; I have made some careful investigations. Anyway, I propose to act on that theory. If we can get into the crypt the murderer may hear us and come to investigate. I want to draw him off from the Campions' rooms. That will then be your job. You must let him pass, and then see that he does not come back."

"We'll see to that," Rob said, grinding his teeth, "but I would like to have a smack at the blighter."

"That would be fatal; Elsie is your first care. Guillet and I will deal with him. There may be more than one, but I fancy only one will be actually in the castle."

Rhodes strolled to the window and drew the blind. "Damn! It's bright moonlight."

"We can't help that. It may be a blessing in disguise, as it gives a false sense of security. We shall have to be careful. Now let's see. You, Rhodes, have a weapon, I know—it's all right, Rob had it the other day. Don't be afraid to use it if absolutely necessary, but wing your man. Rob, what about you?"

"I'll take this stick." He picked up Rhodes' knotted club, which he had carried on the night that he had met Sinclair.

"All right then. And you, Bertrand?"

The doughty Frenchman had lost something of his keenness when the time for action had come. "I regret—I am not armed, and perhaps I had better remain and watch for you."

"Oh no, you don't—I might be wounded or something, and would want your help. You come along with me."

Guillet shrugged his shoulders with a wry smile. "It shall be as you say, Sir Arthur," he said gloomily.

"One can but die once," Sinclair said, grinning at him.

"It is sufficient," Guillet commented in a sepulchral voice.

Sinclair pulled out the first-aid case he always carried, and examined the contents. The sight did not cheer Guillet, whose white face made Rhodes rise with a laugh and place a bottle of whisky before him.

"Now we are ready," Sinclair remarked when Guillet and Rhodes had each consumed a generous dose.

They made a wide detour, through meadowland, hugging the hedges, and approached the castle from the opposite side from Barton. Every detail stood out white and clear in the intense moonlight.

They crossed the road about half a mile from Cantire, and carefully worked their way through the woods till they came close to the north-west corner of the surrounding wall. The moon was behind the trees here, and the spot was in pitchy blackness. They crept forward and stood beneath the wall in a huddled group.

"I say," Rhodes whispered, "wouldn't it be better to find out if your theory is right first before we go over the top?"

"No." Sinclair spoke very low. "I have thought of that, but while I and Guillet could easily account for our presence if the police see us, with four of us it would be difficult. Give me half an hour, and then act."

Rhodes unwound a stout cord he had brought with him, with a three-pronged grappling hook at the end. There was no room to swing it as the trees were too close, but Rob swarmed up a tall beech tree, and from the top branches managed after several attempts to catch the hooks on the coping stones with a firm grip.

He dropped the end down to Rhodes, who pulled on to it tightly, and then, spitting on his hands, went up like a sailor without mishap.

So far so good. Rob slid down the tree and followed Rhodes, and both disappeared from sight. The rope was drawn up to the top of the wall.

Sinclair and Guillet waited for a few minutes, but no sound came from the other side, and the first and less difficult part of the attack on the castle was over.

Now that action had come Guillet, like so many of his temperament, rose to the occasion and followed Sinclair if not with enthusiasm at any rate without hesitation. It was a long business getting through the thick woods without making any sound, but at last they reached the road, and proceeded under the shadow of the wall towards the gateway. The bright moonlight flooded the drive, and they saw the constable on duty pacing up and down. Their task was rendered easier than it would otherwise have been by the fact that one of the sides of the gatehouse—the further one from them—was in partial ruin, and little more than a heap of stones, with enough left to support the heavy iron gate.

The other was completely intact, which alone was suspicious. The pile of masonry was roughly about ten feet thick and seven feet from side to side. And then Sinclair gave a low chuckle and pointed. Their task had been rendered absurdly easy. On the side facing the road was a large board on which were displayed notices of services of buses to Payning, and times of departure, for the benefit of visitors. There was also a notice printed with the instruc-tions that the castle was on view from 10 A.M. till 6.30 P.M. in the summer and till 4.30 in winter, and that the woods were out of bounds. The board seemed to be nailed firmly to the stonework.

"It is fastened on the other side, of course, but we can't stand on ceremony," Sinclair whispered, and produced a formidable burglar's crowbar. He worked as silently and efficiently as any member of that fraternity, and Guillet stood by admiring his burg-larious skill. There was a crack, and Sinclair paused and looked cautiously round, but the officer was at the other end of the drive.

He worked on, and there was a rip, and the whole board fell outward with a cloud of dust, showing a cavity which had un-doubtedly once been a window, about three feet from the ground, and with a rotting iron bar across the centre. Sinclair did not hesi-tate; he slithered into the opening, and only his legs showed for a moment. Then his face appeared, and he beckoned Guillet to pass him the board. Guillet slipped through, fearing to fall into some abyss, but Sinclair's hand guided him, and he stood on solid ground.

Sinclair raised the board, and examined it with his torch.

"As I thought," he whispered, "I have broken the fastening. I'll just fix it roughly in case anyone comes along.

"But our way of retreat—it will be cut short," Guillet ex-claimed.

"There will be no retreat for us," Sinclair said grimly. "There; that will do for the present. Now where are we?"

"They stood in a small room where evidently the porter had been stationed to answer the Abbey bell. In the corner was a spiral staircase winding down, and marks on the walls showed that it had once continued upwards as well. They descended this, and found themselves in a passage, the walls of which were of solid huge stones, and without sign of the wear of centuries.

It must have been about fifteen feet below the ground, Sinclair calculated. The floor was thick with dust, but there were marks of feet that had come and gone, and Sinclair knew they were on the right track, and the crisis was at hand.

He felt his way along, not wishing to use his torch, and counted his steps carefully. He had already measured the distance from the gateway to the castle by the plan and knew roughly how far they had to go. At last they reached a stout wooden door. It was not fastened and Sinclair gently pushed it open. A musty smell came out to meet them, and the roof was higher. Sinclair guessed they had reached the crypt. He took Guillet's hand and pressed it to ensure silence. Then there was a very slight click as he pressed the stud of the torch and flashed the light round. The sight that met them made even Sinclair's heart give a wild beat, and Guillet uttered a cry, "*Mon Dieu!*" for this is what they saw. Coffins were placed round the walls of the place, and squatting on one at the further end was such a creature as the eye of man had hardly seen in his wildest dreams. A huge black bird or bat, all black, with an enormous beak, and fiery red eyes, was staring at them. As they gazed, struck motionless with terror, the thing slowly lifted its black wings and uttered a hoarse cry which echoed dolefully in the silent tomb.

For one moment Sinclair was frozen by horror to inaction. Then he rushed forward, holding his revolver levelled.

In that split second the creature had dashed or flown, they could not see which in the beam from the torch, and disappeared up a stone stairway. Sinclair was after it in a flash, but Guillet leant against the wall in abject terror, muttering long-forgotten prayers.

As Sinclair had already conjectured, the short flight of steps emerged in the chapel, where the stone altar had been merely rolled aside. The moonlight shone down to the inner court as they went through the door. Sinclair fired, and rushed into the court after it.

He heard a shout from the other end, and Rhodes let fly at the figure in the moonlight showing uncertainly in the patch of light cast on the floor. Then he saw what he was shooting at, and Sinclair in hot pursuit.

The thing was trapped, it was caught between the two parties. With incredible speed it turned suddenly, wings wide spread, and

hurled itself on Sinclair before he could fire. The attack was so
unexpected that he was borne back, and fell. The foul mass passed
over him and made for the entrance to the stairway going up to the
Monks' Chamber. The rubble that half blocked the inner court
rendered sight and aim difficult. Stones were falling as Sinclair
rose to his feet.

Rhodes and Rob came running forward, and Guillet came from
the chapel.

"We have him," Sinclair panted. "What of Elsie?"

"You were right," Rhodes said gaily. "Elsie is in the Campions' room, fast asleep. We left her there."

Things moved with breathless celerity.

Sinclair led the way to the chapel.

"Rhodes, you and Rob go up that staircase into the Monks'
Room. Be careful. I am going up that spiral stair."

Guillet sprang forward. He felt he had cut rather a poor figure.
"No! You must not go to face that thing of evil alone in that narrow staircase. Never."

"Leave go, Bertrand," Sinclair said roughly, and shook him off.
The other two were already ascending the wooden staircase. Sinclair disappeared in the spiral stone stairway.

The Monks' Chamber was empty, and Sinclair came out from
the first part of the staircase. They met. Rhodes showed his bared
teeth, and his eyes were flaming with hate and horror. "What is
it?" he gasped.

"Never mind that," Sinclair said brusquely. "Get out into the
courtyard. This staircase ends blindly in the air. I went up it with
Elsie one night, when she was sleep-walking. The secret chamber
is half-way up, but it has crumbled with the tower. There is no
way of escape unless this thing can fly. Quick now."

"Don't go alone, sir," Rob said earnestly.

"Leave that to me; there's not a moment to waste."

The others flew down the stair and through the chapel into the
garden, gazing up with fear at the remnants of the north tower that
looked in the moonlight as though it might fall at any moment.

Sinclair set himself grimly to climb the spiral, going step by
step and listening tensely. He expected a rush at any moment, and
held pistol and torch firmly. Round and round, and at each turn a
shaft of moonlight came through the loopholes.

The three men in the garden gazed up silent and horrified. And
then the blood froze in their veins. The dreadful shape appeared
above the tower, hovering at it were, wings spread. A thing of evil

such as they had never seen. Rhodes' arm was rigid by his side, too paralysed to lift his revolver.

From above they heard a shot—Sinclair was emerging from the stairway. The thing fluttered for one moment, and then flew, with wings outspread, across the gulf and over the wall into the thick black woods beyond. They saw Sinclair's head above the broken tower, and the top of the masonry gave way and crashed down into the court, making the three men dash for shelter.

It was a close call for Sinclair. Had another four feet or so given way he would have been hurled down to the ground below, a broken, bleeding corpse.

More shaken than he had ever felt in his life, he tottered down the stair and staggered into the garden.

"Thank God you're safe, sir, but you are bleeding," Rob exclaimed.

"A mere scratch. Let's go round the other side by the kitchen. I don't feel like facing that inner court again."

A loud knocking came like the sound of doom. Shouts were heard from outside.

"That will be the police," Sinclair said shortly. "You had better let them in, Guillet. I told you the trick of that sliding shutter. Merely say that I am here and will explain. I must go to Elsie."

He turned on the others. "Now, remember our tale. Get this in your heads. We had reason to suppose that Elsie was in the castle and came to find her. That we have done. There was no one else here. No mention of what we have seen should be made, as it is too melodramatic, and would cause a sensation. Leave that part to me." He led the way to the Campions' rooms while Guillet went to the postern.

Elsie was sleeping on the bed which had belonged to the old couple. There was something un-natural about the sleep that Sinclair did not like. Her heart was strong and beating to time, but she appeared to be more in a trance than in a natural sleep.

He made as careful an examination as any doctor could have done, but found no trace of injury or, what he was looking for, of the tiny puncture made by a hypodermic syringe, or something else.

"We must leave her as she is," he told Rhodes and Rob who were waiting in the sitting-room. The sound of heavy footsteps on stone stairs came from outside. Guillet had kept the police in conversation so that Sinclair could complete his examination.

Sergeant Haddon and two constables entered, the former red of face and evidently disturbed.

Sinclair was very precise.

"I am glad to see you, Sergeant. Fortunately no damage has been done, and there is no cause for alarm."

"But the shots, sir? I was coming along with the relief when we heard firing, and thought at first it was in the woods. Bolt thought it was from inside, but the key would not go in, as before, you remember." He looked unspoken things at Sinclair.

"That's very simple, Haddon. There is a shutter, as I will show you, and sometimes it slips down and blocks the keyhole.

"When young Rob came home, and said he didn't know where Elsie was, we had a consultation, and decided to come and see whether she was still in the castle. We found we were right."

The sergeant's jaw dropped. "Alive?"

"Oh yes, and resting in the next room. I didn't bother the police as I didn't want to lead you on a fool's errand."

"But who was firing, and why?" Sergeant Haddon was only half convinced.

"Oh, that—Rhodes here fancied he saw someone and let drive at him. It was tricky in the moonlight."

"You saw a man?" Haddon turned to Rhodes, who answered with sincerity.

"I fancied I did, but it wasn't a man, was it, Rob?"

"No, there wasn't any man there," he corroborated.

"Then how on earth did the girl get here?"

"That we shall find out when she wakes up. I rather fancy she has been drugged. By the way, Bertrand, I left my torch in the chapel. You might get it for me and close the door after you." He gave a significant nod, and Guillet understood that the altar must be slid into place.

"Perhaps we had better have a look round, now that we are here," Haddon said.

Sinclair took him by the arm. "If you wish to, by all means do so, but I should not advise it. There are falling stones, and perhaps something else here which would not be nice to meet."

The sergeant's red face went pale, and he decided that Sinclair was right.

Guillet returned and handed his own torch gravely to Sinclair.

"Lord Wanstead's men will be here tomorrow, and will take over the place from the police. They have arranged to make shanties in the garden so as to be on the spot. The place will then be open, and the mystery will have disappeared," Sinclair announced.

Haddon gazed open mouthed at the detective. "Well, of course, we shall have to get Inspector Gillian's permission for the police to be withdrawn," he said heavily, "but it seems to me, sir, if you will excuse me for saying so, that it was you who wanted the place watched, and now you want it open."

"You see, Haddon," Sinclair remarked with a slight smile, "it was necessary, as long as I thought there was someone hiding here, but we are now convinced that there is no one here at all."

The explanation seemed very weak to Haddon, and more so to Rhodes, but he loyally refrained from comment.

The moon had set and there were greyish streaks in the east. The smell of dawn was in the air.

"I'll just relieve Bolt, and then get back and report. You will let me know, sir, when Elsie can give an account of herself."

Sinclair gave his promise, and the sergeant went off with his supporters, glancing uneasily down the dark inner court as he went.

"Now," Sinclair laughed, "we've got rid of him, and the next thing is to get Elsie to your cottage, Rhodes."

"That's all very fine, sir. We backed you up, and told the tale, but how do we know that the thing we saw won't come back, or even come to my cottage?"

Sinclair looked round at them with a curious expression on his face. "I don't think somehow that you will ever see that thing again. It has vanished into the night. You see," he added cryptically, "now that we have discovered the way into the castle we shall effectually shut it up. And with good, common-sense British navvies about the place, the atmosphere will change."

The dawn came, bright and cheerful after the horrors of the night. Rob had been despatched to the 'Green Man' to get a car.

"Just stay here with Elsie for a few minutes, Rhodes," Sinclair said. "I want to stroll round with M. Guillet."

When they had reached the garden the architect turned an eager face to his friend. "What is the meaning of it?"

"You have, I suppose," Sinclair said with a laugh, "grasped the fact that this horror we saw was no supernatural being."

"But we saw it in the vault! Horrible." Guillet shuddered.

"We saw it all right—and it used the passage for coming in and going out, but you hardly imagine it fetched Elsie from Paris, my friend."

"But it flew—so," Guillet expanded his arms wide.

"That is what I brought you here for."

They had reached the end of the piled-up mass of fallen masonry. "Now, Bertrand—you were out here, and I was inside. When that creature flew away the tower started to collapse. Think carefully—where did the stones fall from that tower?"

Guillet stared at Sinclair. "It is impossible to tell—It was but moonlight, and I was watching it!"

"No you weren't, for it had gone. You were watching the top of the tower to see what had happened to me, was that not so?"

"*Vraiment!* I recollect." He pointed. "There is where I feared the body would fall—your body."

"Cheerful fellow. That's what I wanted."

Sinclair followed the direction to which Guillet pointed, scrambling over the rubbish heap.

He searched eagerly among the ruins, turning over the stones while showers of loose stone and mortar fell in a stream down the side.

Guillet saw him beckon, and climbed the heap, wondering what the detective was after. Sinclair was examining a huge block of cut stone.

"You see, my friend Bertrand," he said in triumph. On the outward side of this stone, embedded firmly in the block, was a huge staple.

"What is that?" Guillet asked, wondering,

"You can't guess?—mind, it was a long shot on my part, and I was lucky to find this. Only you see I was on the top, and had a better view."

"Also you were not frightened so much as we," Guillet said gallantly.

"The thing you saw had a thin strong cord passing through this staple, and tied probably to a tree beyond the walls. What you called flying was merely gliding down that cord and over the wall. Then he would have pulled the cord through and left no trace but this staple, which in the general ruin he might reasonably expect to pass unnoticed. This was the block of stone that was used to hang Musgrave, and has been brought from the chapel."

A look of enormous relief came to Guillet, touched with admiration. "It is wonderful, my friend. You are a marble."

"Marvel, you mean. Come, let's get away before some more falls on us."

They scrambled down to the garden. "Again I ask—what does it mean?"

"Ah, now you are going to ask me to theorize. This is between ourselves, mind. As I see the problem now, Elsie for some reason was brought here, and the person who brought her came through that tunnel. It was also the way the murderers came. I rather fancy that he must have seen Rhodes and Rob, or at any rate have become suspicious. He is a clever scoundrel, for he had this disguise, frightful enough to scare anyone, and had already fooled the policeman with a skull. He had prepared this weird way of retreat in case he was cornered, and, I suppose, knew that Rhodes and Rob were in the grounds. He went down to the crypt to see whether his retreat was cut off, and found that someone was coming that way. He waited till the last moment, and then made a desperate effort to get to Elsie. I hardly dare think of the reason. He was foiled and fled up those stairs. You know the rest."

"Marvellous," Guillet said in a tone of relief. "But why should he not come back?"

"He has now no hiding-place, and Elsie has been found. He knows I am hard on his track."

"And you, my friend—have you no idea of this man or men?"

"I am completely in the dark—that's not very clever, is it?"

"Then nothing can now be done."

"As regards the murder of Colonel Musgrave, the police will continue to investigate; I shall not. I have remained here to safeguard Elsie, because I was sure the mystery centres round her."

"But she is still in danger?"

Sinclair faced Guillet squarely. "If your restoration work goes on, and nothing happens except that Lord and Lady Wanstead come here and take possession, I do not think anything will happen. The past will be buried. That is what I hope."

"You are for me too deep, but I hope it may be so."

Rob had arrived with a car when they reached the Campions' room. Rhodes reported that Elsie was in the same state of trance or whatever it was.

They carried her to the car, and drove to Rhodes' cottage, leaving the postern door wide open.

"Now, Guillet, you had better take the car and get to the 'Green Man'; you look half dead. Have a good bath, a meal and some sleep."

"But you—you are of iron."

"I shall stay here for a little while."

"Hadn't we better have a doctor?" Rob asked with a yawn.

"Not at present—I will attend to Elsie. Rob, you get some strong tea made."

They carried the girl upstairs, and Guillet, only too pleased to get away, drove to Barton.

Wild rumours were floating round, and curious eyes were cast at Guillet as he came in to the dining-room for breakfast.

Seften was sitting alone at a table, and beckoned Guillet to him. Rather unwillingly he accepted the invitation.

"My uncle is coming today," Seften said when they had started their meal. "He is coming at eleven and wants to see you."

Guillet murmured that he would be pleased, though he was longing for sleep.

"I say," Seften said in his nervous, hesitating way, "what's all this about the castle—some cock-and-bull story, I suppose? The police seem to have found something, but won't say."

"You had better ask the great Sir Arthur Sinclair," Guillet said shortly, and turned to his kidney and bacon with the avidity of a hunter.

CHAPTER XIV

LORD WANSTEAD'S DINNER

THE STRANGE TRANCE into which Elsie had sunk gradually cleared away, like the slow awakening after a long fit of delirium. Sinclair sat beside her, as he had done before in the castle, and watched the changes pass over her face as consciousness returned.

There was none of the horror and fright of the last occasion. She simply opened her eyes and smiled at Sinclair. She was back in her own room, and for the moment seemed to have forgotten all that had happened since she left for Paris.

Sinclair took his time. He did not even address the girl. He laid a reassuring hand on her arm, and she took it in her own.

Gradually full consciousness came back. She frowned slightly, and shook her head.

"You are awake at last," Sinclair said brightly.

"Have I been sleeping for long? It all seems so strange. I dreamt of going to Paris."

Sinclair smiled. "What happened there?" he said gently.

"It's not all clear. Yes; now I remember." She sat up and gripped Sinclair's arm. "I was in Paris I remember clearly now. You brought me back?"

"You came with me and Rob to Paris—that's quite true. I left you at the hotel. Do you recall what took place then?"

She shook her head. "Nothing." She puckered her brows. "I do remember now, but it must have been a dream. I fancied I dressed and went out; I don't know where or why. I even remember going in an airplane—how funny."

"Who did you go with?"

She shook her head. "I don't remember; something seemed to drag me to Cantire. Did I go there?"

"We found you there, Elsie. Mr. Rhodes and Rob and I. You were discovered through looking out of the window. Don't you even remember that? Haven't you any recollection of anyone with you?"

"None," she answered again. "Only in my dreams I saw an awful creature, but it couldn't have been real. It was a great bird all black."

And that was all that Sinclair could extract from the girl. She was in no physical danger, and the queer trance was working off.

Sinclair left her, and finding Rob and Rhodes both asleep, took a seat by the fire and lit his pipe.

In the afternoon Lord Wanstead accompanied by Gillian went to the castle. His own men had taken charge, and with the rapidity of action to which Wanstead had brought them in erecting his suburban villas, were already putting together sections of huts in the garden. The sound of hammering filled the place. Others had already begun the immense task of clearing the pile of stones. Lorries stood in the drive, brightly painted with the words—The Eastern Traction Company Ltd.—another name for Wanstead. It was a busy and prosaic scene, that not only destroyed the romance of the place but blew away any element of mystery. Gillian felt that these strong London navvies, if they saw a ghost, would hit it good and hard with a spade.

Lord Wanstead was in his element, going from group to group, hustling and directing.

In a spare moment he engaged Gillian in conversation.

"You had better give up altogether this problem of the murder of my brother-in-law. I don't see the slightest chance of your ever solving it, and as for that crank Sinclair, I don't suppose he will bother any more about it. He hates to be defeated, and will be glad enough to back out of it and get on to something easier."

Guillet was busy at a small table working out diagrams. He looked up angrily, and was going to interrupt, but gave a shrug of indifference. He did not care to quarrel with Wanstead, who was now his employer.

Even Seften, who had come up with Guillet, and was seated beside him, seemed to have thrown off something of his nervous manner, and was watching with interest the restored castle growing up on the paper under Guillet's skilled hands.

He heard his uncle speaking to Gillian.

"My foreman tells me that it will take two months to clear all that stuff away."

"Two months!"

"Every stone has to be numbered and set aside. Oh, we'll get your corpses in time."

That evening Lord Wanstead celebrated the occasion of the starting of the restoration by giving a little dinner at the 'Green Man.' He was the builder again, and had put aside his peerage and coronet.

There was Sinclair as guest of honour, and the rest. Hicks and Gillian and Bertrand Guillet. He could not quite bring himself to ask Sergeant Haddon.

Grimes was delighted at the honour done his house, and got his staff busy.

If there was not to be another Musgrave at Cantire, there was at least to be one on the female side, and a real peer of the realm.

Before the others arrived Wanstead had a word with Hicks. He was in a most affable mood.

"Well, I think things are fairly watertight now, eh?"

"Yes, my lord. The whole thing has gone very well. There is not a breath of suspicion, but if we had not acted quickly it might have been different."

There was a depth of meaning in the simple words

His lordship took a cocktail. "I have—er—decided, Hicks, in what way to reward you for your most valuable services."

The lawyer waited, his heart beating fast.

"You will leave that rotten, old practice of yours—it's not worth much anyway. I want you to devote yourself entirely to my affairs. Now that Cantire is being restored it will be necessary to buy back the old family estates bit by bit. You understand. If it became known that I was trying to get them the price would go up enormously. You must act with cunning, and find out when and in what quantity the property is in the market."

Hicks showed some signs of disappointment. "Then you want me to remain here? I had rather wished to move to Town."

Lord Wanstead showed his teeth. "I know you did, but I would rather have you where I can keep an eye on you. You might be tempted to speak, you see, and that would be awkward for both of us. No; you will stay here and be my eyes and ears. I shall make you a gift for the work you have already done. A substantial sum of"—he paused deliberately and grinned at Hicks—"five thousand pounds."

Hicks turned white. "Five thousand—and when?"

"The day that the building is completed. Come. I hear our guests arriving."

Sinclair had managed to see Guillet alone for a few minutes.

"The matter of restoration is now in your hands, Bertrand. I want to ask you something—it is rather important. Later on, get one or two expert men from France who can't talk English. Then 'discover' the crypt. You take my meaning?"

"Perfectly! It shall be a great find for us." He smiled in appreciation at what he thought was one of Sinclair's jokes.

"Now follow. You will get your men to fasten up the passage that we discovered with old stones. Your own men, mind you. But you will contrive that it can be unsealed if it is ever necessary."

Guillet's eyes became troubled. "We are not to open that secret passage so interesting, no?"

"On no account. I am fastening that board properly, so that both ends will be sealed."

"But why?"

"There may come a time when I shall want to use that tunnel. The game is not yet played out," Sinclair said very gravely.

"I will do what you ask. It can be managed. I shall say I want my own men for the work of more delicate finesse."

"Very well, then. Only you and I and another know of that place."

They joined the others in the dining-room of the inn.

Inspector Gillian thought himself rather out of place, but Wanstead's generous wine thawed his reserve.

There seemed to be an end to the problem on which they had all taken a part. The fate of the luckless Campions was forgotten, and Musgrave had become merely a memory.

In fact, Wanstead referred to the affair in a jocular way.

"I hope," he said, "that all these stories of bogeys and ghosts will now be scotched for ever. I never knew such a village."

Guillet threw a dash of cold water on the assembly. "I do not know. The ghost, he do live with the very stones of the building. He does not go when it is rebuilt."

Wanstead laughed heartily. "You want candle and book, and one of your Catholic priests with incense and incantations. I know the breed."

Guillet shot an angry glance at him. "Perhaps it is not the ghost that you mean, to whom I do refer. There are ghosts in the soul of the guilty man that haunt him for ever," he said solemnly.

"That's another matter," Wanstead said shortly. "Sir Arthur, what are your plans?"

"My holiday is over, and I have enjoyed the air of Devon. I must get back to my work."

A look of relief flitted across Hicks' pale face. "You are still at work, then?" he asked politely.

"People come and ask advice. Sometimes I can help them; sometimes I fail. This time I have not been of much service, except perhaps in helping to get that girl Elsie from Cantire. She should see a doctor. I don't like her condition. She has absolutely no recollection of anything that happened after she walked in her sleep."

The wine was circling freely, and Wanstead was in a genial mood.

"That reminds me. I am glad you mentioned her name. Now that her parents are both dead she will be unprovided for. After all, they were employed by my brother-in-law, and I have some responsibility. I shall take on myself the expense of seeing that she is properly educated. Yes—a boarding school. Perhaps a convent school abroad would be best."

"I am sure that is very good of you," Sinclair said. "As she has no living relatives, I suppose she is a ward in chancery."

"There will be no difficulty for one in my position."

Wanstead said loftily. "I shall get Lady Wanstead to take the matter up."

"That would be the best thing," Sinclair agreed. "Perhaps you know of some school, Bertrand?"

"There are many good schools in Paris," Guillet said. "If Lord Wanstead wishes, I will make inquiries."

Wanstead took refuge in his glass. His suggestion was being taken up too literally.

Seften had not taken any part in the conversation, but, finding his uncle in a genial mood, he ventured to say in a halting manner, "I wonder if you could find employment for that man Rhodes?"

Sinclair looked keenly at him. Perhaps some spark of remorse had come to him for his treatment of Mary Rhodes. It was a strange thing, that had baffled Sinclair. Rhodes had never shown any signs of hatred of Seften. At first Sinclair had watched carefully, fearing that the man was nursing up his grievance until he could take revenge, but as he began to understand him he was convinced that Rhodes was ignorant of the fact that Seften had been the man who had married his sister. She had been loyal to the last, and as she had remained silent in court, so she had held back the man's name even from her brother.

Sinclair's opinion of Seften rose, and he backed up the request.

"I agree with your nephew," he urged. "I have formed a high opinion of Rhodes, and I happen to know that he lost his farm by helping a friend, and not, as the police think, by betting."

Wanstead turned a dusky crimson at the remark, which he understood. "I will certainly do so," he said, with assumed heartiness.

"If I may suggest it," Gillian said ironically, "I should make him gamekeeper. You know the old saying, my lord, about poachers."

"One might do worse," Sinclair observed. "The only difficulty will be with the man himself. He is stubborn and obstinate. Shall I mention it to him?"

"Please do," Wanstead agreed, anxious to get away from a delicate subject.

Guillet broke the silence that followed. He turned to Gillian with a friendly smile. "It is strange, Monsieur Inspecteur, that our names are so near to each other."

It was a simple remark, and would have called for no comment; but Gillian flushed up quite angrily. "It's not really strange at all; that was the original form in which my name was spelt. It sounded rather foreign, so I altered it when I joined the police force."

"That is so," Sinclair said genially. "I have known that for many years, and often wondered whether perhaps you two were related. Inspector Gillian was at the Yard, you know, for some time."

"I thought a country district would suit me better, so came to Devonshire," Gillian muttered.

"Then I will drink the health of my possibly relation, eh?" Guillet lifted his glass and clinked it with Gillian's, who seemed slightly annoyed for some reason.

"I hope on the next occasion we meet," Wanstead said, "we shall be able to celebrate the engagement of my nephew. I must not mention names at present, but I believe there will be an announcement before long."

Nothing more was said, and the party broke up. Wanstead was having a word with Grimes. Sinclair was for a moment alone. He turned, to see Seften, who closed the door and came forward.

"I know you have a very low opinion of me, Sir Arthur, and rightly so, but do you blame me for what you heard my uncle say? I mean, it sounds rotten after what happened, but I am heir to my uncle, and he is very keen on my marrying."

"It is entirely a matter you must decide for yourself. You cannot undo the past. It is not for me to judge."

"Thank you, sir; only, as you knew the story, I thought I would ask your opinion."

"You need not be afraid that I should say anything," Sinclair said stiffly. "I gave you advice once which you would not take. I am giving no more. You have done something in asking your uncle to employ Rhodes, for the whole of his modest fortune went on the defence of Mary. Perhaps you didn't know that?"

"I had no idea. Poor fellow. We must certainly do something for him, then."

Before Sinclair returned to London he had one call to make the following day. He went to see Rhodes and the two young people.

Elsie, rather to Sinclair's surprise, welcomed the idea of going to a school, especially in Paris. Rob's face fell, but he showed a brave front, and congratulated her.

Sinclair got Rhodes alone, and broached the subject of the job.

"I'll see him in hell first!" he said stoutly, as Sinclair had expected.

"Now listen to me, Rhodes. I knew you would take that line, but I particularly wish it. I have other work to do, but the mystery of Cantire remains still unsolved, and you will be most useful if you not only remain here, but take employment with Lord Wanstead. Do it as a personal favour to me, and keep in touch."

After considerable persuasion, Rhodes agreed; and Sinclair left for London.

As his car passed through the Devon lanes he looked back at Cantire from a corner and saw the grim pile in the valley below. He wondered how and when he would see it again, for he was convinced in his mind that this was not the last time.

CHAPTER XV

SINCLAIR'S RETURN

A YEAR HAD ELAPSED since the last dinner at Barton. On his return to London Sinclair had found an urgent request waiting for him from India, where he had served in his early days.

An Indian prince required his services on a matter of such extreme delicacy that he had not ventured to invoke the assistance of the police. He packed up and went off at once, for he had often longed to return to that country where he had made his first successes.

The case took him into strange places and taxed his resources to the utmost. He was nearly poisoned, and had lain ill for weeks, and attempts had been made on his life with dagger and other means. He had brought it to a successful conclusion, avoided a scandal, and earned the eternal gratitude of the Prince, who insisted on rewarding him in such a manner that he was better off than he had ever been in his life. In many of his cases he had actually been out of pocket, and in others he had merely taken bare expenses.

Weak from his illness, he came back by slow stages. He had to allow time to get rid of the saffron from his face. His appearance when he shaved off beard and whiskers was, to say the least, weird; a piebald creature was shown by the glass.

It was spring when he finally reached Paris and sought his friend Guillet.

For months he had been cut off from all news, and was anxious to hear the latest gossip which he knew Guillet would give him.

His welcome was rapturous. He found a prosperous and stouter Bertrand, who embraced him with enthusiasm.

Guillet's house on Montparnasse had been redecorated throughout and there were signs of prosperity that indicated that Wanstead had treated him generously.

They dined together in the open air at a favourite café in the Boulevard du Montparnasse. The air was soft, and the sparkle and gaiety reminded Sinclair that he had returned to civilization. They talked long on the general news and of all that had taken place, and then, as coffee was served, on more intimate topics.

The work at Cantire had been completed to both Guillet's and Lord Wanstead's entire satisfaction. Everything that the architect required had been bought in record time. Wanstead had coolly bought an old manor house in order to obtain the oak panelling and fireplaces, and had ordered tapestries and pictures without regard to expense.

So Guillet had been in paradise. He had never been able to let his art have full sway before. His mind was so full of the work he had done—as he called it banally, his *magnum opus*—that it was late before Sinclair could inquire about persons rather than the building. Nehemiah would probably have been as great a bore when describing his rebuilding of the Temple.

"And now," Sinclair said, with his old laugh, "what about all our friends?"

Guillet became grave. "I regret to say that Lady Wanstead is dead." He crossed himself, and for a moment his flamboyant manner was gone.

"I am sorry to hear that," Sinclair said. "It is the last of the Musgrave family."

"That is what they are saying in the village. It seems that the curse on the family has now died out."

"What did she die of?"

"Oh, my friend, nothing in your line. It was, as they say, the normal. She caught a cold at Cantire, when she came down to see how things were going on, and when she returned to her home the pneumonia attacked her. It has upset Lord Wanstead so, he has gone bald, and looks older. He is going to have the little miss— Elsie, as you call her—to keep house for him."

"Where is she?" Sinclair asked quickly.

"Still at the convent here in Paris, and you would hardly know her. The time he has worked miracles." Guillet rose and fetched a framed photograph. "She has sent this to me only the other day."

He pushed the photograph into Sinclair's hands, and saw a look of intense interest on the detective's face. "It's wonderful what proper surroundings will do for a girl; good food and so on."

Guillet stared at his friend. "But you do not see. Do you not the miniature remember?"

"I have not forgotten it, Bertrand. This photograph is more like that than ever. There is no question now that Elsie's mother was the original. I never had a doubt myself."

"Elsie, if I may call her that, is leaving shortly from the convent and will go to Cantire."

"I see. Lord Wanstead has carried out his promise."

"I am not a detective like you, only a poor artist, but I have seen much of Lord Wanstead. He seems to me like a man who wishes to pay the reparations."

"Yes, I follow you. And that man Rhodes?"

"He is now the manager of the estate, now so big. The lawyer Heeks bought for the Lord Wanstead the property that once was owned by the Musgraves. He was artful, that lawyer, and is getting quite fat."

"And young Rob?"

"Ah, he has not turned out well. He went away to London after Elsie came here with me to the convent, and we heard nothing. He does not write, and I am afraid he has gone to the hounds."

Sinclair was too worried about the youth to correct Guillet.

"I don't think we can be surprised at that," he said seriously. "When Elsie was taken away, and was no longer to be his play-mate, no wonder he was upset. He was quite unfitted for a place like Barton. I shall have to find him."

"Mr. Seften has been trying. He too has changed; he is—how do you say?—stiff in the back."

For a moment Sinclair was at a loss. He thought of lumbago, and then the meaning dawned on him. "You mean he is more of a man?"

"That is it. He has been much at Cantire, and I have grown to like him. He has some secret sorrow, which I know not of, but he has told me he can never marry."

"I can understand that. Perhaps one day he will get over it."

Guillet brightened up. "The Lord Wanstead is, so I have heard, to be made a Viscount. He is taking the title of Lord Cantire."

"Indeed. It shows what can be done in the building trade," Sinclair said venomously.

"That is all, my friend. All goes well and quiet. Lord Wanstead is giving what you call the house-firing party when Elsie goes from her convent to become the chatelaine."

"I suppose you mean house-warming."

"That is so. All are to come."

"Including Inspector Gillian, your namesake."

"He will not be there," Guillet said gravely. "Soon after you had gone he went from Devon. He did not get the credit for that case, and was under the clouds. He went to some other place, I know not where, perhaps to London."

"Poor fellow. He had rather a bad time there, and didn't do very well."

"I traced his pedigree, as you call it, and found he had been in Paris before he went to London. He is a cousin to me on the distant side."

They talked far on into the night, and Sinclair learnt all that had happened since he had been away. He could piece together the bits of Guillet's information. So it was more than a mere boy-and-girl affection on Rob's side. He could picture the despair the young man felt when Elsie was taken away to be made into a grand lady, like a story from a pantomime. He was proud and generous, and would efface himself because he might stand in Elsie's way. Sinclair hoped he had not gone to pieces.

Guillet, he saw, had come completely under Wanstead's dominant influence. Seften looked like becoming a man, and making good. Everything seemed to be settling down, and the mystery likely to remain unsolved.

Sinclair returned to London. He did not wish to bring up the past by seeing Elsie, and hoped he would meet her when she finished at the convent in a few weeks' time.

His flat had been looked after by his faithful servant Buggins, and piles of correspondence awaited his attention.

Still feeling far from well, he decided to postpone the evil day when he must wade through this, and sought sunshine and the feel of London in the spring.

No one, as far as he knew, was aware of his return, and he would not be worried by callers.

He was months behind with the news, and would have to do a lot of reading in his club library.

He was walking up Whitehall, enjoying the fresh May air and feeling the delight a Londoner does in the sights and sounds of the old city. He crossed the Strand, and was making his way past the Commonwealth Building, at the point where the tube goes down to the subway. He paused for a moment to watch the pigeons, and then heard a familiar voice speaking behind him.

"Hullo, Sir Arthur!"

He turned quickly, and saw Rob, but an altered Rob. The year had changed him into a man, and his face was bronzed and healthy.

"I am delighted to see you," Sinclair said, and held out his hand. To his surprise the other lit a cigarette, whether intentionally or not, and ignored the hand.

"How are you getting on?" Sinclair asked. "I would like to hear all the news."

The crowd was thick, as it was just before the lunch hour. Someone jostled into Sinclair, and he turned to apologize, as he always did, for obstructing the way.

"Let's go and have a talk—" he had wheeled round. There was no one there. Rob had disappeared—he supposed, down the tube. It was most churlish conduct, and Sinclair felt it would be undignified to run after him. He shrugged his shoulders and proceeded towards St. Martin's Church. He decided to drop into the Chandos, an old haunt of his, and sample their wine.

It was annoying that he should see the very man he wanted to find, and then to lose him.

He took a seat by the window and ordered his drink.

The pleasant hum of conversation was round him, and the strain of keeping up a disguise was now over. He had determined to devote some of the money he had received from the Prince to Elsie and Rob, but apparently Elsie was now well provided for.

And then he had a shock. The door swung back and Seften and Elsie entered together, but it was a transformed Elsie. She was laughing, and the paleness had gone from her face. She had developed into an exceedingly pretty girl with a springy, light figure, and with the touch that only Paris can give.

Seften looked better in health, and more self-assured than before, and they were evidently on the best of terms.

It was just a fleeting vision as they went upstairs to the restaurant, but in that moment Elsie turned her head and saw Sinclair.

A look almost of horror came to her, and her face went scarlet. She seemed to hesitate for one second, and then went out of sight up the stairs.

It was a most astonishing coincidence. But was it? A sudden thought flashed through Sinclair's mind. Rob was there watching the other two. Then that would account for his sudden disappearance if he had seen them, for he would not want to be seen talking with Sinclair. But Elsie! She was supposed to be in Paris. This meeting must be then a clandestine one. A frown gathered on his face. The old Cantire business was cropping up again.

He took a light luncheon at his club, and then firmly resolved to attack his correspondence.

He conscientiously waded through the mass. There were urgent requests for his services, begging letters and circulars, and also the usual crop of threatening letters from men he had run to earth and who had emerged from prison full of hate. Mostly they were vulgar and abusive scrawls telling him what the writers would do when they got him in a solitary place.

He was used to this sort of thing.

He filed a few letters and threw a number into the waste-paper-basket. Then he opened one letter with his penknife, and gave a start of surprise.

It was from Elsie, and the date was February 15th There were four pages of closely written script in a large but elegant hand.

Coming after the episode at the Chandos, it was particularly interesting, but pathetic. She told him she was in great trouble and wanted Sinclair's advice badly. She mentioned no names, and the hints were vague, but she was dreading something.

Sinclair read it through twice and then laid it on the table. What must she have thought of him? No wonder she had not spoken to him.

Sinclair lit his pipe and stared into the cheerful fire, for he was not yet acclimatized.

Elsie was lunching with Seften, and Rob had evidently been shadowing them. Here was a complication he had not reckoned for, and his mouth set firm.

He was still thinking over the problem. The room was filled with tobacco smoke, and dusk was coming down.

Huggins announced that a lady wished to see him, and Sinclair had little doubt as to the caller. He told his man to show her in, and Elsie entered.

Seen thus face to face, the change in the girl was more apparent. No one now would ever take her for the daughter of the Campions.

She was more certain of herself, and the large dark eyes had a look in them that denoted intelligence and spirit.

She came forward to his desk without formality and spoke. "I want an explanation, Sir Arthur, and I think I am entitled to one."

"Sit down, Elsie, and have a cigarette," he said suavely. "I rather expected to see you after our strange meeting today."

Her eye caught the letter open on the desk, and she gave a gasp.

"Yes," Sinclair said, answering her unspoken question, "I found this among my unopened letters this afternoon. I only returned from India a few days ago, and arrived in London yesterday. I have not had any letters forwarded because the affair on which I was engaged entailed complete loss of identity for a time."

"Then that was the reason you did not answer," she said thoughtfully. "And I thought that you would not have anything more to do with me."

"Why should you think that?" His voice was almost stern.

Before replying, she took the cigarette Sinclair offered and smoked furiously.

"Do you know all that has happened since last year?" she answered evasively.

"I have had a long conversation with Guillet in Paris and have learnt a great deal."

"Have you heard from Rob?" she asked nervously.

"Not a word," he was able to answer truthfully.

"Then he hasn't told you anything?"

"Not a word."

"Poor Rob!" she said. "What must he think of me?"

"I suppose you mean your going about with Seften," Sinclair said at a venture.

Instead of flaring up, as he had expected, she sank her head on her hands.

"Do you still want my advice?" he asked.

"I know what it will be; I can guess," she said miserably.

"Yes; to tell the whole truth to me."

"I can't," she said, white to the lips, "not even to you."

Sinclair was more disturbed than he cared to acknowledge. He rose from his seat and paced the room, while Elsie watched him anxiously.

"Elsie, I am not quite an old fool. I am quite certain you know a good deal more than you will tell me. Come"—he held out his hand—"won't you trust me? I was certain at Cantire. That is why I gave the case up. Now you have complicated matters. Won't you tell me?"

For one moment a frightened look came to her eyes, and her mouth quivered. She was on the point of weakening. It was a crucial moment. He waited, and gradually saw her face harden.

"I can't," she almost whispered. "It's not my secret."

"I won't press you, my dear. But I am going to take you into my confidence. Once, in this very room, I had an interview with a woman who had been as beautiful as you are now. She too was in great distress, and wanted my advice. Shall I go on?"

Fear and horror were chasing each other over Elsie's face.

"Who was it?" She spoke hoarsely, her wide-open eyes glued to his, and her mouth half open.

"My friend Monsieur Guillet, whom you know, had her picture in Paris. He knew her. Shall I go on?" She nodded her head, unable to speak.

"It was your mother, Elsie."

"My mother—but that is impossible!" she cried. "You couldn't have met her. She died when I was a baby."

"You never knew her name?"

"Never. I was brought up with the Campions. I believed they were my parents. Only I was told the truth—" She stopped abruptly and averted her eyes.

"How much of the truth, Elsie? Come, I have told you. Won't you tell me?"

"I was told that my mother was dead, and that I had no relation. I was told another thing"—her face went a deep crimson. "I suppose you must know; I am illegitimate. No one knew who my father was."

"Who told you that?" Sinclair said sharply.

"Lord Wanstead when he adopted me."

An abyss yawned before Sinclair. The scoundrel. So this was the cause of his kindness.

The girl was crying softly, and Sinclair desisted from further questions.

"What can I do to help? I am working in the dark, but I will do anything I can."

She jumped to her feet. "Would you? You are a dear, after my being such a beast. I do want something so badly."

"Tell me, Elsie."

"Will you come to Cantire? If only you can come, I believe you will be able to find out everything. It's all finished now, and Lord Wanstead is giving a sort of reception to celebrate the occasion."

"I have nothing to do, Elsie, and will certainly come if invited."

She gripped his arm, and her voice took on a shrill note. "That's what you mustn't do. Listen. I am going back to Paris today. I got leave by telling a lie. In a few weeks' time I shall be leaving and I want you to take me to Cantire. Will you?"

"With the greatest of pleasure."

"You are a dear!" she exclaimed, with her old vivacity.

"I shall come and fetch you myself," Sinclair said, watching her, "and we call run down in my car."

"That wouldn't do. I must come across, and will call here. No one must know. I will arrange everything."

"Very well, then, Elsie. Will you tell me one thing? Have those fits of sleep-walking gone?"

She turned white to the lips and reeled back. "Don't please mention that. Don't ever!" She spoke passionately, and Sinclair reassured her.

"I will write to you," she said at parting, "only don't run off to India again."

Her hurried departure told Sinclair that she was not going to say another word, and was afraid of his questions.

He turned to the old file of the case and read carefully through. At one point he paused, and gave an exclamation. "Fool that I was! That explains the whole case! And I have been blind for months. Never call me a detective again!"

And there grew round him in the thick tobacco smoke and the rays of the dying sun a picture vivid and real, of that saturnine face of Musgrave as he stood there and told his story.

There was a sharp ring at the door, and Buggins answered.

Sinclair switched on the light. His uncanny instinct told him who his visitor was. Once before, immediately after Musgrave and Seften had gone, Mary Rhodes had called. Now the situation was reversed, and yet the same. Rob came in.

"I'm glad to find you in," he said. "You must have thought me some sort of swine when I rushed off."

"I think I know the reason. I have only just returned to England you must know."

Rob's face took on the stubborn look Sinclair had seen so often on his uncle's face.

"I came to apologize," he said awkwardly.

"I think not, Rob. Sit down, my lad, and let's talk. You ran away because you saw Elsie with Seften."

"That's true. I didn't want to be seen by them," he said, in the surly tone of his uncle.

"What have you been doing with yourself all this time?" Sinclair remarked, to put him at his ease.

"Look here, Sir Arthur. I didn't come here about myself. It's about Elsie. It's all very fine. I've nothing personal against Seften except that I don't like the man."

"You mean that he is trying to cut you out with Elsie?"

"It's so underhand. They meet secretly, but that's not my affair. What is worrying me is that she has absolutely altered. She won't answer letters, and when we have met she has implored me not to see her again. I feel certain it's not that snob stuff with her, and just because that blighter Wanstead has taken her up. Honest, Sir Arthur, I'm glad for her sake, but there's something all wrong. Why should she not want to see me?"

"I can't tell you, Rob, my boy." Sinclair laid a hand on his shoulder. "But I do promise you one thing: that old mystery of Cantire is going to be cleared up very soon, and then perhaps things will all come right. Meanwhile I am going to have a word with Seften that may clear matters up a bit about Elsie."

"I'm ever so grateful. Don't think I'm a rotter. I am earning my living, and getting on fine."

"All right, my boy. Keep in touch with me. And one more thing. Isn't it about time you went and saw your uncle?"

"I'm not keen on going to Cantire."

"I understand that. But Lord Wanstead is throwing a party, I believe it is called, when Elsie comes back from France. Can you manage to go down at that time and stay with your uncle?"

"If you want me to, but—"

"There are no buts, Rob; and believe me, I may want your help. It's not a joke. I have reason to believe that the person who murdered Musgrave will be present at Cantire at the party, though you may not see him or hear him speak."

Rob's eyes showed his sudden feeling of repulsion. "You don't mean that beastly thing we saw?"

"The very same. Now you know why I want you to come—for Elsie."

"I'll be there," Rob said simply.

"You don't happen to know where Seften is staying?"

"I do then. I've had my eye on the blighter. He's at the Ordley Hotel."

Strange how everything seemed to be moving in a circle. The whole affair had started with Musgrave's letter from this very hotel.

"Thanks. I shan't forget that name," Sinclair smiled. "Goodbye for the present. Keep in touch, don't forget."

When Rob had gone, Sinclair laughed to himself, a little scorn-fully. So it had come to this. A murder problem had now become one of trying to straighten out the simple question of Elsie and Rob and their love troubles. It was no new experience for Sinclair, and a pleasant change from the grim business in India, where the slightest slip would have meant a knife stab or a bow-string.

He had a quiet dinner by himself, and then drove to the Ordley. Seften was in, the office clerk told him, and he ascended the lift.

The page conducted him to an expensive suite, where Seften was sitting by a fire alone. He had just seen Elsie off to Paris, as Sinclair had ascertained, and looked up quickly.

Sinclair was the very last man he expected to see, and he greeted him with reserve. Here was the man who knew his past, and he wished that to be buried.

Sinclair was never one to beat about the bush.

"I came to see you, Seften, because I happened by mere chance to catch a glimpse of you today at the Chandos, with Elsie."

Seften coloured up, and his old nervous manner returned.

"I was lunching there. But really, Sir Arthur, I hardly see what business it is of anyone else's."

"Elsie is supposed to be in Paris. In a few weeks' time she will leave the convent; but she was over here. That is not my business, but I came to ask you a question. Do you know who Elsie is?"

Seften wheeled round as though he had been shot. "Whatever do you mean?" he exclaimed angrily.

"You have answered me," Sinclair remarked calmly. "I see you don't. Now please don't imagine I am prying into your affairs, or that I want to rake up the past. Get that clearly out of your head. My question is a very important one."

Seften leant forward, scanning the face of the detective in-tently.

"She is the daughter of Mary Rhodes, your late wife."

The blow was shattering. Seften rose to his feet and leant heav-ily against the mantelpiece. Sinclair thought he would have col-lapsed, but he mastered himself, and turned haggard eyes to him.

"You are sure of this?" he said hoarsely.

For answer, Sinclair drew from his pocket the miniature that Guillet had given him and handed it to Seften.

He gazed long and earnestly at the picture, and his face went grey. "I might have known," he muttered over and over again. "You have known this for some time?"

"I knew it when I first saw her, but wanted proof, and found that in Paris. My friend Guillet knew Mary in Paris long ago."

Seften clenched his fists. "He is not the scoundrel."

"Certainly not," Sinclair said emphatically.

Seften walked across to a table and helped himself to brandy. He was so upset that it was not until he had consumed a large dose that he remembered his manners. "I beg your pardon, Sir Arthur. Will you have a drink?"

"Not just now, thank you. Sit down and let us have a chat. I knew this would be a blow to you."

Seften sat down, holding his refilled glass. He smiled wanly. "Not so much as you think, Sir Arthur. When Elsie was at Cantire last year, of course, I took hardly any notice of her, a mere ragged brat, but when she came back at Christmas, and stayed with my uncle, I was somehow attracted to her and could not quite get her face out of my mind. Now I can see the reason," he went on bitterly. "I was seeing Mary's face all the time. It must have been subconscious."

"Was it fair to bring her over here?"

Seften put his glass down and looked at Sinclair.

"I brought her over here! I am sure I never did. It was the very last thing I would do. She wrote and asked whether she might come and see me. I have her letter." He went to a bureau and produced a pile of letters. "Here you are. Please read it. There is nothing whatever of a private nature."

Sinclair recognized the same large schoolgirl handwriting, and took the sheet from the envelope. It was, as Seften had said, purely formal. She told small details of her daily work, and then said that she wanted to come to London, and could she see him. She would arrive in the morning and go back in the evening, and then followed a request that he would arrange for two days' leave of absence for her. The signature was merely 'yours sincerely.'

Seften watched Sinclair as he read, and when he handed the letter back he said coldly, "I hope you are not falling into the mistake of thinking that I was making love to the girl. I had a most impertinent letter from that young jackanapes, Rob Summers."

"Your interest was purely platonic?"

"Let us understand each other. I know the opinion you hold of me after that other affair, but I am not going into that. My uncle was pressing me to marry again, for the sake of the inheritance, but I could not bring myself to do so. How could I ask any decent woman to marry me without telling her the truth; and if I did, would any self-respecting woman do so? Finally I told my uncle flatly that I would not marry again, and the amazing part of the business was that, instead of cursing me as I expected, he took it like a lamb, and said he thought I was quite right."

"I think you are wise," Sinclair said gravely. "So that Elsie is only a friend. You should have told Rob."

"Is he then keen on Elsie? I didn't know. After his letter I did not wish to see the young blighter again."

"You have no objection to my telling him?"

"I have none; but wouldn't it be a good thing to find out the truth first? Perhaps that black fellow Rhodes may know. He is Elsie's uncle."

He paced the room in great agitation. "What a business! What a tangle it is!" Then he faced Sinclair as a sudden flash came to his mind. "Then I will bet anything that the father of Elsie is the murderer of Musgrave, and the man who abducted Elsie from Paris and took her to Cantire."

Sinclair never moved a muscle. "I think you are very near the truth. But I should not say a word to anyone if I were you. This wants careful handling and the utmost discretion. I understand your uncle is moving in shortly to Cantire, and is celebrating the occasion.

"I know," Seften said listlessly. "I have been requested to be there. I could not quite make out what my uncle was driving at. It seemed a queer thing to do, with his wife dead only a few months ago."

"Perhaps he is doing it for Elsie's sake."

"Have you told him about her?" Seften asked eagerly.

"I shall not do so. I told you because, frankly, I thought you were getting too fond of her. But your uncle has adopted her, and Rhodes either doesn't know or has made no claim. Better for the girl that she should not know. Don't you agree?"

"I am very glad you take that line. I think it is best, and I will tell you another thing that puzzled me. Uncle wrote that he was giving this dinner because he had an important announcement to make. What do you make of that? It could hardly be that he had found out about Mary. That would be the last thing he would broadcast."

"I expect it is something to do with the future of the estate."

"It may be," Seften said doubtfully.

"Then we must just wait. I haven't had the honour of an invitation, but then, I have been so long away. I expect Lord Wanstead will have forgotten all about me."

"I know!" Seften exclaimed. "I've got it! Of course, my uncle's going to be raised in the Peerage to a Viscount. That's the announcement. I'll bet anything. He would think it very important."

"It's quite likely," Sinclair agreed.

"Can't you do anything more to find out who the murderer was?" Seften asked. "I have no cause to love Musgrave, but still, it was a murder."

"I think I can promise that I shall also be able to make an announcement."

"I am pleased to have cleared up this misunderstanding," Seften said, as Sinclair rose to go. "I am hoping to settle down now to a quite uneventful life, and help my uncle, if only you can get hold of this brute."

"You seem to think the man who wronged Mary was the man. But why kill Musgrave?"

Seften looked round the room with the old scared aspect.

"Don't you see, Sir Arthur, he was after us both. You can tell that by the warnings; and I have been afraid all this time he would try to complete his work."

CHAPTER XVI

THE RETURN TO CANTIRE

A CABLE FROM ELSIE informed Sinclair that she had broken up at her convent, and that she was on her way back. Would he meet her at Charing Cross.

It was a hot, close evening in July, and crowds were seeking the country. The station was packed, but Sinclair saw the girl getting out of her carriage alone.

She was dressed neatly in a fawn costume and close-fitting hat, but the look on her face struck Sinclair more than her dress. She had a stern, almost hard look, and even the smile she gave him was forced. He saw to her luggage, and got her away from the crowd as quickly as possible.

Buggins was waiting with the car, and they drove straight to his rooms. He wanted an explanation, and Elsie opened the conversation bluntly.

"You are surprised that I have come before I was expected, and alone? Lord Wanstead had arranged to have me met by his nephew tomorrow, for, as you know, his celebration dinner is fixed on purpose for the day after."

"You slipped off a day too soon then?"

"Yes. I thought I could put up somewhere tonight, and then you and I can motor down early tomorrow and get to Cantire in the evening."

"You also wanted to avoid meeting Seften?"

She looked at him with frank, open eyes. "Honestly, I did. After I saw you the last time, he wrote me a long, confused letter, saying he had seen you, and"—she gave a mirthless laugh—"trying very elaborately to explain that he wasn't making love to me. As though I thought he was!"

"Is that all he said?"

"It was quite enough. I don't know what you said to him, but he positively grovelled in his letter."

"Elsie, I must ask you one question. Seften told me that you had asked to come and see him and, in fact, he showed me your letter. Why did you want to see him?"

"It's so difficult to explain. I knew you would ask me that. I felt I was treating Rob badly, and he might misunderstand. I wanted to tell Mr. Seften that I didn't care for him, except of course as a mere acquaintance. Oh, let's leave it at that. I think he understood, but I made an awful box of it."

"Very well, Elsie, I won't worry you. But you didn't come a day earlier solely to miss him."

"I came because, as you know we arranged before, we could be at Cantire the day before the dinner. I wanted to know who were coming."

Sinclair smoked in silence. Elsie was picking nervously at her handkerchief.

"I think I understand," Sinclair said softly. "Let's drop the subject. Did you see anything of my friend Guillet?"

She brightened up at that. "He called to see me, and came to the prize-giving. It was jolly decent of him, and the Mother Superior was awfully pleased. He gave quite a large sum to the chapel fund."

"Wanstead's bounty," Sinclair commented with a smile. "Come, I suppose you had lunch on the train. I am going to put you up here for tonight. I have a reliable old housekeeper, and am old enough to take charge of a child like you."

"I am so pleased," she said, with a tone of unmistakable relief.

"I have a surprise for you. Rob is coming here, and we shall all go somewhere together this evening."

A look of terror came to her face. "No! Please no, Sir Arthur. I would rather be with you."

"So you shall be. I have no intention of letting you out of my sight. I shall act as chaperon, and"—he paused for emphasis—"as watchdog. Does that content you?"

"Yes. If you are there, I don't mind."

"There he is, I expect," Sinclair said, when they heard a step in the hall.

Buggins entered. "Inspector Gillian to see you, sir."

"I'll go," Elsie said hurriedly. But there was no time, as the man himself entered behind Buggins.

He had grown thinner, the features were sharper and more marked with lines.

He glanced at Sinclair, and then saw Elsie. "I suppose I must believe my eyes, and greet this young lady as Elsie Campion. But how you have changed!" There was genuine admiration in his voice. "How are you, Sir Arthur? You must forgive me for calling. Can I speak to you?"

"You can say anything you wish to in front of Miss Campion; but since Lord Wanstead legally adopted her she has taken the name of Seften from him."

"It was only a small matter. As you probably know, I rather rapped my knuckles over that affair at Cantire. The authorities were not best pleased, and you had gone away somewhere and couldn't put in a good word for me. They transferred me to Durham."

"I am very sorry. I had to go abroad."

"Well, as you can imagine, I wanted to forget all about the case, but Lord Wanstead somehow got hold of my address—I expect through the Yard, he being a Peer of the Realm—and has invited me to go to Cantire for a dinner, of all things, at which he is going to celebrate the restoration, and make some announcement. He asked me to be present. I had to come to town, and thought I would look you up."

Elsie turned to the window and gazed out, but her hands behind her back were tightly clasped.

"I should certainly go. It will be quite a reunion. As for the case of the Musgrave murder, I should not worry about that. Wanstead has a great deal of influence, and I think he was doing a very courteous thing in asking you. I hope to be there myself, and we can have an interesting talk."

"Well, if you think that, I shall try to come. I understand that the place is now habitable."

"The restoration is complete," Sinclair said, with a strange smile. "There will be no more danger after the opening ceremony, which is the day after tomorrow."

"The day after—oh yes, of course, I had almost forgotten the day. If one arrives in the evening I suppose that will do."

"I should not advise you to arrive before that."

Gillian shook hands, gave one glance at Elsie's back, and muttered a good-day.

Huggins showed him out.

Elsie wheeled round sharply. "What is he coming for?"

"Because, my dear, he has been invited, I expect."

"Sir Arthur, I am afraid—desperately. I believe M⁻. Seften is in grave danger of his life."

"I do not think he is the only one," Sinclair said seriously.

The afternoon and evening passed quietly, though in an atmosphere of suspense. Rob was pleased to see Elsie, but very reserved and formal. Questions would keep on cropping up in their minds, questions that they must not put, for Sinclair had sternly forbidden all discussion. They were glad when it came to an end, and Sinclair and Elsie returned to his house. Rob was coming by train the next day.

It was a bright, sparkling morning, and they were up betimes for the long run to Devonshire. There was not a cloud in the sky, and Elsie's spirits revived in the fresh air.

She prattled on about her life at the convent, and of the visits she had received there.

They took a hurried lunch at Taunton, and then went westward. Sinclair stopped the car at a crossroad sign-post. They were on the outskirts of a forest, where the trees met overhead like a great green tunnel, and the sunlight through the trees made a dappled pattern on the road. This was the English countryside, unspoilt as yet by building fiend or advertising vandal.

They might have been back in the early ages, but for the gawky sign-post and its strange hieroglyphics denoting map reference. The road on the left would take them by winding lanes to the seaside town of Torton. Straight ahead their road would merge with the Great West Road running into Cornwall. On the right a valley stretched beneath them, and the spire of Barton church rose above the trees. Far off and misty in the heat haze the Castle of Cantire stood, no longer a ruin, but with all its towers and battlements standing proudly in the wooded background.

The cross-roads seemed almost symbolic of their fateful journey. Elsie glanced at her companion, wondering why he was waiting.

Out of the woods there stepped a man carrying a suit-case. He lifted his hat and bowed low to Elsie.

"You are punctual, as always, Sir Arthur."

"And you, too, Bertrand. Jump in."

Elsie felt that her head was whirling round with the crazy journey.

Guillet took things as a matter of course. "Sir Arthur requested me to meet him here," he said in explanation, as though it were the most natural place in the world.

They drove down a steep rutted road, where the banks were thick with ferns, hart's-tongues and osmundas, and in which two cars could barely pass. The trees grew sparse and a vista of rolling hill and wooded denes rose before them, while high on the skyline was the great plateau of Dartmoor.

They drew up at the 'Green Man,' and old Grimes came hobbling out to meet them with a grin of pleasure on his gnarled face.

"Why, to be sure," he said, "if it isn't Sir Arthur Sinclair. Fancy seeing you again, sir." He shook his hand warmly, and then greeted Guillet. He cast a covert glance at Elsie.

"Don't you know me, Grimes?" the girl said merrily, her courage restored by the end of the journey.

"Well, I never did. If it isn't Elsie; and you used to run here with bare legs for a pint of milk or maybe a quart of cider for— But, lord, how I do run on! Come in and welcome."

Sinclair knew the old man was just going to say 'father,' and stopped in time for fear of raking up a painful subject.

He ushered them in, and called his wife, insisting on their sampling his cider. Sinclair saw a subtle change in the place. It looked smarter and cleaner, and he was not surprised to hear that Lord Wanstead had bought it, and Guillet had repaired it, to keep up the old style.

Elsie went out with Mrs. Grimes, and the old man apologized for his lapse with regard to nearly mentioning Campion's name. He was full of gossip. Lord Wanstead was at the castle. Hicks was getting fat, and was quite prosperous these days.

He had done his work well, Grimes stated. Bit by bit he had purchased field and meadow and wood until nearly all the old estate had been reclaimed. Sergeant Haddon was still about, but hardly ever came out to Barton now. Gillian, as Sinclair already knew, had gone to another district. Grimes shrewdly suspected that his failure over the Musgrave case had been the cause.

"And the Campions?" Sinclair asked, when his flow of small talk had died down.

"Lord, sir, I didn't want to mention it before the young lady, as she is now. They found the bones, and little more, when they got all those stones away. Poor souls, it was only by bits of clothing they could identify them. The crowner said 'twas death by misadventure, whatever that means. The place wasn't safe."

"Well, Grimes, we shall just go and pay our respects to Lord Wanstead, and if he does not wish to put me up I shall stay here, as I have not been invited."

Elsie was summoned, and they drove off. Sinclair stopped the car at the entrance to the drive. It was his first view of the reconstructed place, and Guillet had done his work magnificently.

There was not a trace of any new work to be seen. The castle rose in perfect proportions as it had done four centuries before. The gatehouse had been restored, and Sinclair exchanged glances with Guillet as he saw it, now complete with a chamber in the arch above, with an oriel window. On either side was a room, that on the left in use as a porter's lodge, and that on the right, where the secret passage began, shut up and locked.

Sinclair made no comment, but a smile from Guillet told him that the secret was secure. Elaborate wrought-iron gates from an old manor house stood beneath the archway.

A porter came bustling from the lodge, a gorgeous person quite out of keeping with the place, but Guillet had had no hand in his creation. This was Wanstead at his worst.

Sinclair gave his name, and the great gates were opened. Evidently Wanstead had established the customs of a great feudal lord, as he imagined one to have been.

At the massive doors of the castle another flunkey, also in a sort of uniform, appeared. The gates were exactly as they had been. Any strengthening had been cunningly done by Guillet, and could not be noticed. Sinclair and Elsie were ushered into the old withdrawing-room, now hung with tapestries and beamed with black oak.

Elsie was spellbound. It reminded her of one of those old fairy stories where at the touch of a magician's wand a castle fit for a princess sprang up in a night.

In a few minutes Lord Wanstead came bustling in.

"Why, Sir Arthur, this is a surprise!" he said, with rather an exaggerated boisterousness. He extended a fat, damp hand. "I suppose Elsie brought you." He took Elsie by the shoulders in a paternal fashion. "Why, my dear, you have grown. Welcome to the castle. And Guillet too. I wasn't expecting either of you till tomorrow."

His face suddenly assumed a serious air. "But, you young puss, you have come away a day too soon, and my nephew has gone over to bring you back."

"I am sorry, Uncle"—he had told her to call him that. "We broke up earlier than I had expected. I ought to have let you know, but thought it would be a surprise."

"I suppose Monsieur Guillet brought you back," he said, and luckily did not wait for an answer. "Come along to my sanctum and have a drink."

He led them out into the inner court. "I must show you over the place later on."

Guillet had retained all the old winding stairways, but had cunningly inserted lifts in the thickness of the walls, concealed by oak panelling.

Elsie gave a slight shudder as she passed the door to the chapel and the stairway leading to the Monks' Chamber.

On the first floor, facing down the drive, was Lord Wanstead's palatial study.

A heavy butler in plain evening dress came in answer to the bell, and brought sherry wine, which Wanstead recommended.

"Your friend Guillet has done wonders. I never thought anyone could make such a job of it. There is a magnificent view from the towers." He went on with a detailed description. His enthusiasm was that of a schoolboy for a new toy; only, as he spoke, the veins on his thick neck were pulsating and swollen. The danger signals of apoplexy were there. "Do you know, Guillet made a most interesting discovery."

A slight movement of Sinclair's head alone showed his sudden alertness.

"You remember that chapel, where poor Musgrave was murdered?"

"It is *poor* Musgrave now," Sinclair thought. "I have reason to remember it," he said aloud.

"He found that that altar-stone moved, and that underneath was an old crypt which must have been concealed for many years. There were coffins of old Musgraves there, which I have had removed to Barton church. Guillet placed an altar there, and it is quite the old mediaeval crypt of the pictures."

"An altar?" Sinclair asked innocently.

"He said that was the proper thing. There is a small vesper light burning—of course electric—but one would never know, and it is really quite a feature in the place. You must see it."

Sinclair shot a look at Elsie and Guillet, who were gazing out of the window, apparently uninterested in the conversation.

So Guillet had covered the entrance to the passage with an altar—ingenious!

"You must stay here for as long as you care to," Wanstead said with courtesy.

Sinclair perceived by the warmth of the invitation that Wanstead was glad of company, and guessed that he had fallen between the two stools that a moneyed snob invariably does.

The old friends who had been pals during his rise to wealth he would not ask to Cantire, and the old families who would have accepted Lady Wanstead as a Musgrave had little use for the *parvenu*, whose very gushing praise of his place indicated how unused he was to such surroundings.

"I am sure I shall be delighted. I wished to see the old place, and of course I am most interested, having first introduced you to Guillet."

"You have your suit-case with you?"

"Our luggage is still strapped to the car, but if you prefer it, I can go to the 'Green Man.' "

"Most certainly not. I would not hear of it. By the way, I am giving a sort of celebration dinner tomorrow night. I don't know if they told you."

There was just a shade of anxiety in his voice, and he looked keenly at Sinclair. The latter smiled.

"I did hear something about it," he said indifferently.

"Elsie, would you see about the luggage and tell Mrs. Neegle to have rooms prepared? You will have to learn your duties, you know."

The girl went out, and Wanstead helped himself to sherry.

"I have had the old state-rooms of the Musgraves refurnished in the style in which they were. I occupy the historic Musgrave bed, in which several of them have been murdered." He laughed at his joke.

"I should have thought you would have avoided that room," Sinclair said gravely.

"I am not a Musgrave, and the old curse of the Black Abbot will not fall on me. Come along and I will show you."

A booming sound came from somewhere below.

"We must postpone the pleasure; that is the first dinner-gong. My butler will conduct you to your rooms.

He rang the bell, and that well-fed individual entered like the slave of the lamp.

Wanstead issued his orders. He could organize a staff as well as a business.

They took dinner in the great hall, now roofed and provided with windows. It was a vast, gloomy place for so small a party, but Wanstead would insist on making dinner a ceremonial, at which he could display his plate and his servants. The huge open grate yawned in the middle of one side, and the table appeared tiny in the centre. For a Christmas party with crowds of happy children it would have been suitable in every way. Holly and evergreens festooned from the beams, and a boar's head carried in with song and dance, with a flowing wassail bowl.

All this passed before Sinclair's imagination as he sat there. It was a most uncomfortable meal, and they were all glad when it was over.

"You men will want to have a talk," Elsie announced when they rose. "I have lots of things to do, so I will say good night."

Outwardly she was calm enough, and Sinclair alone saw that her nerve was almost at breaking point. She turned at the doorway and gave him an appealing look, which he answered with a reassuring smile.

They adjourned to Wanstead's study. When coffee and liqueurs had been offered by the butler and two maids, Wanstead opened out.

"I suppose, Sir Arthur, with your busy life, you have given no further thought to the problem that brought you down here?"

"I can't really say that I have; but returning to England and seeing my friend Guillet brought it all back to me."

"Yes, of course." Wanstead seemed to hesitate. "I was just wondering—excuse the question—whether you came down to tell me something, something perhaps of a private nature." He glanced at the architect meaningly.

"I have nothing to tell you, Lord Wanstead, but I fancy you could tell me a good deal if you wanted to."

The words were spoken simply, as though without any ulterior meaning, but Wanstead flinched.

"I? What have I to tell?"

"Why, all about the restoration, and the estate."

"Ah yes, of course. It was interesting to see it grow but our friend here took complete charge, and I only came now and then."

"Restoration always gives one a sense of satisfaction, don't you think? Like righting a wrong."

"Of course." Wanstead rolled his cigar round in his mouth and looked searchingly at the detective.

"I suppose Hicks was keeping a careful eye on you, Bertrand, in case you found any awkward secrets."

"Really, Sir Arthur," Wanstead exclaimed irritably, "you have a strange way of talking. Awkward secrets."

"Well, after all, a murder was done here, and I thought perhaps there might have been some clues found; awkward for the murderer."

"As far as I know," Wanstead said stiffly, "apart from the finding of the bodies of those unfortunate Campions, and the crypt about which I told you, there was nothing else found."

"What a pity," Sinclair said. "And you have no fears in sleeping in that room where the ghost prowls round at night?"

Guillet stared at his friend in wonder. He was completely at a loss to understand Sinclair's questions.

"I am not superstitious," Wanstead said shortly. "It suits me, and has a pleasant aspect. I have had a modern bathroom constructed."

"Then of course," Sinclair said solemnly, "no ghost will come. They object to bathrooms."

Wanstead rose impatiently. "Come, I will show you the room you are talking about. I am not going to sit up late."

He led the way along a corridor, brightly lit with electric light, with suits of armour set at intervals.

At the end was a fine carved oak door, purchased by Guillet. Wanstead flung this open with a grand gesture, and disclosed a truly regal bedchamber in which was set a gigantic four-poster bedstead. The room was hung with tapestry over dark oak. Over the old-fashioned fireplace was a painting of Lord Wanstead in Court dress. Every modern convenience had been installed. It was a room fit for a king.

Sinclair cast his eye round with keen interest. Above the bed was a great hook from which a canopy had been suspended in olden days, but Lord Wanstead had drawn the line at that. He did not want to be boxed in, as those of an older generation were accustomed to be.

"Very nice indeed," Sinclair commented.

"I shall write a few letters here," Wanstead said, pointing to a large desk in the embrasure of the window. "If you will forgive me I will wish you good night."

Sinclair and Guillet took the hint, and retired to the nobleman's study.

Sinclair closed the door, and his manner changed completely.

"That's all right as far as he is concerned," he said tersely. "Now listen to me, Bertrand, and don't make any slip, or all my careful plans will go wrong."

"I wait your instructions, but for me, no more adventures, I hope."

"You will take no risk whatever. I understand you closed that passage up at both ends, as you told me."

Guillet paled. "That passage, *mon Dieu!* You are going to open it again?"

"Never mind what I am going to do. Follow my instructions. The end in the crypt is behind the altar?"

"It is the same stone altar that we found in the chapel. I had it moved. As you know, it slides on rollers. I had a little catch placed on the right side, in case someone with a nose, as you say, should touch it."

"Good! Then that can be opened easily. And the other end?"

"That was my masterwork." Guillet grinned expansively. "How to keep the secret? I said to myself. My own men I used for the gatehouse, and the room where we found the stairs. I asked his lordship. One room only we wanted for the porter. That was always the custom"—he chuckled at his subtlety. "His lordship agreed, as to everything. Then, said I, we shall use the other room for a mausoleum."

"A what?" Sinclair asked.

"A store for the old documents, so precious."

"Museum you mean—I take you. That was ingenious. So all the plans and maps are kept there."

"That is right, in tin boxes, and in the corner is just a wooden trapdoor, so innocent, and below that the stairs of which you know, with the tin boxes on the head."

"Excellent," Sinclair commented; "you have done well. Now you will have to go out. Wrap yourself up, and make any excuse you like. You will go to the porter's lodge."

Guillet's eyes were troubled—he scented danger. "What must I do there?"

"Nothing. I have ascertained that the porter sleeps in the room above, and uses the small one in the day-time. You must tell him you are staying in his room, and that he is not to say a word. Use my name. He is not to come out of his bedroom or show any light. You must wait in the dark until something or somebody comes and opens your museum as you call it."

"But I alone have the key?"

"Poof, man! The person we are dealing with is no fool. He has a duplicate, you can be sure. He will go in there. Now here are your orders. You must wait for five minutes, and then go in."

Guillet's hair nearly rose on his head.

"You will be with me?"

"No, my friend, I shall be somewhere else. If my plans work out as I hope, we shall tonight meet the murderer of Musgrave and the Campions, and the person who made that attack on me in Paris."

"It will be dangerous."

"Naturally, but I will protect you."

"But why all these secrecies? Why not do the arrest at once?"

"Because, Bertrand, I have no proof—that is bad for a detective to say. I have suspicion, and quite a lot of information, but that is not sufficient. We must catch him, as they say in Law, *in flagrante delicto*. That means doing another murder."

"I hope you are not using me for the so-called bait!"

"Have no fear. You will be safe."

"I shall wait as you say."

"By that time he will have gone into the passage. You will fasten down the trapdoor and sit on it. Wait till you hear sounds."

"But he may come back!"

"Exactly, and that is why you fasten the door He will be caught. Now is that all clear?"

"For you I will be brave. I shall do it, as you say. But suppose he does not come?"

"He will come, because this is his last chance. Tomorrow Lord Wanstead is going to make an announcement, and that must be prevented by him. Now don't worry about questions. It is quite simple."

"Had we not better inform the police?"

"Rubbish—they would scare him away and then a pretty fool I should look, besides having to do the whole thing over again."

Guillet shrugged his shoulders. "I will go now before my courage he do fail. I will take some of your Scottish whisky and my pistol."

"By all means."

When he had seen Guillet safely out of the postern door, not locked nowadays, he went to Elsie's room and knocked stealthily. The girl opened the door. She had not undressed, and there was a look of absolute misery about her that went to Sinclair's heart. She smiled bravely at him.

"You know what I have come for?" he said gently.

"I think I can guess," she said sadly. "This is going to be a terrible night."

"It's not going to be a joyride for any of us, but this is the end."

She held out the key of her door to him. "This is what you want, isn't it?"

"I am afraid it must be so, Elsie. I can see no other way. You must be brave, and try to sleep. If you can't, then read."

He held her hand in his for a moment. "Good luck, I know you are going into great danger."

Her hand was icy cold as he took it, and slowly closed and locked the door, placing the key in his pocket. Then he went to his room and changed from his evening clothes into a suit of rough tweeds.

CHAPTER XVII

THE NIGHT OF TERROR

THE CASTLE WAS DARK AND SILENT. Only in the inner court a lamp burned, to preserve the ancient custom, and a night watchman paced up and down in a uniform of Wanstead's own designing.

The hours were struck by a fifteenth-century clock installed in the central tower, which showed the days of the year, the phases of the moon, and other funny things.

Sinclair stole from his room in stockinged feet and made his way round the back premises, through the dining-hall, and so into the chapel. This was now properly furnished and decorated, but in one corner Guillet had, as Wanstead had told Sinclair, placed a wooden screen round the original steps that led to the crypt. These Sinclair descended cautiously and found himself in the crypt itself, where a faint gleam shone from the vesper light. Wanstead, with complete disregard for the meaning of the vesper light, had been content with a small bulb in a red glass, and no oil.

The vaulted ceiling had been uncovered, and the pillars replaced. Sinclair had no time to study the beauties of the architecture, and the place was cold and raw. He advanced to the small altar and with a strange thrill saw that it was the one that had been moved from the chapel above. Truly Guillet was a master at his craft. A movement sideways and the altar slid away leaving the entrance to the passage free. No one, as far as Sinclair knew, had penetrated from this end.

Twelve o'clock had struck from the old clock. In the crypt beneath the chapel Sinclair waited, motionless and watchful. The boom of the strokes came muffled in that drear place. Not a sound broke the stillness. Had all his careful plans miscarried, or had his keen brain played him false and the whole elaborate theory he had built up proved the baseless fabric of a vision? Doubts crept into his mind. He reviewed the chain of links which he had patiently riveted together, and they held true.

And then in the stillness there came a very faint noise. Sinclair became alert. He was standing on the steps leading to the chapel above, able to see what took place in the crypt and remain in deep shadow. A shaft of light appeared like a mere crack, gradually broadening, where the altar stood, and then the whole affair slid back and Sinclair could see an electric torch being waved round. He hastily withdrew himself up the stairs, passing like a silent ghost into the chapel, and closing the entrance behind him. He had seen enough. The assassin had come. Noiselessly he crept along to Lord Wanstead's room and opened the door. The nobleman would not wake. Sinclair had seen to that. Apart from his copious libations at dinner and afterwards, he had swallowed a harmless but effective sleeping draught, inserted by Sinclair into his whisky-and-soda.

Sinclair slipped behind the curtains in the bay window, which he had carefully noted when seeing the room. Here he waited, sure of his game.

A short time passed and then his keen ears heard the sound of a door being gently opened. Sinclair loosened his torch in case the murderer might attempt to work in the dark.

There was a slight click, and the room was illumined by the beam of a torch, and the light passed rapidly round the room, resting on the great bed where Wanstead slept as many a Musgrave had done before.

Sinclair's revolver was between the curtains, trained on the spot behind the light. He could follow the movements. A chair was placed by the side of the bed, and a rope was passed over the hook in the ceiling. The noose at the end came into the beam of light, held by black hands that moved swiftly.

The light approached the bed for the last act.

Sinclair emerged from his concealment and flashed his own torch full on the figure behind the light. The same foul creature of night showed itself, the red and baleful eyes flaming in the glare.

"Put your hands up," Sinclair rapped out. The creature raised two arms from which depended great black wings, and then the torch which he carried was hurled straight in Sinclair's face, utterly unexpected. Instinctively Sinclair fired, and there came a scream of pain.

The thing had wheeled like lightning and fled through the open door. Sinclair grimly replaced his revolver in his pocket. There was no hurry to rush after the murderer.

Cautiously he proceeded down the steps and into the chapel. Wanstead had wakened from his drugged sleep at the sound of the shot, and was ringing violently at the bell.

Sinclair never paused. He went down into the crypt, and saw that the altar had been replaced. He pushed this aside, determined not to be caught napping again, but fairly certain that the creature had made for the passage and escape. He had no sense of horror now, for he knew the truth.

He went along the passage, firmly but with the utmost care, showing no light. And then from the darkness beyond he heard a cry of mortal agony. Wild hands were beating against the trapdoor, which Guillet had closed. Escape was cut off. Doom in the shape of the implacable detective was coming along behind.

A light flashed, and Sinclair had just time to throw himself flat on the ground as a stream of bullets passed harmlessly over his head. At the end of the passage, where the steps led up to the room above, the murderer made his last stand.

He was using an automatic, and had emptied the magazine. There was a momentary pause while he reloaded.

Sinclair utilized this by using an old device. He placed the torch in the left-hand corner, where the passage curved, and hugged the right, prepared to rush when the man fired.

His assailant had recharged, and a stream of bullets shattered the electric torch to fragments, leaving the passage in darkness.

Sinclair was on the point of springing forward, when a welcome call came from above, and at the same time a banging on the trapdoor.

"Hold on; I am coming to help."

Guillet's voice was very welcome.

There was a strange silence in the dark tunnel; the smell of burnt cordite, acrid and pungent, pervaded the place.

A single shot rang out.

"You can come down now, my friend, it is all over."

The trapdoor opened, and a light appeared. Guillet came down the stone steps and flashed his light on a huddled black heap that lay, still quivering, on the ground.

"He shot himself: it was the best way out," Sinclair said after a brief examination. "We must carry it to the watchman's room." They hastily removed the gruesome disguise and covered the body with some sacking.

Then, together, they bore it across the intervening space into the porter's room.

The night-watchman came timidly down the stairs. The shots had been heard very faintly by him, but he was aware that someone was moving in the room below.

"You have a telephone here?" Sinclair asserted.

"Yes, sir, but only to the castle."

"Tell them to call up Sergeant Haddon, at Payning, and tell him to come to Cantire as soon as he can."

The man gazed fearfully at the still figure under the sacking, and with a trembling hand picked up the 'phone.

Sinclair left Guillet in the room and went across to the other room, on the other side of the gateway. He carefully closed and fastened the trapdoor, and locked the outer door. There must be no connection shown between the castle and the lodge.

"I have called up, sir," the porter told him. "The butler says that Sergeant Haddon has already been sent for." He looked unspoken questions at the detective.

"You will stay here," Sinclair said sternly, "and allow no one in this room. Meanwhile, until you are asked by the police or myself, you will keep your mouth shut. Do you understand?"

The frightened man gave his assurance readily.

Sinclair and Guillet proceeded in silence up the drive. Lights were flashing from the windows, and figures passed in shadow on the blinds. The whole castle was a blaze of light, as though fire had broken out inside the grim walls.

"Come with me—we must get into the castle."

"But why not through the passage?" Guillet's teeth were chattering.

"I must leave that exactly as it is for the police. No, we will boldly assault the front gate."

Sinclair spoke almost gaily. Even his iron nerves were feeling the reaction after the strain of the last few days.

In answer to his ring, the night porter drew the bars and unlocked the door. Wanstead had 'phoned for the police, and the man was expecting them. He looked suspiciously at Sinclair and Guillet in their rough clothes into which they had changed, but Sinclair brushed past him. "Wait for me here," he said to Guillet, "or, better, go into the dining-room and have a drink, you need it. I shall not keep you."

Sinclair made his way to Elsie's room and unlocked the door. She was calm now, and merely looked a question at him.

"You need have no more fear now, Elsie. It is all over?"

"He is dead?" she whispered.

"He shot himself when there was no escape."

"Thank God—oh, it sounds awful to say that, but you don't know how I feel."

"I know only too well. I must go to Wanstead. If you feel well enough, come along there. There will have to be revelations."

"I will come."

"Elsie!" He took the girl's hand in his. "We are alone together, possibly for the last time. Tell me; it shall go no further. You knew all along?"

Her clear eyes met his tranquilly. "Yes, I knew. I saw the murder."

"I thought so. Sometime you can tell me, but not now. Rob is coming tomorrow."

He left her there, and went to Wanstead's room, where a frightful scene was being enacted. His lordship was sitting up in bed, storming at the servants who were standing round in a helpless group.

All eyes were fixed on a rope suspended over the hook in the ceiling, and at the ugly noose that dangled at one end. The chair still stood where the murderer had left it.

Wanstead turned bloodshot eyes on Sinclair. "Ah, here you are at last. What the hell is the use of having a detective in the house when murderers are about shooting off guns? And look at that"— he pointed with a frenzied gesture to the rope.

"Quiet yourself, Lord Wanstead, and don't behave like a frightened baby. Please request your servants to withdraw. I must talk to you."

Something in the stern set face commanded obedience, and Wanstead waved the servants away. They were glad enough to escape, for the sight of that rope had filled them with grim forebodings.

Sinclair lit his pipe and threw the match into the grate, and the homely action restored calm. There came a knock, and Sinclair opened the door to admit Elsie and Guillet.

"What on earth are you doing here?" Wanstead exclaimed angrily.

"It is necessary for her to be here. I asked her. Please sit down, both of you."

He faced Wanstead. "I have some news to tell you, as you may guess, which I am afraid will cause you much sorrow, but it must be told now. Tomorrow will be too late. This night an attack was made on your life which I was able to frustrate. The murderer was the same man who killed your brother-in-law, and I think for a similar reason."

There was a breathless hush.

"I am grieved to tell you it was your nephew, Rupert Seften."

Wanstead gave a cry that was hardly human. "Rupert! Impossible. You are dreaming, man."

Sinclair held up his hand. "Silence! I saw it myself, and chased him. Guillet was at the other end of a passage, and finding himself cornered he took his life."

Wanstead turned his face to the cushions, and his shoulders heaved. "Are you certain?" he moaned.

"His body is now in the lodge."

"But you say he killed Musgrave too. Why didn't you—"

Sinclair interrupted.

"I know what you are going to say—why didn't I arrest him. Suspicion is not proof, and I had to have that. I am sorry I used you, Lord Wanstead, as a bait, but there was no other way."

Wanstead looked up, and his face had gone grey. "Rupert! I can't believe it. I knew he was weak, but—"

"That is where you made the mistake; we all made the same mistake. I will explain all that, but not just now."

He turned sternly to Wanstead. "You arranged this party for tomorrow, or rather I should say for today. You were going to make an announcement. After what has happened, I think you had better make it now, but I warn you I know what it is, and I want the truth. You have 'phoned Haddon, and in a short time he will be here, and then explanations will have to be made, and the matter will be entirely out of my hands.''

Guillet had never heard Sinclair speak so gravely.

Lord Wanstead sat up in his bed and swallowed hard. He was labouring under some strong struggle that was going on.

"You are right,'' he said at last, with a simplicity that had belonged to his early days. "I can and will tell you now. I have discovered that Elsie is the lawful daughter of my late brother-in-law, Colonel Musgrave. He married Mary Rhodes when she was seventeen, and afterwards divorced her."

He panted strongly, but there was no pity in Sinclair's face.

"That is the truth, as far as it goes. That is what you were going to announce with a great flourish at a dinner. You told that in a letter to Seften, your nephew, and he determined that that announcement should not be made. That is why he came tonight, to kill you, and then to turn up tomorrow with an alibi."

"I suppose you must be right," Wanstead said, with a sigh almost of relief.

"It is not right." Sinclair's voice was like a note of doom to the wretched being on the bed. "Shall I tell you the whole truth? You and that miserable rat Hicks, who was under your thumb, knew this secret from the beginning. You knew it before Musgrave was murdered.

"Money was nothing to you, but the old estate, like Naboth's vineyard, was what you had set your heart upon, and you were desperately anxious to suppress the truth, because you thought the scandal connected with your nephew's marriage would have to come out."

The stuffing was gone from the proud millionaire. "I am afraid that is all quite true," he stammered, looking anywhere but at Elsie. "Musgrave was in a desperate state of panic—he would not tell us why. I must conclude it was my nephew, if what you say is true. He offered to sell the marriage papers to me for five thousand pounds, and I accepted. We suppressed the papers, and as he was dead, we said nothing about it."

"Until you heard, I suppose, that I was going to see Guillet in Paris, and then you feared I should see the miniature and discover that Elsie was Mary's daughter."

"We didn't know what to do," he answered miserably. "I tried to make what reparation I could, by adopting her, but at last I decided I could not keep the secret—it wasn't fair on Elsie. So Hicks suggested that we had just found the proofs, and I should make a public announcement."

"You are a cad. You let Elsie think all this time that she was an illegitimate child, the daughter of her mother's shame."

"She?" Wanstead asked in genuine surprise.

"You knew all along, didn't you, Elsie?" Sinclair asked gently.

"I knew that Colonel Musgrave was my father; he told me so himself when he gave me the locket. I did not know that he married my mother."

"How can you forgive me," Wanstead whined like a cur.

Sinclair strode up and down in excitement he had not shown when he took his life in his hands. He was thinking hard.

"Answer me two questions. Did you send Hicks out there to Paris to try to murder me?"

"Most certainly not—when he came back he said you had had an accident. I am sure he never attacked you."

"I am inclined to agree with you. He is the type that will steal but shrink from any violence. The other question is whether Hicks had any hand in abducting Elsie."

"This is the first time I have ever heard that she was abducted."

"That is all. Then hear me. We have heard your story, and a pretty rotten one it is. We will have that meeting, and you shall make your announcement. I can see no reason why we should rake up the past. It was by the merest accident that I hit on the truth, though I ought to have guessed. Elsie, I told you that I had once interviewed a poor woman in my study, do you remember?"

Elsie nodded.

"It was your mother, a sweet brave woman, and a truthful one. She let out, owing to the emotional stress under which she was labouring, that she had *married* when she was seventeen, but I was so absorbed in the major problem it slipped my memory until I went over the papers again the other day. Then it all became plain. She had married Musgrave, and I have traced the marriage at Somerset House—it was at Chelsea Register Office. I brought a copy down here, in case Wanstead still tried to hide the fact."

A servant came to announce that Sergeant Haddon had arrived and was at the lodge, waiting for Sinclair.

"Come with me, Bertrand," he said. "The rest of you had better get what sleep you can. We must have a general council, as some things are still obscure."

"What and how much do we tell the gendarme?" Guillet said as they walked down the drive.

"No more than I can help. The murderer is dead, and nothing can touch him further. That he attempted to kill his uncle cannot be denied, and the means whereby he got access to his room must be shown. Beyond that, I do not think we need go. I am sure Wanstead will not wish to."

"Then the murder of that Colonel Musgrave?"

"Is merely conjecture, and there is no one to arrest or to convict."

"Well, sir, what's all this? Have you been killing someone?" Haddon laughed at his joke.

"Someone might have been killed, but this man committed suicide."

"Whew! He shot himself through the mouth and made a hell of a mess. I have had the body removed."

"You don't know who it was?"

"Can't say as I looked much. I knew you would tell me, sir."

"It was Seften, Lord Wanstead's nephew. You remember him?"

"Very well, sir."

"I shall give you a full report tomorrow, Haddon, and explain matters. Meantime, I think the less said about this the better. We don't want a sensation. Monsieur Guillet, here, was with me and is a witness. Seften made an attempt on his uncle's life, and being discovered and cornered, put an end to his own, as you have seen."

"Very good, sir. But I must report the matter."

"Of course. By the way, your old friend Inspector Gillian is coming down here tomorrow. Lord Wanstead invited him."

Haddon was no fool. He stroked his moustache, and looked keenly at Sinclair. "Do you think, sir, that this affair has any connection with the murder of Colonel Musgrave?"

"At present it is impossible to say. You have disposed of the body. You had better come with me and have a drink. The night is nearly gone now."

Haddon, nothing loth, accompanied the detective to the castle, and there, with Guillet as attentive listener, the story was told him of all that had taken place, save only with regard to Elsie.

Haddon's eyes grew large and round. He had agreed that this conversation was confidential, but felt regret that he had not been able to find out the truth for himself.

Dawn had come when he took his departure, having made a formal report to Exeter.

"And now, Sergeant, you must get some rest," Sinclair said, clapping him on the back. "But on your way home I think it might be a good thing if you called in on Mr. Hicks and told him the bare fact of Seften's suicide, and nothing more. It may do him good."

"I never can fathom what you are up to, sir," Haddon said with a laugh. "But I will do what you suggest, and tell you what he says."

"And what he does, Sergeant. Good morning."

CHAPTER XVIII

HOW IT HAPPENED

THE END HAD COME. Nothing now remained but to explain exactly what had happened, and how much it was advisable to make public. The day was spent in uneasy speculations, and the servants had been enjoined, on threat of instant dismissal, to say nothing. The castle was in a state of siege.

Lord Wanstead remained in bed, utterly prostrated by the turn of events, and issuing frantic orders that Hicks should be summoned to Cantire as soon as possible. But Hicks never came. The message delivered by Haddon had, as Sinclair had shrewdly guessed, sent the wretched lawyer packing off. He had wisely made provision for such a contingency, and had his plans completed. The generosity of Lord Wanstead had, with sums he had acquired as commissions in the purchases he had made, enabled him to invest sufficient funds to provide for his future. He had no kith nor kin, and silently vanished away, and established himself in more congenial surroundings. Enough of him!

During the morning Gillian arrived at Cantire, and accompanied Sinclair and Guillet to the police station at Payning where their plans were worked out with Haddon. They were busy all day examining the secret passage and reconstructing the crime.

Another person unobtrusively came to the castle and signalled to someone inside. Elsie saw him, and slipped out into the cool woods, where she and Rob spent the day in the way that reunited lovers do: in explanations, some quarrels, and reconciliation. There was much to explain, and when Rob knew that Elsie was the true owner of Cantire, and a Musgrave, he became frigid and then sulky, and had to be coaxed into a more reasonable frame of mind.

And so it was that the scattered party only came together as evening fell, and Rhodes joined them, as arranged. By a strange series of events, the celebration dinner to which Wanstead had looked forward, in order to make his grand declaration about the recent discovery of Elsie's parentage, became a reality, and they all gathered in the great dining-hall, if not a merry party, at any rate excited at the prospect of hearing the whole story pieced together. For it had been arranged that as soon as the meal was over and the servants dismissed, a full and frank discussion should take place behind sealed doors. How much each knew or had guessed would then be disclosed.

The dinner passed in feverish talk on every subject but the one vital one. There was much to tell, as a full year had elapsed since these had met. Only Rhodes remained sullen and sulky as though nursing a grievance. Sinclair took stock of them all. He noticed, for example, that Elsie and Rob seemed to have some difficulty in eating, as they appeared to be trying to perform the operation with one hand at intervals while the others had mysteriously disappeared beneath the table. Wanstead drank a great deal of his excellent champagne, and it struck Sinclair that in spite of the shock he had received there was a secret sense of relief that things had turned out as they had. Guillet, with his artist's temperament, was delighted that the little romance of Elsie and Rob had terminated as romances should, and that he had played an heroic part in the adventures, and shown bravery of which he had thought himself incapable. Sinclair—the great Sinclair—had told him so, and flattered his soul.

Gillian was merely puzzled and still wondered why he had been summoned. He saw little credit to himself in the matter.

Dessert, cloth, and all signs of dinner had been swept away by the well-trained staff. Only large cut-glass decanters and glasses remained, with ash-trays and boxes of cigars and cigarettes. Guillet had emphatically insisted that this old refectory of dead abbots and monks was the only possible place where they could talk, and Sinclair had agreed. Huge silver candelabra were set at intervals down the table, and the frosted globes shone on the silver plate.

Cigars and pipes were lit, while Elsie and Rob, close together, smoked cigarettes.

Sinclair began gravely.

"We have to clear up a lot of things that are obscure, and I hope there will be an absolutely free exchange of information." He glanced at Elsie, who blushed, but nodded in agreement.

"Very well, then, I'm not going to waste your time with a long yarn of all that happened, because if I had possessed a grain of common sense I should have solved this a year ago. I know it is painful to you, Lord Wanstead, but it is necessary to go into some details with regard to your late nephew, and I am bound to say that I think you were to a large extent responsible for his crimes."

"I take that full responsibility," Wanstead said bravely.

"Very well. Seften was a spoilt child from the beginning. He was left an orphan with no father or mother, and had the free run of his uncle's place and purse. I have verified the facts. At what particular moment he decided on this complete mental disguise we shall never know, but I should imagine that it was when he discovered about Musgrave."

"I am afraid I don't quite follow," Wanstead observed fretfully.

"Let me go back. This is how I see things. I had two clues staring me right in the face and failed to see their vital importance. Mary Rhodes, as she called herself—forgive me, Rhodes, we must go into this—called at my office and told me in conversation that she had married when she was seventeen. I have already mentioned that, and we all know now that it was true."

Rhodes uttered a startled cry. "Mary married at seventeen! She ran away with that blackguard Musgrave."

"Hold your horses, Rhodes. It has only just been discovered"— he looked hard at Wanstead—"that Musgrave did marry her, and Elsie is their daughter."

Rhodes thumped the table with his huge fist. "She never told me. It would have made a deal of difference. I knew Elsie was Mary's daughter, but I was so disgusted with the whole thing that I wouldn't say a word, and it was only after Musgrave's death I thought I ought to do something for her. I was afraid the whole damned story would come out if I said anything."

"I guessed that," Sinclair said, "and that was my second clue. When Seften arrived here, simulating intense fear because of you, when he knew that Mary had never mentioned his name, I was taken aback by your apparent ignorance of his having married Mary. It ought to have told me everything."

"All I knew," Rhodes broke in, "was that Mary had gone off with this Musgrave. I found that out. They had simply vanished. I drew the conclusion that he had seduced the girl and she had gone off somewhere with him. When her trouble came, and I saw her, I still thought that it was Musgrave, and had determined to murder him if I got the chance, but Seften seems to have done it for me. I still don't know why."

"This problem was complicated by the conduct of Lord Wanstead and Hicks the lawyer, although I was quite certain neither of them was the actual murderer." Sinclair said.

"Perhaps I ought to explain," Wanstead put in, but Sinclair stopped him.

"Wait; we shall come to that in time. Now, as I see things—and we have to fill in gaps—Musgrave had got rid of Mary by trumping up some charge and divorcing her. We have, then, Seften, a young idle man with no ties and plenty of money, and not happy with his aunt—am I not right?"

"My poor dear wife could not stand him. She resented that we had no child of our own, and with her family pride hated the idea that I had often discussed with her of buying Cantire, so that when I was gone Rupert should inherit. We both wanted him to marry well socially, and it came as an awful shock to hear he had married a widow older than himself and of no family."

Rhodes looked angrily at the risen builder, but caught Sinclair's eye and remained silent.

"Here is another bit filled in," he said cheerfully. "We can follow what happened. Lord Wanstead wanted to get his nephew away from his wife. He made those terms we know of, that they should not meet for a year, under pain of cutting off all supplies. Is that right?"

"That is so," Wanstead said guiltily.

"He placed his nephew in charge of his brother-in-law. Why?"

"My wife suggested it—she said he might train him into being a gentleman."

It was bitter for Wanstead to have to reveal these family secrets, but he knew he was entirely in Sinclair's hands and must tell the truth if he hoped for mercy.

"We have a gap here," Sinclair continued. "My opinion, for what it is worth, is that Musgrave discovered that Seften's wife was the woman he had treated so shabbily, and he was in desperate fear of meeting her. He rushed Seften off abroad and kept him there. But Seften must have discovered the secret. Instead of having it out with Musgrave or leaving him, his warped mind, warped by his early training, conceived the subtle plan of torturing him. He undoubtedly wrote those threatening letters himself, and made the attempts on Musgrave's life, and *Musgrave had guessed it*. He was in desperate fear, but pride prevented him from going to the police. He came to me." Sinclair smiled sourly at the recollection of that interview.

"We can follow the rest. Seften had been down here when the first restoration was going on and undoubtedly discovered the secret passage, the knowledge of which he kept to himself. He even faked that scene in a dungeon, of which you told me, Guillet. But Musgrave found that Rhodes, Mary's brother, was here, and went off as though the fiend himself were after him. When the tour was over, and they came back, Musgrave found himself without a penny. I think by this time he must have guessed the truth about Seften, and when Mary took her life he saw vengeance hard on his track. He had only one asset, the fact that he had a daughter who was the heir to Cantire. The property he could not sell. We know that now he sold the proofs to Hicks the lawyer."

Rob looked up quickly. "So that was it—but who was the man in the other room with whom Hicks kept on communicating?"

"The man who had the money," Sinclair said firmly, and went on: "Musgrave dared not show his face in Payning or Barton, and his only place of concealment was in Cantire. He had discovered with our friend Guillet here that outlet into the garden. It was known only to those two and Elsie, and he thought the secret safe. So it was, but Seften knew of the other passage, and came on him that night. He had acted very cleverly, as men with one mania of revenge generally do. He played on the superstitions of the villagers and the village police."

"But that does not explain how he did the murder," Gillian commented as Sinclair stooped to light his pipe from the fire.

"No; and for the moment I have finished. Elsie, I must ask you now to tell us the whole truth."

Her face was very white, and she was holding Rob's hand convulsively in her own.

"Very well, Sir Arthur. Where shall I begin?"

"You saw Colonel Musgrave."

"I have already told Sir Arthur Sinclair that I saw Colonel Musgrave and this gentleman, M. Guillet, in the garden, at the entrance to the conduit. He told me then that he was my father, but never to breathe a word to anyone, or his life would be in danger. He gave me a locket with the family arms on, and said that would be proof."

"That is clear," Sinclair said as the girl stopped, "and then I think the next thing of importance was that Seften came to your bedroom."

The girl gave a gasp. "How did you know that? I had thought the conduit was rather a fine discovery, and used to meet Rob by that way. When Mr. Seften came, I naturally concluded he had entered that way. I was too frightened to ask him anything. He said that if I ever breathed a word of his being in the castle, or about him, he would kill me."

"Why didn't you go to the police?" Gillian asked impatiently.

"A child that age—I can understand it," Wanstead said nobly.

The white of Elsie's face turned to a bright red. "It wasn't that," she stammered. "I would have told Sir Arthur, but Mr. Seften had told me that if I breathed a word he would kill—" she paused—"Rob."

"He did, did he?" that young man exclaimed fiercely.

"Then he made some funny passes over my face, and said that if he ever called me, I must come to him."

"I thought as much," Sinclair muttered.

"Then Colonel Musgrave came," Elsie went on hurriedly, as though to change the conversation. "He told me he was hiding, and I took him food. I dared not say a word to him about Mr. Seften, but I pulled up that rope in the shaft so that he could not get in."

"That was clever of you," Sinclair said, "but unfortunately he did not come that way."

"I saw him in the chapel," she said fearfully. "I went to warn the Colonel, but it was too late. He came down those winding stairs from his hiding-place and entered the chapel. I was hiding. Mr. Seften had a rope . . . I can't go on." She sank her head on her hands.

"I think I can," Sinclair said grimly. "When I saw the body I could reconstruct the method. It has been done before. He had the loop dangling in that dark place in the wind. Musgrave would naturally have his torch turned to the floor to pick his way. He was going off, having taken advantage of the storm for a getaway. He ran right into the noose, and Seften kicked that huge stone from the steps."

"You didn't see it?" Gillian asked Elsie.

"I ran back into the inner court, not knowing what to do. There was no sound, and I plucked up courage to go back and look. I hoped they had missed each other, but when I got to the chapel door I saw that awful thing that you saw afterwards, as Rob has told me. A vast bird, as it looked, with flaming eyes."

"That was a clever disguise in case he were seen. You naturally shrieked—I don't wonder."

"I rushed back to Mr. and Mrs. Campion's rooms—I knew then they were not my parents."

Sinclair took up the story.

"The rest is simple, but devilish clever. He waited, knowing that Campion would come. Luckily for the old man's sanity he did not see that awful figure. He frightened him to silence, and then cunningly spread a false trail, by that fake of a party of gangsters with a fire and cigarette and pipe ash, probably Musgrave's. He had plenty of time; and when he had done, he retired to the secret passage, where he hid Musgrave's things, including the five thousand pounds."

"Not all of it," Rhodes growled in anger. "Musgrave had the damned impertinence to send me five hundred pounds in notes with a note, to say it was for Elsie. I was on the way to Cantire to fix him when I met you, Sir Arthur."

"That is quite clear. Now, Elsie, I am afraid you must finish."

"Certainly," she said calmly. "I was afraid for Rob, and went to live with them. I didn't know what to do for the best, and then you came and took us away to Paris."

"I did, Elsie, but it turned out badly. I was even at that time convinced that you knew far more than you had told me, and was afraid you were in danger. I wanted to see Guillet because he had, years before, told me about your mother. I wanted him to see you and confirm that fact."

"At the hotel," Elsie went on, "I saw Mr. Seften outside my window, beckoning to me, and I had to go. He took me to an airplane and brought me back here to Cantire. He said again that he would kill Rob if I said a word."

"What was his object?"

"He told me he had killed you, Sir Arthur—stabbed, you from behind, and that Rob would go the same way. He was afraid you had learnt some secret—I suppose that was who I was—and he kept me here in the Campions' rooms. I looked out once when I thought no one was about, and saw Mr. Rhodes. Then Mr. Seften showed a skull at the window to frighten the constable, so that he could get out in the moonlight by the passage. When you all came, he must have slipped into the passage and taken me to the crypt. I was frightened out of my life nearly. He went somewhere and left me. Then the following night he gave me some nasty stuff to make me sleep, and I believe he was going to leave me there or take me right away, but you came."

"That was the close of the chapter," Sinclair said solemnly. "By that time I was nearly certain that Seften was my man, but hadn't a shred of proof. The attack in Paris had shown me the man was desperate, but I felt Elsie's life was safe as long as there was no revelation about her identity. Seften had set his mind on the estate, as his moral fibre had gone. He had murder on his conscience, and an attempted murder on me. He could not quite descend to killing a girl. But then came the climax. Lord Wanstead had written to him telling him the truth and that he was going to announce it publicly—wasn't that so?"

"I did. I told him that Elsie would come into the property, but I would make ample provision for him."

"That letter nearly caused your death. I had to act, and act quickly. I was certain he would come the night before, and by that passage. But to arrest him there would prove nothing. I had to catch him in the act, and I am afraid I used Lord Wanstead as a bait. We know the rest. I thought he would try hanging, as he had done before, to spread the superstition about Cantire. It would appear as a family curse, and be put down to suicide."

"There is one point you have omitted," Gillian said. "What about the Campions?"

"That we may never know. They must have seen him, or how did they get the note that Hicks had given Musgrave? Either they tried to escape in panic, having seen that awful creature after them, or he induced them to try the shaft to get away, and then hurled them to their deaths. We may only conjecture."

There had been complete silence in the old hall while they had spoken. Sinclair reached over and helped himself to a brandy-and-soda, and the familiar sound of the soda water fizzing into the glass seemed to relieve the tension.

Gillian laughed. "A most extraordinary story, Sir Arthur, but what I want to know is why I was brought here, except to show what a fool I was."

"Not so simple as all that," Sinclair said with a smile. "I am afraid I made use of you. I had an interview with Seften, where I had to exercise my utmost tact, and it was touch and go. One breath of suspicion and he would have changed his plans. I managed to insinuate that you were the murderer, and that I was on your track and had got you to come to Cantire. He was, as you see, completely deceived, and must have thought me a great idiot."

A gust of laughter greeted the statement—strained nerves found relief.

"Well, I'm damned." Gillian grinned at Sinclair.

Wanstead rose a little unsteadily. "We are, I am sure, greatly in Sir Arthur Sinclair's debt. I, as well as others, owe my life to him. I know he is a man who will never accept anything by way of personal reward, but I ventured to ask him what I could do in any other way to show my gratitude, and he made a request that I am only too pleased to grant. Elsie, of course, is the rightful heir to Cantire, and will inherit the property I have bought after my death, and I shall make over all that I have bought to her as soon as possible." He paused for effect, and then went on, "This is but just and fair, but not the request that Sinclair made. I wish Elsie, and I am quite sure it is her wish as well, to marry our young friend Rob Summers, when they are a little older perhaps, or now if they wish it. The whole cause of Rhodes losing his farm was his generous attempt to defend his sister when in trouble. I have already bought his old property, but he is too proud to accept it, and will remain here as my trusted steward; but Rob shall have it, and until such time as he comes to live here, after my death, he can be in his old heritage."

Wanstead thought he had put it very well and tactfully, but there was a stubborn look on Rob's face. Sinclair hastily intervened. "I am sure that will be a very happy conclusion. You need not mind taking the farm, as it is mine—that is to say I took it as my fee. I shall be mightily offended if you don't accept, and shall refuse to come to the wedding. Meanwhile"—he solemnly walked round the table—"I am going to claim an old man's privilege of congratulating the bride-to-be."

Elsie sprang from her seat and threw her arms round his neck. "You are a dear," she said, tears in her eyes.

Sinclair placed one arm round her and took Rob's hand.

"I saw how it was," he said whimsically, "when I first met you, Elsie, in bare legs and one garment. Take her, you lucky fellow, and release my arm so that we can all drink your health."

Guillet was not to be outdone. "I loved your so beautiful mother like Plato, as you say—I shall love you likewise."

He kissed the blushing girl and then lifted his glass.

RAMBLE HOUSE's
HARRY STEPHEN KEELER WEBWORK MYSTERIES
(RH) indicates the title is available ONLY in the RAMBLE HOUSE edition

The Ace of Spades Murder
The Affair of the Bottled Deuce (RH)
The Amazing Web
The Barking Clock
Behind That Mask
The Book with the Orange Leaves
The Bottle with the Green Wax Seal
The Box from Japan
The Case of the Canny Killer
The Case of the Crazy Corpse (RH)
The Case of the Flying Hands (RH)
The Case of the Ivory Arrow
The Case of the Jeweled Ragpicker
The Case of the Lavender Gripsack
The Case of the Mysterious Moll
The Case of the 16 Beans
The Case of the Transparent Nude (RH)
The Case of the Transposed Legs
The Case of the Two-Headed Idiot (RH)
The Case of the Two Strange Ladies
The Circus Stealers (RH)
Cleopatra's Tears
A Copy of Beowulf (RH)
The Crimson Cube (RH)
The Face of the Man From Saturn
Find the Clock
The Five Silver Buddhas
The 4th King
The Gallows Waits, My Lord! (RH)
The Green Jade Hand
Finger! Finger!
Hangman's Nights (RH)
I, Chameleon (RH)
I Killed Lincoln at 10:13! (RH)
The Iron Ring
The Man Who Changed His Skin (RH)
The Man with the Crimson Box
The Man with the Magic Eardrums
The Man with the Wooden Spectacles
The Marceau Case
The Matilda Hunter Murder
The Monocled Monster

The Murder of London Lew
The Murdered Mathematician
The Mysterious Card (RH)
The Mysterious Ivory Ball of Wong Shing
   Li (RH)
The Mystery of the Fiddling Cracksman
The Peacock Fan
The Photo of Lady X (RH)
The Portrait of Jirjohn Cobb
Report on Vanessa Hewstone (RH)
Riddle of the Travelling Skull
Riddle of the Wooden Parrakeet (RH)
The Scarlet Mummy (RH)
The Search for X-Y-Z
The Sharkskin Book
Sing Sing Nights
The Six From Nowhere (RH)
The Skull of the Waltzing Clown
The Spectacles of Mr. Cagliostro
Stand By—London Calling!
The Steeltown Strangler
The Stolen Gravestone (RH)
Strange Journey (RH)
The Strange Will
The Straw Hat Murders (RH)
The Street of 1000 Eyes (RH)
Thieves' Nights
Three Novellos (RH)
The Tiger Snake
The Trap (RH)
Vagabond Nights (Defrauded Yeggman)
Vagabond Nights 2 (10 Hours)
The Vanishing Gold Truck
The Voice of the Seven Sparrows
The Washington Square Enigma
When Thief Meets Thief
The White Circle (RH)
The Wonderful Scheme of Mr. Christopher
   Thorne
X. Jones—of Scotland Yard
Y. Cheung, Business Detective

Keeler Related Works

A To Izzard: A Harry Stephen Keeler Companion by Fender Tucker — Articles and
   stories about Harry, by Harry, and in his style. Included is a compleat bibliography.
Wild About Harry: Reviews of Keeler Novels — Edited by Richard Polt & Fender
   Tucker — 22 reviews of works by Harry Stephen Keeler from *Keeler News.* A perfect
   introduction to the author.
The Keeler Keyhole Collection: Annotated newsletter rants from Harry Stephen
   Keeler, edited by Francis M. Nevins. Over 400 pages of incredibly personal Keeleriana.
Fakealoo — Pastiches of the style of Harry Stephen Keeler by selected demented mem-
   bers of the HSK Society. Updated every year with the new winner.
Strands of the Web: Short Stories of Harry Stephen Keeler — 29 stories, just
   about all that Keeler wrote, are edited and introduced by Fred Cleaver.

RAMBLE HOUSE's OTHER LOONS

Invaders from the Dark — Classic werewolf tale from Greye La Spina.

Jack Mann Novels — Strange murder in the English countryside. *Gees First Case, Nightmare Farm, Grey Shapes, The Ninth Life, The Glass Too Many.*

Jake Hardy — A lusty western tale from Wesley Tallant.

Jim Harmon Double Novels — *Vixen Hollow/Celluloid Scandal, The Man Who Made Maniacs/Silent Siren, Ape Rape/Wanton Witch, Sex Burns Like Fire/Twist Session, Sudden Lust/Passion Strip, Sin Unlimited/Harlot Master, Twilight Girls/Sex Institution.* Written in the early 60s and never reprinted until now.

Joel Townsley Rogers Novels and Short Stories — By the author of *The Red Right Hand: Once In a Red Moon, Lady With the Dice, The Stopped Clock, Never Leave My Bed.* Also two short story collections: *Night of Horror* and *Killing Time.*

Joseph Shallit Novels — *The Case of the Billion Dollar Body, Lady Don't Die on My Doorstep, Kiss the Killer, Yell Bloody Murder, Take Your Last Look.* One of America's best 50's authors and a favorite of author, Bill Pronzini.

Keller Memento — 45 short stories of the amazing and weird by Dr. David Keller. Huge!

Killer's Caress — Cary Moran's 1936 hardboiled thriller.

League of the Grateful Dead and Other Stories — Volume One in the Day Keene in the Detective Pulps series. In the introduction John Pelan outlines his plans for republishing all of Day Keene's short stories from the pulps.

Marblehead: A Novel of H.P. Lovecraft — A long-lost masterpiece from Richard A. Lupoff. This is the "director's cut", the long version that has never been published before.

Master of Souls — Mark Hansom's 1937 shocker is introduced by weirdologist John Pelan.

Max Afford Novels — *Owl of Darkness, Death's Mannikins, Blood on His Hands, The Dead Are Blind, The Sheep and the Wolves, Sinners in Paradise* and *Two Locked Room Mysteries and a Ripping Yarn* by one of Australia's finest mystery novelists.

More Secret Adventures of Sherlock Holmes — Gary Lovisi's second collection of tales about the unknown sides of the great detective.

Muddled Mind: Complete Works of Ed Wood, Jr. — David Hayes and Hayden Davis deconstruct the life and works of the mad, but canny, genius.

Murder among the Nudists — A mystery from 1934 by Peter Hunt, featuring a naked Detective-Inspector going undercover in a nudist colony.

Murder in Black and White — 1931 classic tennis whodunit by Evelyn Elder

Murder in Shawnee — Two novels of the Alleghenies by John Douglas: *Shawnee Alley Fire* and *Haunts.*

Murder in Silk — A 1937 Yellow Peril novel of the silk trade by Ralph Trevor.

My Deadly Angel — 1955 Cold War drama by John Chelton.

My First Time: The One Experience You Never Forget — Michael Birchwood — 64 true first-person narratives of how they lost it.

Mysterious Martin, the Master of Murder — Two versions of a strange 1912 novel by Tod Robbins about a man who writes books that can kill.

Norman Berrow Novels — *The Bishop's Sword, Ghost House, Don't Go Out After Dark, Claws of the Cougar, The Smokers of Hashish, The Secret Dancer, Don't Jump Mr. Boland!, The Footprints of Satan, Fingers for Ransom, The Three Tiers of Fantasy, The Spaniard's Thumb, The Eleventh Plague, Words Have Wings, One Thrilling Night, The Lady's in Danger, It Howls at Night, The Terror in the Fog, Oil Under the Window, Murder in the Melody, The Singing Room.* This is the complete Norman Berrow library of classic locked-room mysteries, several of which are masterpieces.

Old Times' Sake — Short stories by James Reasoner from Mike Shayne Magazine.

Prose Bowl — Futuristic satire of a world where hack writing has replaced football as our national obsession, by Bill Pronzini and Barry N. Malzberg.

Red Light — The history of legal prostitution in Shreveport Louisiana by Eric Brock. Includes wonderful photos of the houses and the ladies.

Researching American-Made Toy Soldiers — A 276-page collection of a lifetime of articles by toy soldier expert Richard O'Brien.

Reunion in Hell — Volume One of the John H. Knox series of weird stories from the pulps. Introduced by horror expert John Pelan.

Ripped from the Headlines! — The Jack the Ripper story as told in the newspaper articles in the *New York* and *London Times.*

Robert Randisi Novels — *No Exit to Brooklyn* and *The Dead of Brooklyn.* The first two Nick Delvecchio novels.

Rough Cut & New, Improved Murder — Ed Gorman's first two novels.

Ruled By Radio — 1925 futuristic novel by Robert L. Hadfield & Frank E. Farncombe.

Rupert Penny Novels — *Policeman's Holiday, Policeman's Evidence, Lucky Policeman, Policeman in Armour, Sealed Room Murder, Sweet Poison, The Talkative Policeman, She had to Have Gas* and *Cut and Run* (by Martin Tanner.) Rupert Penny is the pseudonym of Australian Charles Thornett, a master of the locked room, impossible crime plot.

Sand's Game — Spectacular hard-boiled noir from Ennis Willie, edited by Lynn Myers and Stephen Mertz, with contributions from Max Allan Collins, Bill Crider, Wayne Dundee, Bill Pronzini, Gary Lovisi and James Reasoner.

Satan's Den Exposed — True crime in Truth or Consequences New Mexico — Award-winning journalism by the *Desert Journal*.

Gelett Burgess Novels — *The Master of Mysteries, The White Cat, Two O'Clock Courage, Ladies in Boxes, Find the Woman, The Heart Line, The Picaroons* and *Lady Mechante*. All are edited and introduced by Richard A. Lupoff.

Sam McCain Novels — Ed Gorman's terrific series includes *The Day the Music Died, Wake Up Little Susie* and *Will You Still Love Me Tomorrow?*

Sex Slave — Potboiler of lust in the days of Cleopatra by Dion Leclerq, 1966.

Shadows' Edge — Two early novels by Wade Wright: *Shadows Don't Bleed* and *The Sharp Edge*.

Sideslip — 1968 SF masterpiece by Ted White and Dave Van Arnam.

Slammer Days — Two full-length prison memoirs: *Men into Beasts* (1952) by George Sylvester Viereck and *Home Away From Home* (1962) by Jack Woodford.

Sorcerer's Chessmen — John Pelan introduces this 1939 classic by Mark Hansom.

Stakeout on Millennium Drive — Award-winning Indianapolis Noir by Ian Woollen.

Strands of the Web: Short Stories of Harry Stephen Keeler — Edited and Introduced by Fred Cleaver.

Suzy — A collection of comic strips by Richard O'Brien and Bob Vojtko from 1970.

Tales of the Macabre and Ordinary — Modern twisted horror by Chris Mikul, author of the *Bizarrism* series.

Tenebrae — Ernest G. Henham's 1898 horror tale brought back.

The Amorous Intrigues & Adventures of Aaron Burr — by Anonymous. Hot historical action about the man who almost became Emperor of Mexico.

The Anthony Boucher Chronicles — edited by Francis M. Nevins. Book reviews by Anthony Boucher written for the *San Francisco Chronicle,* 1942 – 1947. Essential and fascinating reading by the best book reviewer there ever was.

The Best of 10-Story Book — edited by Chris Mikul, over 35 stories from the literary magazine Harry Stephen Keeler edited.

The Black Dark Murders — Vintage 50s college murder yarn by Milt Ozaki, writing as Robert O. Saber.

The Book of Time — The classic novel by H.G. Wells is joined by sequels by Wells himself and three timely stories by Richard A. Lupoff. Lavishly illustrated by Gavin L. O'Keefe.

The Case of the Little Green Men — Mack Reynolds wrote this love song to sci-fi fans back in 1951 and it's now back in print.

The Case of the Withered Hand — 1936 potboiler by John G. Brandon.

The Charlie Chaplin Murder Mystery — A 2004 tribute by film scholar, Wes D. Gehring.

The Chinese Jar Mystery — Murder in the manor by John Stephen Strange, 1934.

The Compleat Calhoon — All of Fender Tucker's works: Includes *Totah Six-Pack, Weed, Women and Song* and *Tales from the Tower,* plus a CD of all of his songs.

The Compleat Ova Hamlet — Parodies of SF authors by Richard A. Lupoff. This is a brand new edition with more stories and more illustrations by Trina Robbins.

The Contested Earth and Other SF Stories — A never-before published space opera and seven short stories by Jim Harmon.

The Crimson Query — A 1929 thriller from Arlton Eadie. A perfect way to get introduced.

The Curse of Cantire — A classic 1939 novel of a family curse by Walter S. Masterman.

The Devil Drives — An odd prison and lost treasure novel from 1932 by Virgil Markham.

The Devil's Mistress — A 1915 Scottish gothic tale by J. W. Brodie-Innes, a member of Aleister Crowley's Golden Dawn.

The Dumpling — Political murder from 1907 by Coulson Kernahan.

The End of It All and Other Stories — Ed Gorman selected his favorite short stories for this huge collection.

The Ghost of Gaston Revere — From 1935, a novel of life and beyond by Mark Hansom, introduced by John Pelan.

The Gold Star Line — Seaboard adventure from L.T. Reade and Robert Eustace.

The Golden Dagger — 1951 Scotland Yard yarn by E. R. Punshon.

The Hairbreadth Escapes of Major Mendax — Francis Blake Crofton's 1889 boys' book.

The House of the Vampire — 1907 poetic thriller by George S. Viereck.

The Incredible Adventures of Rowland Hern — Intriguing 1928 impossible crimes by Nicholas Olde.

The Julius Caesar Murder Case — A classic 1935 re-telling of the assassination by Wallace Irwin that's much more fun than the Shakespeare version.

The Koky Comics — A collection of all of the 1978-1981 Sunday and daily comic strips by Richard O'Brien and Mort Gerberg, in two volumes.

The Lady of the Terraces — 1925 missing race adventure by E. Charles Vivian.

The Lord of Terror — 1925 mystery with master-criminal, Fantômas.

The N. R. De Mexico Novels — Robert Bragg, the real N.R. de Mexico, presents *Marijuana Girl, Madman on a Drum, Private Chauffeur* in one volume.

The Night Remembers — A 1991 Jack Walsh mystery from Ed Gorman.

The One After Snelling — Kickass modern noir from Richard O'Brien.

The Organ Reader — A huge compilation of just about everything published in the 1971-1972 radical bay-area newspaper, *THE ORGAN*. A coffee table book that points out the shallowness of the coffee table mindset.

The Poker Club — Three in one! Ed Gorman's ground-breaking novel, the short story it was based upon, and the screenplay of the film made from it.

The Private Journal & Diary of John H. Surratt — The memoirs of the man who conspired to assassinate President Lincoln.

The Secret Adventures of Sherlock Holmes — Three Sherlockian pastiches by the Brooklyn author/publisher, Gary Lovisi.

The Shadow on the House — Mark Hansom's 1934 masterpiece of horror is introduced by John Pelan.

The Sign of the Scorpion — A 1935 Edmund Snell tale of oriental evil.

The Singular Problem of the Stygian House-Boat — Two classic tales by John Kendrick Bangs about the denizens of Hades.

The Stench of Death: An Odoriferous Omnibus by Jack Moskovitz — Two complete novels and two novellas from 60's sleaze author, Jack Moskovitz.

The Time Armada — Fox B. Holden's 1953 SF gem.

The Tongueless Horror and Other Stories — Volume One of the series of short stories from the weird pulps by Wyatt Blassingame.

The Tracer of Lost Persons — From 1906, an episodic novel that became a hit radio series in the 30s. Introduced by Richard A. Lupoff.

The Trail of the Cloven Hoof — Diabolical horror from 1935 by Arlton Eadie. Introduced by John Pelan.

The Triune Man — Mindscrambling science fiction from Richard A. Lupoff.

The Universal Holmes — Richard A. Lupoff's 2007 collection of five Holmesian pastiches and a recipe for giant rat stew.

The Werewolf vs the Vampire Woman — Hard to believe ultraviolence by either Arthur M. Scarm or Arthur M. Scram.

The Whistling Ancestors — A 1936 classic of weirdness by Richard E. Goddard and introduced by John Pelan.

The White Peril in the Far East — Sidney Lewis Gulick's 1905 indictment of the West and assurance that Japan would never attack the U.S.

The Wizard of Berner's Abbey — A 1935 horror gem written by Mark Hansom and introduced by John Pelan.

Wade Wright Novels — *Echo of Fear, Death At Nostalgia Street, It Leads to Murder* and *Shadows' Edge*, a double book featuring *Shadows Don't Bleed* and *The Sharp Edge*.

Through the Looking Glass — Lewis Carroll wrote it; Gavin L. O'Keefe illustrated it.

Time Line — Ramble House artist Gavin O'Keefe selects his most evocative art inspired by the twisted literature he reads and designs.

Tiresias — Psychotic modern horror novel by Jonathan M. Sweet.

Totah Six-Pack — Just Fender Tucker's six tales about Farmington in one seek volume.

Trail of the Spirit Warrior — Roger Haley's historical saga of life in the Indian Territories.

Ultra-Boiled — 23 gut-wrenching tales by our Man in Brooklyn, Gary Lovisi.

Up Front From Behind — A 2011 satire of Wall Street by James B. Kobak.

Victims & Villains — Intriguing Sherlockiana from Derham Groves.

Walter S. Masterman Novels — *The Green Toad, The Flying Beast, The Yellow Mistletoe, The Wrong Verdict, The Perjured Alibi, The Border Line* and *The Curse of Cantire*. Masterman wrote horror and mystery, some introduced by John Pelan.

We Are the Dead and Other Stories — Volume Two in the Day Keene in the Detective Pulps series, introduced by Ed Gorman. When done, there may be as many as 11 in the series.

West Texas War and Other Western Stories — by Gary Lovisi.

Whip Dodge: Man Hunter — Wesley Tallant's saga of a bounty hunter of the old West.

You'll Die Laughing — Bruce Elliott's 1945 novel of murder at a practical joker's English countryside manor.

RAMBLE HOUSE

Fender Tucker, Prop.   Gavin L. O'Keefe, Graphics
www.ramblehouse.com   fender@ramblehouse.com
228-826-1783   10329 Sheephead Drive, Vancleave MS 39565

www.ingramcontent.com/pod-product-compliance
Lightning Source LLC
Chambersburg PA
CBHW030321020726
47493CB00004B/1119